MY FRIEND SAM

MY FRIEND SAM

A Novel

Charles A. Reap, Jr.

iUniverse, Inc.
New York Lincoln Shanghai

MY FRIEND SAM

iUniverse books may be ordered through booksellers or by contacting:

iUniverse
2021 Pine Lake Road, Suite 100
Lincoln, NE 68512
www.iuniverse.com
1-800-Authors (1-800-288-4677)

Because of the dynamic nature of the Internet, any Web addresses or links contained in this book may have changed since publication and may no longer be valid.

This is a work of fiction. All of the characters, names, incidents, organizations, and dialogue in this novel are either the products of the author's imagination or are used fictitiously.

ISBN: 978-0-595-44262-1 (pbk)
ISBN: 978-0-595-68617-9 (cloth)
ISBN: 978-0-595-88592-3 (ebk)

Printed in the United States of America

This book is lovingly dedicated to
my always helpful and
sweet wife, Betty

CHAPTER 1

The Urgent Call

Ring!

"Now, who in the heck can that be at this hour?"

Ring!

"Well, answer it!"

I got up and walked across the room to the phone, which was resting on the end table beside where my wife was sitting.

"Hello?"

"Hey, Hank."

"Sam!" I immediately recognized the voice, walked back across the room and sat back down in my chair.

"Yep. Sure is. Come over here. I want to show you something."

"Come over there now?"

He sounded cheerful. "That's what I said. You've gotta come on over."

"Dammit Sam. Don't you realize what time it is?"

"Sure. But it's not very late. Were you still up?"

"Sam, do you realize that it is pouring rain outside?"

"'Course I know that. But it's slacked off a little now. Anyway, it's not far, you know. And besides, it's important. I want to show you something I got in the mail today."

I said, "Let me get this straight. You received something in the mail—which we both know arrives around ten in the morning—and you've waited until now to ask me to come over there?"

He seemed to hesitate a tad. "Well, I just got around to it. I've got a big surprise for you. C'mon, I'm waiting."

I thought to myself, *Sam waiting for me? That'll be a first.*

Barbara, my sweet wifey, whispered to me, "What's the jerk want this time?"

I covered the mouthpiece with my hand and whispered back, "He wants me to come over to his house now."

She continued her whisper, "He's crazy."

"Sh-h. He might hear you."

"I don't care. He's got a lot of nerve asking you to go over there at this hour. And with all that rain outside."

"Sam," I said in a somewhat resigned voice. "I'll be over there in a few minutes." I looked over at Bobbie. Her face expressed her disdain. "But it sure better be important." I hung up and went to don my rain gear.

Barbara's face twisted even more. "That darn friend of yours! Honey, I just don't know why you take so much guff from him. He's always telling you to do things for him. He never asks. I don't like him taking advantage of you like that. He's a know-it-all nitwit. In addition, he never even thanks you for all the 'favors' you do for him. I just knew it'd be like this when he moved next door."

"Well after all," I said back to her as I opened our front door. "I'll bet he'd come over here if I called and said it was important. And besides, he's my best friend."

Barbara was saying as I closed the door, "Best friend, my eye …"

Little did I know that even though my friend had moved next door to us about a year ago, this phone call would set off a series of events and emotions that would control my life.

Indeed, it was a dark and stormy night. In fact, the rains had been falling for nearly four days, almost without let up, and of course, the ground was soaked. Nobody in his right mind would have ventured out without a darn good excuse. A thunderstorm had just passed by a half hour ago, and the rain was still coming down in sheets. You could still smell the ozone from that lightning. I couldn't even hear any insect or frog sounds; maybe it was too wet even for them. Yet, here I was, trodding, or should I say waddling, through the squashy mud path beside the road to Sam's house. The darn town has failed—so far—to install concrete sidewalks along this street. At least the road is paved.

His real name is Adolphus Josephesus Thompson. I think I'm the only one in town that knows his first and middle names. It's my understanding that he began calling himself Sam as soon as he was old enough to talk and learned what his parents had named him. Sam's now in his early fifties and I have to wonder sometimes if he'll make it into his sixties. This of course, makes me approaching forty. Barbara would shoot me if I mentioned her age, so let me just say that she's "fairly close" to my age.

Oh, I didn't mention my name. It's Rogers. Harold Eugene Rogers.

Anyway, because he'd called me on the phone, and told me to come over, I went. He rarely asks, just tells. Or, is it "demands?"

By the way, could you guess that Bobbie doesn't think much of Sam? Seems to think he "uses" me. *Yeah, maybe.* I have to confess that I allow him to do some of that, but I do consider him my best friend and sort of like a big brother, so I do whatever I can to help him. In spite of this, I have to admit he can be somewhat trying at times. Maybe he can't help it. I suppose the shrinks would call him "narcissistic." I suspect Bobbie would add "idiot" to that label. I'll relate to you a little more about Sam's and my personal relationship later.

At any rate, there I was, on my way over to his house in all that gooey mud and downpour. The streetlights on the far corners don't quite illuminate this particular stretch of road and there was too much traffic to safely walk on the pavement. Incidentally, his house is what I call "next door," but it's a right long way—on this particular night at any rate. I never have measured it with my car odometer, but it must be over a quarter of a mile. Of course, tonight it seemed more like ten times that. Normally, it is too short a distance to drive, but as I trudged along, I wondered if maybe I should have driven anyway. I didn't like it when that dang car full of laughing kids drove by and splashed a puddle of water on me.

Anyway, after a few minutes I got over to Sam's house, and climbed up all those fourteen front steps of his. I stomped as much mud off my boots as I could before going up. Arriving on his front porch, I parked my umbrella and carefully took off my still-muddy boots. Naturally, I got the mud all over my hands doing that. I had to stick them out in the rain just to rinse them off. But of course, I didn't have anything to use to dry my hands, so I just pulled up the edge of my wet raincoat and dried my hands on my pants legs. Now my hands were more or less dry, but my pants legs were wet. Go figure.

I pushed the doorbell button. Nothing. Pushed it again. Nothing. Then I finally remembered that the last time I'd been over at Sam's, he'd told me that his doorbell was out of order and that he needed to run into town and get a new button. Seems like some Halloween pranksters had pushed a screwdriver or something into it last fall and broke the darn thing. As many times as Sam has told me he had been to the hardware store over the last few weeks, you would think he'd have planned to get a new one. I'd have made a list of things I needed if it'd been me. But Sam's never been one for lists. I guess he figures his brain is strong enough to remember the important things. He must not have figured the doorbell button was too important. I haven't noticed that he gets many unexpected visitors.

I knocked on the door a couple of times, even banged and yelled, but there was no response. Now that peeved me a little because he knew I was coming. Finally I heard Sam call out to me from somewhere in the rear of the upstairs.

Friend Sam finally arrived at the door, and let me and my wetness in. He was wearing the "uniform" that he usually dons when he's banging around his home. It consists of a stained, slightly ragged old blue shirt that was a nice dress shirt in its previous life. He told me that his neck outgrew it, and since he knew he'd never wear it again as a dress shirt, he converted it into a standard work/casual shirt. With all the old paint and varnish drippings on it, I don't suppose he ever wore it out in public anywhere. Probably not—he looks like a bum in it. His pants were the standard beat-up faded blue jeans. His old deck shoes showed no socks. He told me one time that he wears this outfit a lot, because all he has to do is throw the stuff in the washing machine when it's dirty and then dry it. Then he can put it back on without any ironing or special care. Incidentally, maybe it was unintentional, but somehow he apparently poured some bleach in his washing machine along with his liquid soap, so now those particular jeans are somewhat splotchy.

Standing there in the foyer on the old wide-board oak flooring, I asked, "Sam, why in the hell did you ask me to come over? It's a mess outside."

Sam turned his mouth sort of sideways and squinted one eye at me as if to say, "You idiot, don't you know?" Instead, he grinned in a silly way and said, "Guess what?"

"What?" I had to wonder if he was starting on one of those childish 'guess what' games.

"I'm gonna get married again. What do you think about that?"

Now that just about floored me. I've known Sam a long time and, of course, knew that he dated from time to time, but I never chose to ask whom he was seeing. Didn't care, really. I guess I assumed that he was not going with anybody in particular—just a variety of ladies that I supposed he thought were reasonably attractive, and that could maybe tolerate his interminable lectures.

On the other hand, maybe they never discussed their personal problems with him, so they didn't get any lectures from old Sam. Or, maybe they had sense enough to drift away from him.

Well anyway, once I recovered my senses, I took off my raincoat and just dropped it in a corner. He didn't have a knob or anything else to hang it on. Then I followed him through the open double glass doors into his great big sitting room.

My friend is going to get married again. What a real shocker. Who woulda thunkit?

"Yep." Sam said that in one of his "excited" voices. To him, that meant "again."

Now, let me take a moment to mention that Sam has a bunch of different types of voices. I know this because as I said, I have known him a long time. I'm kind of a student of human nature, so I tend to notice things about people. You know, things that are maybe just a little bit different from how other people are.

Well, anyway, Sam has this "excited" voice where he sort of talks through his nose. His early morning "grumpy" voice is usually pitched so very low, and he barely opens his mouth, so you can hardly hear and understand what he's trying to say. It gets a little bit better after his second cup of coffee. He also has what I call his "angry" voice, and I have heard that a few times. In addition, he has one voice that he has also used on occasion that goes way beyond what I would call anger. Maybe it'd be called his "rage" voice. I'll mention his special profanity a little later.

Sitting there, I said with my own inquisitive voice, "Now Sam, what in the world's going on that you're suddenly gonna get married again? I didn't even know you were dating anybody around here enough to say you were going steady." I'm sure my questioning frown showed as I spoke.

"Well, I'll admit it is kind of sudden," replied Sam with that foolish-looking grin on his face, "but it just happened and I thought you might be interested. By the way, try not to let your wet raincoat run on my floor. When the floor gets wet the varnish gets spotted and it's a devil getting the floor all the same color again."

"Sorry," I said. "Where's a paper towel? I'll wipe it up for you." I stood and moved toward where I'd left my wet raincoat. I picked it up and tossed it out onto the front porch. It's painted and I presumed impervious to wetness damage.

"Stand by," he said, glancing at the small puddle. He's a nice, considerate host—didn't even ask me to fetch my own towels.

After Sam got back from the rear of his house with the towels, and I dried the floor, we moved back into his big sitting room and sat down again. I just continued to hold the wet towels in my hand, kind of hoping to spot a wastebasket, but I didn't. As many times that I've been over to Sam's house, I don't believe I ever noticed a wastebasket.

He continued. "You know, old buddy, this was somewhat of a surprise to me too. I've been corresponding on the Internet with this little lady out in Wichita Falls for a couple of months. That's in Texas, you know. Up near the Red River. Not too far from the Oklahoma border. There's a big Air Force base about four miles up the road from the city. Anyway, her given name is Rowena, but she goes by Clemmy." (I might add here and now that I was never told and never figured out why she had a perfectly decent real name and a different kind of nickname.) At this point Sam hesitated a brief moment as he obviously noted my right eyebrow drop a little while I pondered her name. Then he continued. "She's originally from here in North Carolina, but has been out there living with a recently-widowed aunt. Anyway, I was rummaging through the Internet one night and got into a chat room with her. One thing led to another and now suddenly, we're going to get married. We haven't set a date yet, but I guess she'll want to do that when she settles on what's going to happen with her aunt."

"My gosh Sam," I exclaimed in all seriousness, "This doesn't seem like you at all. You're really going through with this?" I hoped my questioning his decision was not going to make him mad at me.

Oh, yes, by the way, when Sam is angry, watch out, because he just might go into that real loud "angry" voice of his and then a temper tantrum. I've never seen him hit anybody or anything like that, but once I did see him throw a small coffee cup right out a window. And boy, what a fling! Now, I know that Sam never played professional baseball, but that night, you'd have thought he was pitching in the majors. What accuracy. Moreover, real hard, too. Didn't hit the edge of the window or even that bush outside. I heard it bump into a tree and shatter into what must've been ten thousand pieces. Glad I wasn't in the way! We were having coffee one evening and poor Sam became incensed because he had already gotten three of those very annoying suppertime telephone calls in the span of half an hour. You know the kind: the ones where some person on the other end of the line, whom you don't know and doesn't know you, calls you by your first name in a real friendly voice and tries to talk you into buying a new phone system, or set of compact disks, or swamp property, or something stupid like that. Well, this fourth call came in while Sam and I were trying to have a real serious conversation about fishing. Well, actually, he was doing the talking—I, the listening. Sam loves to fish, and I like it pretty good too. Maybe not as much as he does.

Anyway, Sam listened to about five seconds of that person's voice, slammed the receiver down on its cradle and let out a howl. My blood ran cold when I heard the viciousness in his voice and saw the wild-eyed expression of wrath on his face. I really didn't know what he was going to do. He grabbed his cup that fortunately was empty and really gave it a toss right out the open window. Now that seemed to relieve his anger, because then my buddy turned right back to me as if nothing had even happened, and continued, "and you give it a twenty-pound-test leader about thirty feet long, and then tie on your number five swivel. You've already hooked on your Clark spoon, remember."

I just can't understand how he was able to do that. It really flabbergasts me—blows my mind, don't you know. He went through that entire explosion of anger—red-faced, glasses almost falling off and everything. He fired that cup and then continued as if nothing more had happened than a fly had landed on his ear and he needed to flick it away. Things like that make Sam a pretty interesting guy in my book.

"You know," Sam continued philosophically after he threw that cup, "if they're biting, it's pretty easy, but sometimes you can fish for several hours, using every technique known to man and not snag a thing. You may lose a planer or a rig or two on occasion also, but after all, that's part of what makes deep sea fishing."

I knew all this, of course, because I've been deep sea fishing a bunch of times. Besides, Sam had given me this same lecture twice previously in the past year. Nevertheless, he's my buddy, so I let him repeat it again. Friends do that, don't they?

My own opinion is that, of course, going out on a turbulent body of water and bouncing around on a boat for several hours without anything like a decent fish to show for it might not really be considered much fun by some folks. I guess it's a "guy thing." Sorta macho, you know.

Speaking of "macho," I met a niece of Sam's down there at the docks in Wilmington, North Carolina, one time. He told me that she was a real-life sea captain; had her Coast Guard captain's license, her own commercial fishing boat and everything. Seemed like a feminine kind of person to be doing what the average individual would think is a rough man's job. She was a pretty thing—very prissy, nicely made up with blush, lipstick, painted fingernails, fancy hairdo and all. She certainly didn't look like most of the fishing boat captains I'd ever met. Frankly, I'd never met a woman charter-boat captain before. Didn't even know they made 'em. Now, I don't know for sure, but I don't think she even chewed tobacco. At least that one time I didn't spot any telltale brown dribble around the corners of her pretty mouth. I suppose she must have enjoyed running a fishing boat, though. It's a living, as they say.

So anyway, back to my story … that rainy night over at Sam's. We were just sitting there on two of his couches facing each other and I continued, "Sam, my good friend, this doesn't sound like you at all. Now just tell me why you're going to marry this girl. Am I to understand that you haven't actually met her in person yet?"

"No, not yet," he said. "But we're going to try to meet about halfway in the next few weeks. Somewhere between here and there, maybe some place like Nashville. That's over in Tennessee, you know. That's really closer to me then her, but I figure that this is one way to see if she is really serious about us doing the thing. You know, you just can't tell about people. They might say one thing and really mean another. I want to find out if she's really a nice person or just stringing me along."

"Do you know much at all about her? Have you even seen what she looks like?" I was still trying to figure out what to do with the wet paper towels in my hand.

Sam became withdrawn (unusual for my friend). "Well, she did send me a photo. That's what I got in the mail this morning. It mostly shows just her face. I think it must have been cut off a group picture of some sort. She said it wasn't a recent one, but it was the only one she had. Wanna see it?"

"Yeah, sure." What else was I to say?

With that, Sam got up and went upstairs to retrieve it. I wondered why, if it was all that important to drag me over to his house late on a rainy night, he didn't bring it down stairs with him when I arrived.

Now, Sam's been married before. Twice, to be exact. Moreover, my wife, Bobbie, and I met both of those women. Joyce, the first one, was a dilly! That woman needed a darn lion-tamer instead of a husband, if you ask me. To say she was hot-tempered would be like calling the Mississippi a creek. I'm not sure how she ever got Sam to marry her and I'm surprised that their marriage lasted eight years, what with her terrible temper, as well as that of Sam's. Of course, their three kids seemed to have turned out okay. Looks like it to me, anyway. One is a veterinarian in Raleigh, and the other two are schoolteachers—one up in Asheville and the other in Greensboro.

Sam came into my office one time before he and Joyce had separated, with scratches and little plastic bandages darn near all over him. Seems like Joyce didn't like Sam going out and buying a pickup truck. (This was in the days before pickups were the rage.) Apparently, he just decided to do it and then went and bought the thing. Didn't even ask Joyce about it beforehand or anything. He traded in their one-year-old gold-colored Cadillac convertible for it. (They were pretty much into the country club set at the time, had a nice split-level right beside the eleventh hole, and you "needed" a Caddy just to fit in with that crowd.) Seems to me he should have at least mentioned his thoughts to her beforehand. But then, what do I know? Anyway, either the pickup truck or the fingernail scratches seemed to end that union. Sam never showed any desire to want to talk about it much. Maybe he's embarrassed that something he tried didn't work. Incidentally, he sold that truck about two months later. Something about it being underpowered, if I remember correctly. Then he bought a big light green Lincoln Continental.

Well now, wife number two was Carol and she was a real winner. What a gorgeous doll! And so sweet! At least that was my impression of her. She was always real nice to my wife, Bobbie, and me anyway, and always seemed to try to cater to Sam's every wish. (I expect that would be somewhat difficult.) Now this time Sam definitely did his wife wrong. No doubt about it. Here he was, with what I think would have been a fantastic wife. He should have been quite happy with their union, but he went out and had a stupid affair with some young thing he met over at the Middle Carolina Junior College here in Aquaville. For some dumb reason Sam escorted this coed to a big rock and roll concert there on campus. At least a dozen of Sam's acquaintances spotted them. Four, as I understand it, called Carol that evening before he even got home. Sam had told Carol that he was going out to a men's social club where he was a member. So much for marriage number two. Sam never has seemed to want to talk about that one either.

I don't know … I try to have a lot of respect for Sam. After all, he is my friend, and I still think he has a lot of smarts, but he does seem to go off on some really idiotic tangents sometimes. I'll tell you about some of them in a little while. Non-thinking, strange, idiotic, zany, foolish and stupid might be reasonable descriptions of some of them. Nevertheless, to repeat, he is my friend so I guess that I'm supposed to stick by him through thick and thin and be a good buddy. That's my life's obligation I guess.

After a couple of minutes, Sam came back downstairs with his prize.

"Here she is. It's sort of a small photo, but you can get an idea of what she looks like," said Sam as he proudly shoved the picture into my dry right hand. "What do you think of her?"

I'll tell you one thing: I was so stunned, that I darn near dropped the snapshot. I almost dropped the wet paper towels, too. Now here was this picture, not much bigger than a postage stamp, and it showed a rather round face with absolutely no eyebrows. At least not that I could see anyway. She wore long, long dangling earrings, hanging down way beyond where I suspect her shoulders would have been. I figured that if she turned her head sideways real fast, those darn things would smack her right in the mouth. And she had a couple of doodads stuck in the top part of her right ear and what looked like five or six running down in a sort of "S" curve in her left ear. It's a wonder she even had any ear tissue left where holes could be punched! Moreover, she had pulled her hair back so severely that her ears stuck out pretty far. My guess is that those ears of hers were pretty darn easy to pierce, jutting out as they did. It was a black and white photograph, so I couldn't tell what color her hair might be, but it looked kind of dark. Matter of fact, her forehead was so high, I wondered if she was beginning to develop male pattern baldness, but maybe it was just an optical illusion because of those missing eyebrows.

You know, I've always had this thing about teeth. Maybe that's why I became a dental laboratory technician. I don't know why exactly, but I've always felt that while a woman might may not have a particularly pretty face, if she has a nice smile, it kind of tempers things down pretty much. Know what I mean? Anyway, this woman was obviously missing her left second top tooth! Nothing there in the photo but a dark spot. Gone. Moreover, she was smiling real broadly. I just can't understand it. Shouldn't have cost too much for a dentist to stick *something* in there for her. Shoot, I might have done it for her for nothing—just to help her smile out a little bit. Overall, I must admit that her photo simply grossed me out! However, I'd never tell Sam that. He's my friend.

"Well, Sam," I said in all seriousness, "from what I can see with this little photo, she looks like a very healthy and interesting person." I was right proud of my tactful response to him.

"Yeah," he replied with a peculiar gleam in his eye as he nudged up beside me and looked over my shoulder. "She's quite a looker, isn't she?"

(I couldn't help but think to myself, *"hooker" rather than "looker" would be more likely.)*

"Now Sam, my friend," I said with some trepidation. "I'll have to be honest with you. She doesn't look like the kind of gal that I'd have expected you to get latched up with." I sucked in my breath, wondering what kind of response I might receive from my buddy. "I mean, you don't really know much about her at all, do you? I'm not so sure you ought to go through with marrying her. You said you haven't even met her in person. Deciding to marry somebody you've never even met sounds scary. Especially in this day and time."

"Now you listen, Hank," retorted Sam emphatically. His face developed a stern look with several creases across his forehead. "I know a lot more about her than you might think. You can tell a lot about a person just by exchanging e-mails." With that said, he took the photo back from me rather abruptly. He didn't snatch it exactly, but let me know in no uncertain terms that I no longer had any use for it. He looked down at the picture again. He presented a *Mona Lisa* smile. "Hank, the marriage is going to happen. And, for the next while, you're gonna see me spending a bunch of my time around here fixing this place up for her." He grinned while still peering at the photo. "You just watch. This place'll really show some nice changes. I've got a lot of great ideas."

A lot of great ideas. That statement made me cringe. As I said earlier, Bobbie and I had seen some of Sam's "great" ideas turn to chaos. I'll tell you about a few a little later.

Actually, his house had been vacant for a long time before he bought it. He got it at an auction for a pretty good price. Before that, he lived in a small efficiency apartment across town following his divorce from Carol.

Then he promptly stood, turned and walked upstairs, saying over his shoulder, "I'm heading to bed. Want something to drink? You know where the fridge is."

Being that I usually go to bed around eleven at night and it was now twelve-thirty in the morning, I graciously declined. Kind of rude, I thought, to just up and leave me like that. Anyway, I yelled up the stairs at him, "No, Sam, but thanks. I'm heading on home now. Guess I'll see you tomorrow."

"Okay, g'night old buddy," he spoke down from his room. "Hey, turn out the lights down there when you leave and lock the door behind you."

"Yeah, sure," I said. "Keep me informed." With that in mind, I went to the porch and put on my raincoat. Then, reaching back inside the front door, I snapped the latch, flipped off the lights, and then proceeded to pull on my still slightly mud-caked boots. Kind of hard to do in the dark. Humph. Wrong foot. I should have put on my boots before I turned out the light. I got my hands muddy again, but since I was still carrying those wet paper towels, wiped the mud off on them and carried 'em home with me. Threw 'em in my own trash can.

Big deal, locking his front door. Sam's house has these great big windows that almost go from floor to ceiling. Moreover, they don't have any locks. A six-year-old kid could easily get in if he wanted to. Maybe Sam figures there will not be any six-year-olds trying.

I went home that night pondering: Is Sam crazy? Maybe he's just flipped. And, what is he finally going to do with his house and yard? I'll bet Bobbie and the rest of the neighborhood will be real happy to see some decent improvements over there. I had to think, though, that maybe Sam's idea of improvement might not be like the rest of the community. Time would tell.

I thought I really knew Sam. I'd seen him do some pretty weird things in the past, but little did I know what was coming; utterly astounding things—almost unbelievable, in a way.

CHAPTER 2

Sam, Bobbie and Me

Now, Sam's my best friend. Or at least, I like to call him that. Actually, maybe I should say he's more like a big brother. My father passed away when I was only ten years old, so my only sibling, Terry, who was eighteen when Dad died, was forced to become the "man" of the family. In effect, he became the one male I could look up to and try to emulate. And did I ever admire my brother, Terry! Why, in my youthful eyes, he could just do no wrong. And he was very patient with me when I goofed something up. Just like a father.

Terry and Sam were best buddies back then while I was growing up. They went just about everywhere together, played on the high school football team together (Sam played right end and Terry, defensive back), double dated frequently, and were college roommates over in Chapel Hill at the University of North Carolina. Our town of Aquaville is about a hundred miles southwest of there. After their graduation, Terry and Sam had even planned to set up a business together, but it didn't work out. Unfortunately, Terry was diagnosed with leukemia two months following his college graduation, dying four months after that.

I held his hand that last horrible night. Gasping for breath, Terry said, "I've talked with Sam … and … he has agreed to take over … for me as your … 'big brother.'" So for that reason, I gradually switched my allegiance from Terry to Sam. Wasn't the same, really.

Sam's father was a financial advisor and according to Terry, was a self-centered soul that ordered the entire family (two older sisters, both now passed away) around like he was a king or something. Apparently he didn't even allow

Sam's mom to speak out with her thoughts or advice much at all. Maybe that's why Sam became like he is; you might say, "bossy." I suppose my pal figured it was reasonable to do just like his dad did.

Consequently, Sam kind of automatically became what I guess could be called my best friend. On the other hand, I suppose I should say, if I really had a best friend (not including my wife), it'd be him. Maybe I don't really have a "best friend" if you want to call a best friend somebody that you can really unload on. You know, talk to about your concerns, mistakes, foibles, et cetera, and he'd just nod and say, "Yeah, I understand. That's okay, buddy."

You know what I mean when I say, "unload"? It is when you sort of unburden yourself of some concerns that you cannot really bring yourself to talk about with just anybody. It seems to me that this kind of friend would lend a sympathetic ear and not castigate you for something you said or did. There are times when you want to clear the air concerning your own personal feelings and thoughts without any fear of somebody throwing it back at you later. This is where I think a "best friend" would come in.

Seems like whenever I get the urge to unload on my good old pal Sam, and I tell him something that I did that maybe I shouldn't have done, he winds up giving me the old "tsk, tsk" and a stern—and usually lengthy—lecture on why I should not have done what I did. This kind of stuff sometimes makes me feel like I'm a little boy again and my daddy's scolding me. Nevertheless, he's the closest person I have to talk to, so I do it anyway.

Luckily, Sam inherited quite a bunch of money from his deceased dad's estate. He has a degree in accounting from UNC, but I don't think he's ever given any thought to working at it as a business. Personally, I can't help but think that he'd be a lot better off with a steady job. Maybe he'd have less time to go off on his never-ending screwy schemes. I'll tell you about a bunch of 'em in a little while.

Now, Sam's a nice clean-cut sort of person. About an inch over six feet tall, square-jawed, with a kind of sharp nose, high cheekbones, medium build, and bifocals. He suffers from a moderate case of alopecia. (That's actually "male-pattern" hair loss of course, but he prefers to call it by its scientific name.) His hair used to be almost jet black, but not anymore. A couple of years ago—before he moved next door to us—he tried to grow a beard. It, in my humble opinion, looked awful. It was real splotchy-appearing—with a little gray here, a speck of pure white there, and the rest black. I told him it didn't look very good that way and he got real mad at me. He said snappily, "It's none of your business. Period." However, I did notice that when I saw him a week or so later, that beard had transmogrified itself into a thin, Clark Gable-like mustache. He looked foolish with that also, but I declined to speak to him about it. He was clean-faced when I saw him about six weeks later. He did finally admit to me that he seemed to be having trouble getting dates during that time. Of course, now into his middle age, he's getting that typical spread; his chest has now slipped down to around his waist.

Sam's pretty intelligent and likes to give intensively detailed lectures to just about anybody that will listen. For instance, Sam and I were in a hardware store last week and I just happened to make a casual comment to the store-owner about the problem of inadequate parking out on the street in front. I suggested to him that maybe the town could rearrange the parking spots on the street, and that might make for more availability for cars. However, Sam proceeded to spew forth a fifteen-minute dissertation on how *he'd* run the town. He took a blank piece of paper from off the counter and outlined how the traffic patterns and parking arrangements should be adjusted, where new stoplights needed to be, and how many cops should be out on the street at which hours of the day and night. The store clerk was obviously flabbergasted, but yet, remarkably patient, and just stood there speechless. I guess things like this make Sam feel good. Or superior, or something. I've often suspected that he's really just a very insecure guy and does all this talking just to try to prove to himself, as well as others, that he's as good as anybody. I can't prove that, though.

Even though I've always liked Sam, and would like to consider myself one of *his* closest friends, I've never been able to get him to unload many of his difficulties on me. I would personally like it if he did, because that would show me that he trusts and respects me. I wonder sometimes if he just can't accept the idea that I'm a grown man. Okay, I might lack some of his experience, but by darn, I still have a reasonably sharp mind. Maybe he just can't get away from that "big brother" relationship he has with me, and as a result, has little confidence in anything I might say to him because, after all, I'm almost nine years his junior.

On the other hand, maybe he thinks that he never did anything wrong. Or, maybe he'll never admit—to himself, or me—that anything he ever did was wrong. Somehow, he just grew up with an attitude of supreme confidence or arrogance or something. Nevertheless, a lot of things I have seen him do make me wonder a little bit about him.

Bobbie says, "That boy has entirely too much time on his hands." She declares that he badly needs a wife to point him in better directions. I thought *it's probably Bobbie's wifely pressures that help keep me from getting in trouble.*

By the way, as I have mentioned, Bobbie is my sweet wifey. Her real name is Barbara Anne, but "Bobbie" works best. (Except whenever I might be somewhat upset with her, and then she becomes "Barbara Anne!") We've been happily married for quite a number of years now, and mutually decided not to have any children. Sometimes I sort of wish we had some kids, but on the other hand, it does give us a chance to go to places almost whenever we like, rather than having to find a baby-sitter or such.

Bobbie likes to help other folks, and she does some baby-sitting for some of her friends on occasion. She comes from a long line of medical types. Her uncle was a physician, her mother and grandmother, nurses. In fact, her grandmother served as a nurse over in France during the first World War. Her dad was a mechanic at a local Buick dealership.

Bobbie has a couple of nieces working on their nursing degrees at the UNC Nursing School over in Chapel Hill. She volunteers at the nursing home across the street from our house fairly often, too. Since she knows that I don't care too much for that kind of stuff, she usually doesn't drag me along.

Bobbie and I were high school classmates, but we didn't marry until we both finished our college work. She hasn't changed much since then. Her beautiful hair remains a lovely auburn, but I think it was her gorgeous eyes that originally attracted me to her. They're the most striking shade of blue that you'd ever see. Her smooth-textured face is in perfect symmetry. In fact, now that I think about it, her entire body is about as perfect as I would want. And thank goodness, she knows just what kinds of clothes to wear and in what circumstances. She makes me so proud. Oh, I do love that lady.

She never has cared much for Sam. She says she sees right through him—doesn't respect him. She says he is a "blow hard." I think I know why, but I like him anyway. (I have wondered sometimes in a few spells of melancholy if it wasn't that I *needed* him, rather than liking him.) Terry probably assumed that I would readily accept him as my "big brother."

Bobbie and I've had quite a few "discussions" about my relationship with Sam. I guess I can call them discussions. Actually, we've had some of our worst arguments of our marriage about my relationship with him. At the height of her anger she's even accused me of having "an improper relationship" with my pal. She wondered aloud about Sam's masculinity. Needless to say I surely had to defend both myself as well as Sam from that assault. About all I could do was say to her, "Look at the number of lady friends he has had. Besides, you know me and how I feel about things like that." Although that seemed to put an end to it, coming from a quiet, conventional family as she did, I guess there's no way that she can understand why I accept Sam as I do. She never had to endure a parent's death so early in life as I was forced to do. I felt a deep need to grasp whoever I could—and Sam was it.

After high school, I went to technical school over in Durham, North Caro-lina, and became a dental laboratory technician. I worked at my trade for a while, but when an opportunity opened up to buy a dental laboratory, I took the plunge. Glad I did, because my business has thrived. I now have nine employees and this kind of enables me to take things as easy as I desire. In fact, maybe you could say I'm already retired. My wife often says that maybe I ought to spend more time at the lab. I think that's just because she gets tired of hav-ing me hanging around the house so much of the time. What the heck, she's got plenty of friends and hobbies to occupy her time, so why should I not play "lazy" once in a while … okay, a lot?

Now, of course, even though he knows my name is actually Harold, Sam has always called me Hank—from day one. I really don't know why, unless it is because he knows nobody else calls me Hank and maybe he figures that makes him more special. Seems to me that Hank would be short for a name like Henry or maybe even the French-style Henri or something like that, rather than short for Harold. A few folks call me Har (rhymes with "hair"), some Harold, and most people just call me Harry. But Sam calling me Hank? Oh well, it's okay, I suppose, since he's my buddy.

I used to hate it in elementary school when my so-called pals would call me "Har-Har" (rhyming with "car-car"), and then laugh about that name until they nearly split their sides. I would try as hard as I could to figure out some silly names I could call them back that might even up the score, but I never could. Except for "Looney Tunes" Johnson. Poor kid was slightly slow. Really, it was pretty mean of us fourth graders to call him that, but we did it anyway and he just accepted it with a childish grin.

But, then there was the class bully. Oh boy, you sure did have to watch your step—and hang on tight to your lunch. Or anything else that you happened to value. Sheer terror in the halls of learning. This bully apparently had a rather strong inferior complex and picked fights with numerous classmates—nearly always winning and bloodying some noses. That scary thing even chased me home once. I barely got there in time to avoid a serious thrashing. I was pretty good at running through narrow openings in shrubbery. Her name was Beulah

Belle Baldwin, and she was at least a head taller and fifty pounds heavier than anyone else in our group. The school had held her back a couple of years, and Beulah obviously hated everyone in our room. Maybe she hated everybody, period. (Can't say I'd blame her.) Therefore, we quickly learned to avoid her if at all possible. She always seemed to have it in for me—teasing me and often jerking my pants up in the rear—and there was not a thing I could do about it.

She had this little singsong saying about me: "Har-ry, Har-ry, sweet potat-ee." I knew it didn't make sense, but she liked it, so what was I to do? I saw her at a high school class reunion five years ago and she was no longer the tallest one around; broadest, yes, just not the tallest. I expect she weighed in at over four hundred pounds. Must have been a good eater. Said she'd already been married four times, had seven young ones, and was looking around for a fifth idiot (my word, not hers) to marry.

By the way, I'm five ten, weighing in at—shall I say it?—one sixty. Near that anyway. My hair color changes magically by the seasons. And no, I do not use hair coloring. I'm more or less a red head in the winter months and then I lighten up to close to blond during the summer. Figure that. And yeah, I have a few facial freckles. So what? I started my instrumental music in elementary school, stopping briefly after Terry passed away. Actually, I stopped nearly everything for a while. When I finally came around, I developed numerous hobbies that kept my idle hands and fingers busy. For instance, I carved small animals out of cakes of soap … without cutting myself … well, not very often, anyway. I didn't realize it then, but maybe I was practicing using my fingers so that I could get into dental lab school later. You need pretty nimble fingers to do dental laboratory work.

I'm already wearing bifocals, My ophthalmologist tells me it's a little early for my age bracket, but I suppose it's because I work at so much minutiae in my lab. I fully expect to add hearing aids to my armamentarium some day. Either that or maybe I can train Bobbie to learn to raise her voice level even when she's not angry at me.

Oh yes, both Bobbie and I retain all our natural teeth.

❦   ❦   ❦

Working with artificial teeth gives me a chance to have a little fun some-times. Once four years ago, the local country club was holding a big New Year's dance. The directors hired a ten-piece dance band—promising a lot of slow tunes. Bobbie and I like dancing to slow "goldie oldies." Well, Sam and I got to talking about the upcoming dance and he said he wanted to play a trick on his date. We went over to my lab where I took an impression of his mouth. After that, I made up a set of real weird-looking false teeth that fit right over his natural ones. Man, I really outdid myself, too. I mean, when he slipped that appliance into his mouth, you'd have thought he was a monster from Hollywood. He loved it, and told me he knew he'd really have fun displaying it at the party.

Well, things didn't quite go as he had planned that night. Bobbie and I met him and his date—an attractive blond lady named Patricia something—there at the club, and we shared a table. She seemed kind of reserved, but I presumed it was her first date with Sam. Bobbie and I liked her right off; very personable—with us anyway.

Well, as the evening went on, old Sam started imbibing perhaps just a bit too much for his own good.

After a while Sam leaned over to me and said, "Here goes. Let's see what happens. Fun time!" He slipped the appliance out of his pocket and into his mouth. Grinning broadly, he exposed it to Patricia and Bobbie. Both screamed. Then he rose and went around the room grabbing as many of the women that he could, trying to kiss them. He got some real good wild-eyed expressions and screams, I'll say that. Some of the single guys thought it pretty funny. However, one of the married fellows saw what Sam was doing and yelled, "Get the hell away from my wife!" Sam backed away from her slightly, still grinning and looking foolish. However, maybe her husband had been drinking excessively also. He stepped up to Sam and knocked him down right in the middle of the dance floor. It stunned him and bloodied his nose. That action caused the band to stop playing and everybody stopped dancing, standing around as if waiting to see if an actual fist fight was eminent. The angry guy grabbed his wife and pulled her out of the room. Sam's actions embarrassed poor Patricia so much that she immediately called for a taxi and left.

Bobbie and I helped Sam up off the floor, tended to his nosebleed, and ushered him out to his car. After a few minutes, I checked with him and he said he felt that he could drive home to his apartment okay. Bobbie and I decided to follow, just to make sure he made it safely. I don't approve of driving after drinking, but at that moment, he did seem to be pretty much in control. Maybe the knockdown blow helped sober him up.

Bobbie said, "I'm not so sure about this."

The roads were still a little slick from a rain earlier in the evening, but it had now stopped and things didn't look too bad. However, as we were driving along behind him, a deer suddenly popped out from the trees right in front of

Sam's car. He swerved to avoid the animal, but his car skidded off the highway, and turned over in a muddy ditch thick with undergrowth. Just about the time we got our own vehicle stopped, flames started breaking out from under the hood of Sam's car. I jumped out and ran over to his aid. I saw right away that he had a big bruise on his forehead and was a little dazed, but otherwise he seemed okay. I reached in, popped his seat belt, and began to tug him out, just as the flames started expanding towards both of us. I was scared to death that his car might blow up and injure Sam as well as me. Well, me, mostly. Luckily, he was fairly limp, so I could manage him pretty well. I dragged Sam back along the side of the road and propped him up against our car. His continued to burn, but fortunately didn't explode. Bobbie got out a small hand towel we always carry in the car, and wiped off his face. His nose had started bleeding again and he was pretty muddy from the ditch.

Some other passersby had apparently called the police, because it wasn't long before the sirens started wailing on their way to the scene. We quickly stuck Sam in the back seat of our car and took him to his apartment before the cops arrived at the wreck. They could have had a real good time with him, since he had alcohol on his breath. I knew this was probably illegal, but after all, Sam's my good buddy, drunk or sober.

Sam telephoned and talked to the police about the accident the next day, and got everything worked out. They didn't even give him a ticket. Sam has always been a great talker. Maybe he should have become a politician, the way he can use his mouth. I mean, my friend Sam can smooth-talk just about anybody; well, not Bobbie.

You want to know something? Sam has never thanked either of us for what we did to help him that night. Never even said a single word about our heroic actions. Sort of makes me wonder why I bothered. Makes me kind of angry, in fact.

I got so muddy that night that I tracked reddish-brown mud all over my car's floor rug. Even the auto wash never could get it all out the next day. The floor rug still had mud stains on it when I finally sold that car two years later.

And poison ivy! Oh, yes. I'm very allergic to the stuff. I've even been downwind from a burning brush pile that obviously contained some poison ivy or poison oak and caught "the itch." I got a good case of it from scrambling around in that ditch that night. I'm telling you, I had such a swollen face, neck and wrists that I could barely move for two weeks. My doctor gave me some kind of shots to help relieve the itching, but it was pretty rough for me for a time.

But, nope—no thanks from Sam for saving his hide. Zero. None. Nada. Zip. Bobbie said, "See?"

CHAPTER 3

Sam's Old House

We live in an area of town that includes many older homes that have histories tied to them. There are a lot of these up and down our street. One elegant mansion is on the other side of Sam's property, and four more are across the street and down the block a way. We have an absolutely gorgeous street and we're (Bobbie and myself) quite proud to live on it. A lot of yard work has been done by our neighbors, so that—particularly in the spring—it's like something out of the movies. We have a dazzling display of white as well as pink dogwoods up and down the block. With a great deal of pride by the owners, yards are kept manicured like golf course greens. One owner's older father-in-law, that lives with them, actually goes out and hand-picks dandelions one-by-one from that yard.

Most of our neighbors are bankers, doctors, financial advisors. A dentist lives on the other side of Sam. All the yards are kept immaculate, to say the least. All of these houses are fronted with Azaleas of various colors. Yep, really pretty in the spring. Bobbie selected ours—pure white—and planted blue ajuga all around the beds. Simply magnificent in my opinion. Then, she, as with most of our neighbors, stuck real pretty rows of yellow and purple pansies all along our driveways. No doubt about it, the pride our neighborhood takes in appearance is outstanding. And in the fall, the multitude of oaks, poplars, and maples continue the trend with their magnificent explosions of color.

I'm not sure of this, but I don't think George Washington slept in any of these homes. Maybe Robert E. Lee, though.

The town ladies (no gentlemen, interestingly) have brought together an organization called "The Aquaville Preservation Society." They've designated certain residences as "historic," if they are either at least seventy-five years old, or are located within certain boundaries of our town. If a residence has received the said "historic" designation, the Society has determined that it would need to be preserved in pretty-much its original state.

Our own home is included in the bunch of course, and Bobbie and I have spent a moderate sum having the outside trim properly painted and re-roofed over the years.

Bobbie has the green thumb in our family, certainly not me. I do keep our lawn mown, and I'll dig an occasional hole for one of her plantings, but if I so much as stick a plant into said hole, it's sure to die. She, however, can almost take a dry twig and bring forth a lovely flower; magical.

When Sam bought his house next door, everybody assumed that he'd restore it to its original elegance. He could certainly afford it. It would have been a nice touch, but Sam declined to improve it to its proper state. This, as you might imagine, irritated the Society a great deal. They sent him letter after letter and one Sunday afternoon even gathered right out front and picketed. It so happens that Sam and I were sitting on his front porch chatting when they gathered with their bull horn and signs. Their leader had a chant for them to holler: "Hey, hey, hey! Can't, can't, can't! Paint, paint, paint." They even brought out about a dozen wheelchair-bound residents of the nursing home across the street from our house. It disturbed and embarrassed me, but ol' Sam just sat there grinning, rocking and sipping on a cold beer. He waved at them. The group didn't seem to appreciate that.

Sweet Bobbie, a long-time member of said preservation society, knowing the plans to picket Sam's house, declined to appear. Wise lady, my sweet wifey.

The Society's founder and President For Life, the widow Clareece Hopkins Simpson, actually tried to have the town's Board of Aldermen declare the entire area a "Designated Preservation Zone." That would have made it a lawful requirement. I must say, the five gentlemen on the Board were quite polite and patient with her. However, they declined to make such a declaration. When she stormed out of the room that night, she slammed the paned door so hard that the glass shattered.

❦   ❦   ❦

Sam's house is one of the oldest in Aquaville. It was probably the finest at one time. It has two additional stories on top of that high first floor I told you about. One of those levels is a big attic that is filled with all kinds of the weirdest stuff you would ever find. Sam told me that the junk ("junque"?) preceded his ownership. Maybe he bought the house just to get his hands on all the various objects up there. I can't figure out why he'd want any of it, though. Frankly I don't know why he'd even want such a big old house in the first place. All that for one person. Such inefficiency. I went up in that musty old loft with him one time and had an opportunity to just look at and poke around in all the stuff. Darn, whoever lived in this house before Sam sure had some strange ideas of what to buy. But maybe it was stuff that was given to them, and they didn't know what else to do with it. Perhaps the house had multiple owners. I do know that the house remained vacant for at least fifteen years before Sam bought it.

While we were up there, I spotted several old trunks, just filled almost to overflowing with nineteenth century clothes—well, maybe early twentieth—and a bunch of ancient dried-up leather high-topped women's shoes. And in a beat-up crate lying in a dusty corner, I found a complete World War I second lieutenant's uniform. Made out of brown wool, it was sort of a surprise to me that it was not full of moth holes. Shuffling through it, however, I did find two small remnants of mothballs lying in the bottom of the box. It actually had an original "Sam Brown" belt with it. And by golly, an old German soldier's fancy helmet, also from that war, I think. The darn thing was made of leather of all things, and also dried out of shape. It was the type that had a sort of metal spike on top. That pointed top probably didn't do the German soldier much good, but maybe it looked good in parades.

There was also a big box full of some 1930s and 1940s era sheet music that must have belonged to a big dance band of some sort. I don't know why they (whoever "they" were) didn't carry it with them whenever they moved from the house. Since I play saxophone and clarinet a little bit, I was somewhat interested in the music. It was for saxes, trumpets, trombones, guitar and drums. As I glanced over those various sheets, I had immediate pleasant memories of some rather halcyon evenings listening on my radio to dance band concerts—"from the Blue Room of the such-and-such hotel in New York City."

They were for some nice tunes. Those music sheets would play a role in my life a little later.

It just occurred to me that maybe I have never gotten around to telling you about the rest of Sam's house. Describing it, I mean. Well anyway, it is an old, sort of ante bellum-type structure. It has of course, this nice wrap-around porch where he and I have spent a lot of time rocking and talking. The big wide porch goes around on both sides to about a quarter of the way toward the rear. He has a smaller screened-in porch on the back, just off the kitchen. I think that before the introduction of running water to our town there was a hand pump down to a well under that little porch. This house had the first floor built up higher than you'd normally expect for some reason or another. Maybe to increase the height of the basement without digging so far down into the ground? But, what do I know? Anyway, there are those darn fourteen steps up to his front porch. Lining said porch are six fancy columns. Real pretty except for the chipped paint. The tops of them have very detailed hand carved (I guess) filigree around them. Real pretty stuff in its day, I'm sure.

Anyway, you go in his front door and you are in a pretty big hallway or foyer. At least twelve-foot high ceilings all over. The steps to upstairs are just across the foyer and go up for a little way, then swing a dogleg left to the second floor.

Downstairs though, immediately to your right is his big three-couch sitting room that I will get back to in a moment.

To your left off this hall is his never-used dining room. I say "never-used," but I really didn't quite mean it that way. It's used all right; just not for dining. No table or chairs in there. Just a rather bland chandelier hanging down in the middle of the room. Obviously, this room was at one time a rather elegant spot in the house because centered on the ceiling was about a six-foot diameter bas-relief ring surrounding the place where the chandelier hangs. All plastered to look as if it were hand-carved ivy. Darn pretty stuff if you ask me. In there he keeps a multitude of old magazines—stacked all over the floor. I'll bet he has over a thousand of those things. I spotted copies of *Life, Colliers,* and *Saturday Evening Post.* Also, *Newsweek* and *Time* and a few on boating and fishing stuff. I've often wondered if he ever read them before he started stacking them up in there, or ever heard of recycling. On real humid days you can catch the smell of aging paper when you first enter Sam's house.

Moving straight on back, bypassing the stairs, you come to the kitchen on the left and his downstairs bathroom on the right. Somebody in the past has remodeled the kitchen, putting in the latest and nicest utilities you would ever need. I think the realtor had it done, so as to more easily dump the big house on somebody. He has this big stainless steel doublewide refrigerator like the ones you may see in all the elegant home-remodeling magazines. And of course, there is the typical center console stove with all the copper-bottomed pots and pans lining one wall. Triple stainless steel sink, and all the rest. The countertops and floors were done in an elaborate Southwestern tile motif. Boy, I'll say it is a nice kitchen. Sure doesn't look like it fits the rest of the decor in Sam's house, though. Not really being a cook or chef, I'll say it looks nice anyway. I expect Bobbie would appreciate it more than I do.

Upstairs, is his master bedroom, with its sitting area over in front of the nice bay window. That's where he keeps his computer, and incidentally, it faces our house and yard. Maybe that's how he always seems to know when I'm home and out in my hammock. Somebody rebuilt the upstairs slightly so that the master bath opens directly off his bedroom. Then there are two more large bedrooms upstairs, a smaller guest bath and a closet-like opening to the narrow stairs up to the attic.

However, he did add something inside his house that sort of makes me wonder. He installed not one, but two ceiling fans in his master bedroom. They are set in such close proximity that they barely miss each other. I've never gone to the trouble to ask why he mounted them that way, but let me tell you that when you're in there and both those darn things are turned up on high speed at the same time, boy, you've really got a blow going. I was up there once last summer and I guess he'd forgotten how he had 'em set, because when we walked in, he hit the fan switches simultaneously. (They are mounted beside the light switch.) They both went on full blast and blew a whole mess of papers right off his table. It almost looked like it was snowing in there. Sam's face got red and he started using some strange-sounding cuss words. I'll tell you about those a little later. I didn't understand what he was saying, and at that moment, was not about to ask him for a repeat. After he turned the fans off, I helped him pick up his room. Sort of a mess, as you might expect. He said something about having to re-sort all those papers. Must have been about two hundred sheets. Oh well. I went on home after that incident.

Now, back to his sitting room on his first floor. This is the biggest room in Sam's house, and, as I said earlier, is just to the right as you walk through the front door into his foyer. This room is a real nice one, probably thirty-five by forty feet in size, painted a sort of robin's egg blue. It has very light pink curtains adorning each of the great big windows. A huge old three-tiered crystal chandelier hangs from the center of the ceiling (with six bulbs blown and two missing entirely.) This ceiling doesn't have a bas-relief thingamajig. I found that peculiar. There's a nice oriental rug on the floor that more or less ties the room's decor together. The room has at least eight scattered end tables and elaborate old floor lamps parked around randomly. Two of these have ornamental strings hanging down all around them real fancy-like. I can't recall which era that design came from, but know it was before I was born.

I figure it was actually just what most people would have called a living room, but Sam calls it his sitting room. He has three, count 'em three, full-sized sofas all arranged in more or less a triangle, so that whoever was sitting in one would easily be looking at the individual in either one of the other two. I think that's kind of efficient. Of course, if you ask me, none of the patterns and colors on these sofas matched the others—or anything else in the room for that matter. But, I'm not really an expert at things like that. I don't think I'd have arranged the room that way, but there was plenty of room and that is the way Sam decided to do it.

He also had a short-legged round solid teak coffee table about four feet in diameter parked right smack in the middle of these three couches. I commented on it once. Sam said, "A friend gave it to me. Seems like that expensive table had been parked out in my friend's garden for several years." He stopped speaking momentarily while he cleared his throat. "My friend—his name was Jonathan—moved away several years ago. He lived over on Eighth Street, down at the bottom of that big hill over there. Ever been over there? That's the hill where all us kids used to skate down." Sam was off on one of his long dissertations. "I remember how scared all of us were. We were afraid not to try it, though. Your brother Terry was usually the first one to go down. Sometimes there'd be three or four of us skating down holding on to each other's waist. We thought we were a train. I made it all the way down a few times, but one day my skate came off when I was almost at the bottom. Skinned my right knee pretty bad. Did I ever show you the scar?"

"No Sam, I don't believe you ever did." I was beginning to wonder if he'd ever get back to the original subject of the teak table. He pulled up his pant leg and displayed a faint scar right over his knee cap. Bravely, I said, "But back to the table?"

Pulling his pant leg back down and taking a sip of his sherry, he continued. Sam told me, "Jonathan—actually everybody called him Jon—told me that he used it out in his garden to rest potted plants on until it was darn near ruined and coming to pieces. That's when he asked me if I wanted the thing just for the teak wood. He knew I was into boating and, you know, boats require a lot of good teak." He sipped again. "You know that teak doesn't rot as fast as most other woods, don't you?"

"Yeah. I believe I read that somewhere."

"It's official name is *Tectona grandis*, but not many people know that."

"I didn't," I admitted. I didn't really care, either.

Sam continued with his lecture. "Yep. Using teak for furniture was started before the 19th century." He paused. No more words came forth. Was his mind working? "With the Victorian era."

"Oh."

"You know (I didn't) a lot of people think it's mainly grown in rain forests, but that's wrong. Actually, most of the teak used for furniture these days comes from tree farms." He looked over at me to see if I was still listening, or had fallen asleep. I wondered if many people fell asleep during one of his long, boring lectures. He continued, "Java has a lot of teak tree farms. Most of them were started by the Dutch in the early 1800s."

"Okay."

Oh, he was on a roll now. "Down east here in North Carolina, lots of boat builders use white oak for framing and top it off with pretty teak. They can't use red oak because it rots too fast. Much faster than white oak. Did you know that?"

"Nope."

"It all depends on the specific cellular structure of the particular wood. Want me to tell you about it?"

Uh-oh. Now I was in for it. How could I tell my pal that I wasn't interested, without hurting his feelings? Could I get the subject changed? I said, "You really did a good job refinishing that table."

Well, anyway, Sam took that old table, refinished it, and made it look just like new. I mean it's simply beautiful. It's sort of oriental looking. One thing that you couldn't help but notice, though, was that it was only about four inches high. Kind of low for a coffee table, I think. Sam told me he didn't have enough teak to make it higher as he was refinishing the table, and so he made do with what he had. I'd bet that some interior decorator would say it didn't fit with the rest of the decor in the room. But so far as I know, no decorator has ever been in Sam's house, so I suppose it really doesn't matter what's there. What with the blue walls and pink curtains, I'm guessing that a former owner was of the female persuasion.

Oh, by the way, there is not a regular closet in Sam's entire house. He's got all these great big rooms on the two main floors, and that large attic, as I explained. Also a huge basement, but not a single closet. Not one! I don't know who drew up the plans for that crazy house, but I'd have sure fired him when he showed the plans to me. No closets. What a crock! I can't believe a lady lived in said house without a single closet.

When I told Bobbie about that, she said Sam probably needed to get himself some armoires. I suppose he didn't think of that, though, because instead, he suspended a long galvanized one-inch diameter pipe from the ceiling and hung his clothes on that. Didn't look too great, but it did serve my friend's purpose I suppose.

Now, you really ought to see down in Sam's basement sometime. Well, maybe not, because you can't see very well down there. There's only one little twenty-five watt light bulb hanging down from the middle of the entire room. Note now that this basement is the size of the entire floor space of his house. Not even a single window to the outside even though the house was built up so high off the ground. And would you believe that there are (what else?) fourteen dark and steep steps down to the bottom? Some basement! It has a solid concrete floor. Well, mostly solid. Over on your left by the steps, you gotta be a tad careful, because there are a lot of broken pieces of cement. Looks to me as if somebody sometime or another decided that they wanted to change the floor or add something. (I don't think it was Sam, and I'll tell you a little later about his cement work.) Maybe a drainpipe for a basement toilet? I really don't know, and never asked Sam. Anyway, I guess when they got started banging on that old hard concrete floor, they figured that it was too hard to break up, or at any rate, too much trouble, so they just quit after a few dozen strokes. It left the floor sort of rocky in that one area, but the rest is okay. Of course, in reality, you can barely find the floor most of the time due to all the boxes of stuff that Sam has stored there. Even if you can't see very well without a flashlight, you can quickly get a good idea of what's there. Those boxes present a penetrating smell of damp, moldy, and rotting cardboard. I think, if it were me putting my things down there, I'd have built me some shelves first. Or at least, put some planks down on top of some bricks or concrete blocks, just to keep the things off the damp floor. Never have seen any sign of rats or, heaven help us, snakes down there, but then, I really don't usually go hunting for such animals in somebody else's house.

I'm not real sure what Sam has in all those boxes. It seems that, while you might not call Sam a "pack rat," maybe he is. I can't remember ever seeing him throw anything away. Maybe he figures that someday he will find a use for some of it. Personally, I kind of doubt that he remembers what all he actually has down there. Like I said, he's not one for keeping lists. Not that I know of, anyway.

Okay, back to the main level. Whenever I'm over there and have to use the toilet, I take advantage of his first floor bathroom. Now let me say, you really ought to see that room! First off, it's painted a real dark red with gray trim. Right pretty except where the gray paint is kind of wearing thin on the lino-leum floor. Doesn't match up color with anything else in the entire house. Nat-urally, it has the usual amenities, but in addition, Sam had a regular men's urinal put in for himself. Pretty darn handy, if you ask me. Wouldn't be such a bad idea if he'd tell his weekly cleaning woman to take a little more time to freshen up the toilet, though.

The old tub in there has the typical (I guess) eagle's claws on it. You know, I've often wondered why they use those things. Who decided that? Why not use horses' hooves? Or chicken's feet? Or pigs' feet for that matter? And naturally, it has the old-timey separate hot and cold faucets, now with lots of bronze exposed after years of scrubbing. Of course, the constant slow drip from the tub's faucet has created a big rusty-looking stain around the drain. Probably never would be able to bleach that brown away. If it were in my house, it'd be an embarrassment and I'd replace that darn tub.

I'm guessing the house was originally built over a hundred years ago. Of course, as I've pointed out, there was some remodeling. Sam even added a shower to his master bathroom tub. The tub is just like the one downstairs, water stains included. He did all the work and plumbing himself. It's kind of quaint, I suppose you could say. I think he is real proud of his work. He ran two pipes—hot and cold—about six or so feet up from the back of the tub, with an upside-down "T." From there he positioned a six-inch-diameter shower outlet right over the center of the tub. Didn't add a shower curtain at all, so I suppose he has to be sort of careful not to splash too much water over the sides.

On the other hand, I know for a fact that my good friend Sam has various and sundry female visitors staying overnight at his house on occasion, so maybe he set the darn shower head up that way so it'd work better over two people. Boy, I will bet that splashed a lot of water on the walls and floor! Just a thought. Wonder who cleaned up all that water—and when.

Funny, now that I think about it, I don't believe I've ever met more than a couple of Sam's lady friends. Don't know why, because he's usually pretty good about calling me over to have a beer or soda when he has some guys over at his house for some general rapping. That the right word? Anyway, for guy talk. I sometimes wonder if Sam feels like his taste in women is not up to what he thinks my standards are. However, Sam's usually so authoritative about every-thing and everybody, it's not like him to care about my feelings and thoughts. I think that's a fault, but I've never brought up that subject to him.

Sam's house has two original great big chimneys going up both sides of the house, with a smaller one beside the kitchen. Of course, it's now nicely heated and air conditioned with the original fireplaces blocked off.

We were sitting on his porch one day and out of the blue he said, "Hank. I think I'll build me a barbeque grill."

"Yeah?" I said. "I thought you already had a pretty nice one. You keep it under the back porch, don't you?"

"Yeah, but that's kinda shabby. I've had something else in mind for a while." He said no more.

I suppose at this point he thought I could read his mind.

We were quiet for a time and watched a few cars drive by on the street in front of his house. I waited, presuming that Sam'd start back up after a while. Situations like this make me think about old country stores with a pot-bellied stove in the back with several old timers sitting around it jawing. One, fre-quently the main speaker, would inevitably be chewing tobacco and have to stop and spit into an old tin can of some sort. Then conversation would recommence.

Getting somewhat uncomfortable with the silence, I said, "What'd you have in mind?"

Sam still said nothing. Four more autos and a big moving van passed by.

At long last he said, "Been thinking about building a brick one and hooking it on to one of my chimneys."

"Yeah?"

"They're not being used for anything any more, so I figure one of 'em ought to make a good smoke stack."

I'm not an engineer. I wondered, *why not?* I said, "Ever done any brick work?"

"Nope, but it doesn't look too hard."

"Okay." With that, I decided to head back home for lunch.

Sitting across the table from Bobbie, I relayed Sam's idea.

"Boy, I'll bet that'll turn into a big dud, just like most of your friend's stuff."

"We'll see." I bit into a delicious tuna fish salad sandwich she had fixed for me.

The following week Sam had a big pile of red bricks and several bags of mortar sitting beside the chimney closest to our house. I just had to go over to observe the master bricklayer at work.

He had previously borrowed my twelve-pound sledgehammer and punched a pretty big hole through the outside bricks on the chimney. I kind of felt that he broke away too many bricks, but I said nothing as usual.

Sam grinned as I arrived. He was just completing his bottom row of bricks. I was immediately struck by the fact that these new bricks didn't come close to matching the old ones on the chimney. I said, "Sam, I thought you had to lay a supporting foundation of thick concrete before you put on the bricks."

His grin turned into a deep scowl, as he said, "I'm not doing it that way."

"Okay." I continued to watch. Sam seemed pretty sure of his actions, so maybe he'd read about bricklaying sometime. He was mixing his mortar in a wheelbarrow. It looked awfully runny to me. I thought he'd poured in too much water, but after all, it was his baby. I went back home.

The next day when I ventured over again, I saw that he'd almost finished the whole thing. It really wasn't very attractive, in my opinion. I'd have scraped away the excess mortar between the bricks so it would have looked more professional. Maybe his mix was too loose. Not only that, the darn bricks were only about an eighth of an inch between layers. All the other brick buildings I've ever seen (well granted, this wasn't supposed to be a building) had their bricks a minimum of nearly a half-inch. The whole thing looked kind of squashed down too much. I was tempted to go home and get Bobbie to see it. However, realistic thinking prevailed and I judiciously decided that might not be a good idea. Maybe some evening when we could sneak over surreptitiously. Even then I might be afraid she'd laugh too loudly and alert Sam that we were there.

He looked over at me and, proudly said, "How do you like it? Isn't she a beauty?"

I was hesitant to offer any criticism, even though I thought it looked lousy. One other thing I noticed was that instead of a pattern of alternating bricks as I've seen in buildings, Sam had apparently gotten mixed up and had several horizontal lines with no alternating. It was brick above brick above brick. Peculiar.

I said, "Interesting job, buddy. When are you going to have it ready?"

"I'll call you." He didn't seem to want to talk to me any more, so I left.

He let all the mortar harden for about a week and then came the big trial—cooking on his grill. He had judiciously placed an iron grill that he got someplace in town on which to place the food. It was already badly rusted. See-ing that, I gathered he found it at Tom's Junk Yard on Elm Street. He was using charcoal and after splashing the lighter fluid all over the charcoal bricks, and setting fire to them, he quickly learned that his grill didn't quite do right. In other words, the old punched-in chimney didn't draw, and the darn smoke just sort of blossomed up all around the grill and on both of us standing there watching.

Sam said, "Damn!" He went into his house, brought out a newspaper, and started fanning the smoke, trying to make that old chimney start sucking. Didn't work. So, he and I "enjoyed" some well-smoked hot dogs that evening. I told him that if he got a big old washtub and put over the grill, he could prob-ably have himself a real good fish and crab smoker. He got mad at that, so I left.

The next day he had a professional chimney sweep clean the two bird nests out of that tall chimney. I watched him from my house as he tried it again the following evening. It still didn't do right.

Sam never did figure out why his chimney wouldn't draw the smoke up out of his grill, and never tried to use it again. I think I spotted a buzzard flying out of that chimney one time. My friend and I have never discussed it.

Sam painted the house himself when he moved in. At least he painted most of it. He couldn't reach parts of the upper floors, so he just left those parts the previously painted beige. He probably figured on coming back and finishing those parts someday. Maybe that's when Bobbie started disliking my pal Sam so intensely. When he moved in he painted what he could of it light green with white trim. Although I'm not certain about it, I think he used too much thin-ner, because by this time, the green had faded badly and lightened up some-what. I really didn't think it was all that bad, frankly. Also, the previously-painted beige had weathered and mildewed so much that it more or less blended in with the green, looking a little like a big wide trim around the top.

Out back, are a garage and adjoining shop. These were painted dark tan—nearly brown. I've never had the nerve to ask him why he didn't paint these outbuildings that same (mostly) color as his house. I'll be discussing his shop later.

On our side of his yard is just a big field of weeds. Although it's his property, he doesn't ever cut those weeds down, so it looks pretty sloppy. Bobbie's not at all thrilled with that kind of stuff next door to us. Thank goodness, she has never (yet) asked me to cut down Sam's collection of weeds for him. The tall weeds keep Bobbie from seeing Sam's ridiculous-looking "grill," so maybe things aren't so bad after all.

CHAPTER 4

The Artificial Trees

After I got home the night that he told me all about his impending nuptials, I told Sam's story to Bobbie and figured she'd be happy to hear that he was going to fix up his place for his new bride.

What she responded with was, "Yep. He's crazy all right, marrying somebody he's never even met. But at least, finally, maybe he's going to restore his house. The ladies in the Preservation Society'll be awfully glad to hear that."

Now, I've always tried to admire and look up to Sam and he's shown me a lot of what I call friendship over the years. As I've mentioned I guess I've tried to sort of model myself after him because I think he's so intelligent and all. But I swear, some of the things he does do make me wonder. I mean, how about both of those screwed-up marriages? The crazy grill, his activity at the dance, and now, this business with this new lady. At any rate, even if he hasn't had very good luck with choosing women to marry, at least I'm sure he's been pretty successful with his business investments. I don't know his income, but it's pretty obvious that he handles his money well. Most of the time, anyway.

During a late breakfast one morning, Bobbie and I were sitting there at our table and I glanced over at Sam's yard. Oh-my-gosh! We saw that he went out somewhere and bought himself four huge artificial trees. And I mean big! I've never, ever seen any that big before in my life—didn't even know they made 'em. I've no idea where he was able to find them. But, there they were, just lying there on their sides in his front yard. I could see from the leaves, even that far away, that they were simulated white oak trees with trunks at least ten to twelve inches in diameter. Sam has told me he always liked oaks, especially white oaks. He has several big old red oaks in his backyard, but I've never spotted a white oak over there.

Bobbie sat there speechless.

But let me tell you what he did. He went out a little later that beautiful sunny morning and rented one of those back-hoe-type of tractors, dug four great big holes in his front yard, two on each side of his walkway, and darned if he didn't "plant" those big artificial trees right there! He did. He bought a bunch of pine straw and sort of covered the bare dirt around their bases real nice and neat. Unbelievable! I mean to tell you, those artificial trees sure did look nice there, too. Each of them must have been nearly twenty-five feet tall. Gave off real good shade. Bobbie simply stared with her mouth gaped. I didn't ask her for her opinion. However, she said, "Damn!"

Sam showed that he was real proud of those trees too—for about two months.

A couple of days after his planting, I saw a lady from the Preservation Society stop her car right in front of Sam's house. She got out, took some pictures, got back in her car and sped off. I figured she was collecting evidence of some kind.

Maybe Sam didn't quiz the guy that sold him those trees, because after about five or six weeks of bright sun and rain (I think it hailed once), those fake leaves sort of bleached out and turned brittle. Darn near all of 'em fell right off. Here it was in the beginning of summer, and all of a sudden, and he had four big discolored trees with no leaves. Oh, I almost forgot to mention, they also developed rather severe lists.

Well, Sam had been on a trip someplace returning (I assume) after dark. The next morning I saw him come out on his front porch with his coffee cup and look at those things. I mean to tell you, although I live maybe a couple hundred or so yards from him, I could see him jumping up and down and I swear I heard him scream like he'd been shot. I decided right then and there that it was not a particularly good time to go over to his house. I just casually sat in my lawn chair under my own (real) white oak and watched my good friend. I saw him go into his shop, get a shovel, and darned if he didn't excavate all around those four fake trees. Boy, you could sure tell that he was mad, by the way the dirt was flying.

He finished his digging pretty soon—not any roots of course—and went into his house. About half a minute later I heard my phone ring, and since Bobbie was over across the street at the nursing home, I jumped up, ran in, and answered.

"Hey Hank," said Sam's commanding voice over the phone. "Come over here a minute," he said emphatically. No request, just more like an order. Boy, you could tell he was still pretty mad.

So, I grabbed a soda from my fridge, and like any good friend, walked over, highly suspecting what he wanted with me. I'd have bet money it'd not have been to talk about his impending nuptials.

Yep, just as I figured, he needed my help to pull those dreadfulnesses the rest of the way out of the ground. So, he provided a five-eighths inch nylon mooring line that I guess he had for one of his boats. He's always very specific about things like thicknesses. Somehow though, this fact didn't seem to apply to his brick laying. He said, "Hank, I've got lines in my shop that are one inch thick, three quarters, one-half as well as three-eighths. But I figure this five-eighths line will do us best." I've no idea why he told me that bit of information. He tied it around the trunk of the first artificial tree about two feet above the ground, we tugged, and up it came, immediately flopping over toward me. I'm not sure I'm stronger than Sam, but maybe I just gave it more effort. Naturally I jumped and it missed me. Probably would not have hurt even if it had hit me 'cause its limbs were just flimsy plastic. It did have seven leaves left on it. Not a pretty sight. Then, we did the same thing for the other three.

Well, Sam and I dragged those things around back behind his garage. He looked at me and solemnly said, "Thanks." He thanked me? That's all. Nothing more. I was discharged and free to go back home. Hmm. But, after all, he is about my best friend, so I guess it's okay to accept just that.

He burned them that afternoon and you should have seen the thick black smoke. Luckily Bobbie was up town at the time. I don't think she'd have liked seeing that next door to us. I expect she'd have said, "Damn!"

CHAPTER 5

The Roof Job

For informational purposes, Sam's house has a high, steeply slanted roof, covered with badly eroded asphalt shingles. My assumption here is that while it might not be the original covering, the house had needed a new roof applied several years earlier. Bobbie said it was trashy.

One day I was casually talking over the phone to Sam. Well, in reality, I was listening to a oft-repeated lecture about boats. I glanced out my side window and noticed a big flatbed delivery truck backing up into his yard. The guys in it unloaded what looked to me to be a bunch of two-by-four boards and a lot of packets of something. I couldn't see too clearly from where I was at that moment because of the high weeds in his side yard. After learning that the boats he was discussing didn't sink, I said, "Sam, what's with the big truck? What's going on?"

"Need a new roof."

Maybe these old eyes with corrective lenses aren't too bad off after all. Those packets contained roof shingles.

Well, I just figured that Sam had hired himself a professional roofing contractor to come over and redo his roof. After all, I'm sure that he could afford it.

But no, no, no. That didn't seem to fit into my friend's life plan. Before he hung up, Sam told me that he had watched a couple of roofers do another house down the street one time, and that it looked simple enough, so he'd do it himself. Of course, the other house had a fairly low roof, and here, Sam's house had a tall peaked one, but that was only a small detail.

I don't remember Sam ever mentioning a leaky roof, but maybe he just wanted a different color or something. I wondered if maybe that Clemmy woman had talked to him about his roof color. Now that would have been a really strange conversation to have with a woman you'd not yet even met in person.

Let me tell you, though, I presumed at that time that Sam'd never again try to do himself what should really be a professional production. Actually, I hate to chide a good friend, but it really almost proved to be his undoing. On the other hand, many of the things that Sam sets out to do never cease to amaze me … and Bobbie.

Later, as I watched from my yard, I saw him run his tall ladder up to the edge of the roof. His house didn't have gutters. I saw that his ladder didn't quite reach to the roof. He went into his shop for an hour or so, while I ran an errand for Bobbie.

Settling myself comfortably back into my trusty hammock, I saw that he had built a sort of box with some of the two-by-fours and some plywood. He sat that down on the ground and put his ladder on top of that. Frankly, it looked pretty precarious, but I guess Sam figured that it'd serve him well. I'd not have done it that way. I'd have rented a longer ladder, but then, what do I know about such things? Sam always figures these complicated things out pretty well in advance. One of the things I've always liked about Sam is that he's shrewd.

Anyway, he got that ladder propped up as high as he wanted it and I saw him laboriously lug several of the rest of those two-by-fours up onto the roof and, one by one, nail them onto the roof horizontally, to act as foot rests. I told you he was smart. Then, he muscled those shingle bundles up there and propped them on the boards so they wouldn't slide off. Lot of work, but my buddy's pretty strong.

Just about the time when he finished doing that was when things started to go wrong. I'd been watching from my yard, but pretty soon I saw some clouds working themselves down toward our neighborhood. I'd just barely made it onto my front stoop before the bottom dropped out. Boy, what a downpour! I saw Sam scramble down safely and run into his house.

However, I found out the next day that the nails Sam had used to secure those two-by-fours had gone all the way through his original roof, and darn near every one of 'em had allowed rainwater to leak into his attic and eventually down onto his second floor. Ruined several feet of good ceiling plaster and, catch this: soaked his bed in the master bedroom. I mean, all the way through his mattress and box springs. I'd have bet that he wouldn't be taking a date up there for the next little while. Actually, I saw the mattress and box springs out on his back porch the next day, drying out, so I guessed maybe he had a big date lined up for the next couple of nights. I didn't go over, but I do know he has beds in his other bedrooms, so maybe he slept there for the duration of the drying time.

You'd think that maybe he'd have stopped dating other girls after becoming engaged to the "Monster from the Internet," as I came to call her. Never mentioned that nickname to Sam of course. But anyway, he didn't. Maybe he wanted to cover all his bases and keep a few irons in the fire just in case the impending marriage didn't work out. Is that optimism or pessimism?

Back to the roof job. After things had dried off, Sam once again went up on that steep roof of his and started nailing in those shingles. A slight problem that I noticed right away, but maybe he didn't see, was that somehow a couple of the batches were of a slightly different color than the others. Maybe you couldn't notice it unless you were some distance away from the house and the daylight was just right.

I guess the secret to a good roofing job is to start the shingles in a straight line; and maybe start from one end or edge of the roof. Well, Sam apparently figured that technique would be for dummies, and that after all, he was a pretty sharp guy, and he said he'd seen it done.

Oh yes, I noticed something else as he was working away. There must be some sort of knack to placing shingles just right so that the roof looks good when finished. Knowing my friend's presumed flair for accuracy, I figured that what I was seeing was an optical illusion, but I later realized that it was not that at all. Sam must have let the first shingle slip just a little, because after he had about half the side he was working on done, I could notice from my yard that they were all at a slight angle, not perfectly horizontal at all. I mean, frankly, it really looked awful. He must have noticed as he was working that the lines didn't quite work out right. You could tell that he was trying to fudge a little bit and straighten things up since he had already nailed down a big bunch of those off-color shingles. As a result, the roof began to look almost like an unfolded Japanese fan. Not a good sight at all. Bobbie told me she didn't like it.

I don't suppose I need to tell you what happened next. Well, I will anyway. It happened. A couple of days later, Sam was about halfway up that propped-up ladder, lugging a bundle of shingles on his shoulder, and his foot slipped. Suddenly he found himself about to lose his manhood, what with one leg on one side of a ladder rung and the other leg on the other side. Needless to say, he dropped that batch of shingles pretty quickly and tried to grab onto the ladder. Not only were the shingles thoroughly broken, but he pulled on the ladder so hard that it came away from the house. It slid off the big box, and both he and the ladder came crashing down to the ground still with one leg on one side of a rung and the other leg on the other side. Maybe that fall is what saved him, though. I started to get out of my lawn chair and trot over there to see if I could help. But then I realized that his predicament just might embarrass him, so I stayed put. I spotted him stealing a little glance over in my direction.

He came out of it with only a badly sprained ankle, but at least he kept his manly parts intact. Of course, I have to mention here that during that time we also had several more days of rain. Need I say more?

A couple of weeks later, I saw two trucks from Aquaville Roofing Company ("We Cover The Town") pull up into his yard, and two days later a nice-looking new roof adorned Sam's house. Bobbie was so happy. Maybe Clemmy would like it, too.

I'm his friend, so I've never mentioned the incident to him. It might upset him, and good friends simply don't do things like that. Besides, I figure it'd do no good.

CHAPTER 6

The Sod Experiment

Incidentally, Sam's yard was not really doing very well at all. He said, "I want to provide a real nice place for Clemmy." This must have been about the tenth time he'd mentioned that. "She told me she's about ready to come, but I put her off for a little longer. I don't quite have my home and yard like I want it. It'll be real nice by the time she gets here." I thought, *yeah, maybe.*

It seems that Sam was off somewhere and somebody got him interested in sod. He said, "This is the stuff where you grade out your yard pretty much like you want it, and then the sod company will sell you enough pre-grown grass in strips or sections to just lay down on top of your dirt. This provides 'instant' grass."

I said, "Yeah Sam. I believe I heard some of the guys out at the golf course talking about it." I hoped that this might head off some of his repetitive declarations. Didn't work.

He continued, "Most of the yards I have seen done this way are real pretty. I mean, the grass all grows at about the same rate and, properly done, these yards look almost as nice as our golf club's practice putting green."

I guess Sam wondered why he should pay somebody to put all this beautiful sod down when he was perfectly capable of doing it himself. So, he rented a small riding lawnmower-size tractor one day, scraped off all his sparse fescue grass, and more or less leveled up the dirt underneath.

Then he ordered the sod. They brought it on a big flat bed eighteen-wheeler and the man off-loaded a three-wheeled front-end loader and the driver plopped a bunch of piles of pre-grown sod right there beside Sam's bare dirt. I don't know how many sets of stuff he ordered, but there were several big piles. Each bunch of sod appeared to be two or three inches of dirt with grass growing on it maybe an inch or so high. Pretty stuff.

Well, I don't know how much sod costs, but apparently Sam figured that he'd cut his expenses a little bit more. What he did was to kind of lay out the darn stuff sort of checkerboard style, with these squares of sod all laid out by hand with about twenty-four inches between each square. Then, he kind of filled the open areas in with some pretty well cultivated dirt, nice and smooth. I saw him using a cement trowel for that process. I think he figured that the grass in each bundle would grow and spread over to the next one so he could get by with fewer bundles of sod and would have saved himself a bunch of money. I may have mentioned Sam's always been pretty sharp with his dollars. I admire a man that can handle his money really well.

Anyway, unfortunately, there was more of that bad weather I told you about that sort of interfered with Sam's plans. It seems that the rain washed away all that nice soft cultivated dirt between each section of sod, and Sam's yard now consisted of various and sundry squares of nice grass interspersed with *accurately measured* rectangles of red clay mud. I guess it wasn't too bad if you were experienced in hopscotch as a child. You could sort of step from plot of sod to plot of sod, and if you were reasonably careful, you wouldn't even get much muddy water on your shoes at all.

Interestingly, I was watching Sam's once-a-week cleaning lady arrive over there once and darned if she didn't really take a tumble. I don't think she got hurt, but you could sure as heck see that she muddied herself up pretty good. She was not very tall and it kind of looked like she was jumping from one square to the next, and the next one hadn't grown down attached to the solid dirt beneath it quite enough yet and it slipped out from under her. Sort of like a throw rug slipping on a slick wooden floor. Boy, I will bet she was really mad.

Sam apparently located another cleaning lady pretty soon. Personally, I'd have left the old hard-packed dirt walkway like it was before, but I think Sam wanted to get a real good stand of sod grass all over his yard first and then establish a new walkway.

The next day I saw Sam out in his front yard with a hammer and some pretty long nails, nailing each square down into the dirt underneath. Seemed to be a reasonable idea to me. I guess he was lucky not to get sued by somebody coming to visit his house. I'll have to tell you, my good buddy is awfully smart, but he does get into some very interesting difficulties from time to time.

When Bobbie saw what he was doing she said, "Damn!"

CHAPTER 7

Sam's Dam

I don't think I have ever mentioned it, but Sam's property is quite a bit more expansive and larger than ours. Originally, I think our entire neighborhood consisted of ten acre sections. However, a few years back, I sold my back nine to a guy on the next block. He paid me handsomely for them, and proceeded to fence it all off. He and his second wife now have eight kids and he turned it into a safe, giant playground for them. Bobbie and I can hear them across our back fence just having a delightful time. They have enough room to play a lot of soccer and touch football over there. Fortunately, the parents, Mr. and Mrs. Jay Miller, have controlled them very nicely and they shut down all noise around eight o'clock every night.

Sam continues to own the original ten acres, as compared to our now single one. His front part out by the street, is like ours, pretty flat and even, but back towards the rear of his acreage the land has a deep gully with a spring, which feeds a little stream. Lots of woods with fairly large trees, pines, elms, oaks (red) and hickories are there, along with lot of underbrush. He has done a little bit of clearing back there and keeps talking about doing some more serious landscaping sometime.

We were chatting on his front porch one evening, watching a few cars and one motorcyclist pass by. From where I was sitting I could watch the swarm of insects buzzing away around the street light out beside the road. I'd already fetched myself a soda and him a beer. Remarkably there were no bugs out around us yet, which was a blessing. Those darn things don't seem to bother him as much as they do me. I really get tired of talking and swatting and sipping and slapping. Hey, that sounds almost like words for some country/western song. Maybe like one of my favorite titles: "I Get Tears in My Ears from Lying on My Back Crying over You." Ever heard it? Don't know who wrote that thing. Maybe it made him or her a million dollars and he or she retired from public life. Yeah, fat chance.

Anyway, just as I heard a small plane fly over, Sam pops up and says, "You know that little stream I have on my back acreage?"

"Ahh. Yeah. I think I know where you mean," I said. "What about it?"

"I figure that Clemmy might enjoy a fishing pond back there. She says she likes fishing."

"Yeah?"

"Yep," he said. "If I dam up that little stream, I expect I'd get a real nice pond. You agree?"

"I guess so. Do you think it'd be much trouble?"

"Nah," Sam replied. "I've got it all figured out."

About this time I began to wonder when Clemmy was coming. She and Sam had been "engaged" for several months by now. He still talked glowingly about her, even though I showed absolutely no enthusiasm to him about their plans. Personally, I thought maybe he had completely lost his mind, getting mixed up with someone over the Internet the way he did with her. Maybe one of these days I would tell him and try to bang some sense into his thick skull. Maybe.

I have often thought that some of our ancestors must have done something rather offbeat with beavers at one time. Ever seen a little boy that didn't like to dam up small flows of water? I have no idea why it is, but I'm pretty sure all us male types like to do that. Never saw a girl that had such interests. Maybe it gives us boys and men unexpected delusions of grandeur, building dams and such. Yet, only a few become engineers when they grow to manhood and get the chance to construct a real, honest-to-goodness big dam. Just standing in a puddle of water and splashing up and down in it seems to make good sense to little boys. I guess girls somehow got left out of that part of the gene pool. Tough luck for them, I think.

Anyway, my good friend said, "I'm going down to that stream tomorrow and start building. I don't think it'll take more than a few days."

I only said, "It sounds like it might be a lot of fun." In my own mind I figured that it might even be something I would enjoy, except for all the hard digging and shoveling that I could imagine. "Maybe I'll come over and watch while you work."

"I'm going to build it all by hand because I don't want to have a bulldozer come on my land. That would require cutting down a bunch of trees and destroy part of my forest." I'd already realized the bulldozer part before he mentioned it. Still, as I said, most little boys think building a dam would be a lot of fun.

Since Sam was such a good and close friend, I asked, "Do you mind if I come over and fish in it when you get it finished?"

"Of course not." I didn't really know if it'd automatically be stocked with fish by the birds flying over it and accidentally dropping fish or gobbled-up fish roe into it. Or, maybe Sam would stock it himself. Judging from the size of the area I didn't think he'd ever have it large enough for boating. But when my buddy starts to do something, he usually plans for it to be pretty nice, so you never know. He was obviously trying real hard to fix his property up for Clemmy.

Well anyway, after I spotted him heading in the direction of his gully the next day, I walked over to the top of the hill above where he intended to build his dam. I was very careful not to carry a digger or shovel, or else I'm sure old buddy Sam would have invited me to help him with his project. I sat down on an old oak log. Unfortunately I failed to notice the ants crawling on it. Pretty soon I decided to stand and watch. He went on down to the stream and started digging into the side of the hill there. This was apparently where he was going to get his dirt for the dam. Then he shoveled his production into the middle of that stream. Although there was not much water flowing down his stream that particular morning, he and I could quickly see that the water was already beginning to back up. Yeah, boy! I suppose he could already visualize the future and see Lake Mead beginning right there in his own back yard.

Well, he dug, shoveled and worked until he had built that earthen dam to a level where the upstream water was about three feet deep and the "pond" ran back up the deep gully about ten feet. Things looked pretty good at that point. I'd gone back home in the middle of his digging and brought back some anti-ant spray and a couple of sodas—one for the worker and one for the "supervisor" (me). He seemed to appreciate my interest while he took his break. He failed to thank me for the soda. Too busy thinking about his work, I guess.

While we were up on the ridge, casually sitting there on the now-ant-free log and observing nature, I noticed a hawk circling overhead. Maybe it had already spotted a nice fish in Sam's pond. Sure! But what Sam noticed was that the water had reached the top of his earthen dam and was spilling over. This of course was beginning to wash away some of the dirt he'd just put there. For some strange reason this didn't sit too well with my buddy. His face kind of reddened even more in spite of his sweating. He uttered something that I will not repeat here, went down, took his digger, sliced right down the middle of his dam, and released all his water. It made a right pretty flow from where I was sitting, although Sam's shoes got pretty muddy—and even the bottom of his pant legs.

I said my goodbyes and went home. Sam's not particularly fun to be around when he's upset.

The next day I saw my friend carrying a long PVC pipe and a valve of some sort down to his project area. Naturally, being somewhat curious, I soon positioned myself on my regal observation post above him.

I yelled down, "What're you doing with the pipe and stuff?"

"Watch." I guess he just forgot that he'd need some sort of way to manage the water level. He placed a release valve on the end of that big pipe and carefully put it at the bottom of the gully. "It's my water level control. Now I can continue unabated." Let me tell you, he really made progress that second day after placing his control pipe. I suppose it was because of his extra determination since having to backtrack from the first day and the fact that he already had a fair amount of previously dug dirt (mud) to use. So, this time he didn't even let water back up behind his dam while he was building it. He had graduated to a hydraulic engineering expert by this time, I guess. He labored pretty much the whole day and got that pile of dirt up to about five feet high. I thought to myself that now he really had things going and we'd get to see a real nice pond.

Just as I was about to head home, Sam closed his valve so that water would begin to collect overnight and he climbed up the hill and stopped where I was sitting. He was just puffing and gasping for breath after all his hard work and climbing the steep hill. I will say that my buddy was pretty darn dirty and smelly by this time. Which was all right I suppose; a good day's work will frequently make one dirty. I don't see how he could ever get his shoes clean though, what with all that red-clay mud caked on them. Probably added a couple of pounds to his normal weight.

I could hardly wait overnight so I could go out the next morning and see his beautiful pond. Bobbie didn't show much enthusiasm with his project when I described it to her. I don't know—she never does seem to have much confidence in my friend's numerous projects. But after all, he is about my best buddy and I like to show my friend encouragement and reinforce his decisions whenever I can. Pals do that kind of thing, don't they? I just knew it'd be all the way to the top of his dam and maybe even have water lilies already growing in it. I will admit, though, that I was not sure how he'd do his spillway. If the water overflowed again like the first time, it'd probably mess his dam up again. I'd stopped by Sam's house on my way to the overlook and as he and I were strolling towards the dam site he said, "I've cut myself a spillway on the far edge of my dam. This way I can control my water flow better." This time I also noticed that Sam had gone to town and bought himself some high-topped boots to work in. He was wearing those same dirty pants he had on yesterday, though. I didn't say anything, but he had begun to smell just a little bit—sort of sweaty-like. Sort of? What am I saying? He stunk like a filthy wet boar! And his trouser legs looked pretty stiff from the hardening mud.

But Sam seemed very determined to have his nice pond completed before Clemmy arrived. Oh, he was working hard.

Uh-oh! When we got to the edge of the hill and looked down, we expected to see a nicely formed pond. Unfortunately, however, we could only see a small amount of collected water. Both of us went down that steep embankment this time and when we got to the dam we spotted his (not mine, thank goodness) problem. Seepage. Or was it leakage? What's the difference anyway? Maybe it has something to do with volume. Anyway, the water was oozing through the dirt of his dam so much that it couldn't back up much water. Instead of a nice dam of solid dirt, it was more like a big mud pile. Water had not been contained, but rather, had continued to seep through the dirt that he had piled up there. It didn't do it the first day, so my guess is that when it got to a certain higher level or volume and the backed up water had a certain amount of weight behind it that the dirt simply was not packed hard enough to withstand it and thus, seeped or leaked, or flowed through—or whatever. Does that sound scientific? Now I realize that while most boys like to play in the mud, your typical grown man does not. I even knew what would come out of my buddy's mouth before he uttered some of his infamous profane words. Now let me say that there was a little bit of water backed up, maybe about two feet deep. But not enough so that you could really say that he had a pond. Maybe not even a pool.

So, after looking at his situation for a few moments and rubbing his chin a couple of times in deep thought, he said "I'll see you later, Hank." In other words, he wanted me to leave. I suppose it was so he could have a few moments of quiet solitude and meditation. Maybe not.

I have to tell you that although I consider Sam as my best friend and I like to assume that he thinks of me as a good friend too, sometimes he treats me sort of rudely. I mean, after all, I wasn't going to tease him about his darn seeping dam or anything like that. I wasn't even going to offer him any suggestions. I was just going to sympathize and empathize with him. After all, that is what friends do, don't they? Maybe he just wanted to be alone in his difficulty at that point.

Anyway, I said "so long" to him and went on home. There I got a nice soothing glass of minted iced tea and carefully positioned myself in my trusty hammock. I intentionally didn't contact Sam for about a week, and, I might add, he didn't call me. That didn't bother me too much, because I was still kind of perturbed at him for being rude to me—his friend.

When I finally strolled over there, I found that he had been doing some real serious work on that dam. When I say serious I mean that he had switched from dirt to concrete!

I asked him about that.

He turned his head toward me and said, "I figure that I didn't have my dirt packed hard enough, and concrete is not as likely to leak."

Lo and behold if he hadn't gone and made himself some plywood forms and hand-mixed up a bunch of concrete in his wheelbarrow and now he had a concrete dam. I couldn't help but notice however, that in my opinion he had reversed the shape of his construction. I mean, don't most professionally built dams sort of curve up toward the pool of retained water? His didn't. It curved all right, but away from the pool and I suppose it suited him to be different. Maybe he didn't plan it out very well. Or, maybe he thought it'd look snazzy that way, and impress his darling Clemmy. I really don't know why he shaped it that way and I'd be darned if I would've quizzed my buddy about that particular point. Maybe he just figured that as long as he had a concrete dam and it was not scheduled to be any larger than he wanted it to be, that it'd be strong enough. Just as long as it held the water. I did notice that he had stuck some steel rods in the concrete, (I think they're called "re-bars") supposedly for additional strength. Anyway, it looked pretty much like any small dam, about three inches thick, except for the outward curve. He had piled a big bunch of the dirt on the downwind side of the concrete—for additional support, I suppose. Besides, at this point the concrete was about five feet high and the dirt sort of provided an easy walkway along the backside of old Sam's three-inch-thick Hoover dam.

Problem! When I scooted down to where Sam was continuing to shovel that dirt, I noticed that although he was finally getting a fair amount of water backed up, he was still getting seepage—right through that backfill dirt he had placed below the dam. He had piled more and more dirt over the seeping areas, obviously packed it down as firm as he could, and all he had to show for it was more mud. And I could see that he was becoming more and more agitated and frustrated. Or maybe his face was that red was because of his working efforts. Maybe. Sam didn't seem to be in a talking mood at that moment, so I left.

While watching from my yard several days running I could not help but gather that old Sam was still having difficulties with his project. What I mean by this is that three separate times I saw him coming across his back yard from the direction of his dam, just as muddy as could be. He had apparently fallen down in his mud puddle. I will say that whenever I was over there observing him and his digging and shoveling, I saw him slip several times and almost fall down into the mud. Yet, agile as he is, he caught himself each time. Got a little water splashed up on his pants, but that apparently didn't bother him particularly. Of course a red face and a few cuss words, the regular kind, seemed to handle his concerns at that point. I wondered if he'd get tired physically and then not be able to keep from sprawling flat out. But he didn't fall completely anytime when I was there watching. Maybe he was just extra careful, knowing he had an observer.

Once, I spotted him from my house and got out my binoculars, just to confirm in my own mind what I suspected. Yep, there he was, almost totally covered with reddish-brown mud, just moving his mouth as if to be talking to himself. More likely, though, he was expressing his anger in Vietnamese as he rapidly walked back toward his house. Sam has some special cuss words that he uses when he is really, really raging about something. Actually they sound kind of oriental to me, so I guess he learned 'em while he was over in Vietnam during his tour of duty there. Luckily it was summer at that point because he used his garden hose to rinse himself off before going up his back steps. I will bet he filled those work boots of his up with mud too. If it had been in the winter I guess he'd have had to either rig himself up a hot shower in his back yard or else he'd start disrobing completely there behind his house. I'm glad he didn't go that route.

Bobbie just had to look at him through those field glasses after I told her what I'd seen. She really enjoyed that scene! She said "Ha!" That is all, just "Ha!" Although she'd never gone over to see his production, I'd certainly told her plenty about it. In fact, although I thought he'd begun a pretty nice project, she didn't seem to have much confidence in his ability to complete the dam and pond. She's a real "Doubting Thomas" when it comes to my pal. Personally I felt like he'd eventually be able to overcome that continual seeping problem that kept his pond from filling up to something of decent size. Sam's pretty smart and I figured he'd come up with some solution sooner or later. However, I couldn't help but be curious as to how he was going to do it.

Sitting on Sam's front porch a couple of evenings later he got sort of nostalgic during our conversation. His dad had a farm when Sam was growing up and had wanted to build himself a dam there on his farm so he could have a source of water for his cows. "Well," Sam said, "Dad never could get that dam to hold water either. Apparently the dirt was too full of tiny pebbles and so, porous or something." I gathered his dad didn't try to go the concrete route with his though, or else Sam would probably have mentioned it.

As he was telling me this I couldn't help but notice that my buddy was spending a fair amount of time scratching various parts of his body. Naturally, being his friend and all, and showing my concern for him, I inquired, "What's with all your scratching?"

He looked over at me, put his beer down, scratched over his shoulder and said, "I've been almost eaten up by a bunch of chiggers." At this point I could quickly realize that a lecture was coming forth from ol' Sam's mouth. He continued, "You know, they're from the *trombiculidae* family of insects. Some people call 'em 'redbugs,' and others, 'jiggers.' In some parts of Africa the darn things carry disease, but not around here." He stopped and sucked on his beer. I took the opportunity to sip on my soda. "As you know I have to walk through a bunch of weeds down to my dam site and this is where they like to stay." He glanced over at me to see if I was still listening to his scientific lecture. I was. "They like to attach themselves to human skin wherever there's not a lot of tight clothing. You can't usually see them because they're so small." I knew that. "Since we had a fairly mild winter their larvae weren't killed off, so they're now out in force."

I instantly recalled that I picked up just one on one of my casual visits over there. And boy, did that spot under my right knee itch. For days! I guess Sam must have had at least ten on him the way he was redirecting his scratching onto various places of his body.

I suggested, "Maybe you should consider buying a can of insect repellant and spraying your clothing pretty thoroughly before venturing down to the dam site."

He didn't respond, so I said, "Heading home now. Bye."

I don't know if he took my advice or not, but I did notice him still scratching ten days later. We're also kind of bad for ticks around here in North Carolina, but so far I have managed to evade those little pests. I especially hate the deer ticks. They're only about the size of a pin head, and red, so they're awfully hard to spot on your body until they suck out enough of your blood to fill up. The regular ticks can be caught fairly easily with a normal body inspection.

Anyway, a couple of weeks later I again ventured over, and quickly noticed that the pond was still only about five feet deep, but his dam was thicker than before. Sam had presumably determined that his concrete was seeping and that by making it thicker, he could control it and get some serious water volume. He kept telling me that he wanted the dam to be about ten feet high at its completion. Didn't work out that way, though. I don't really know how many bags of cement he mixed and put on the front of his dam, but after a while I will bet it was over a foot thick instead of the three inches he started with. It wasn't getting any taller—just thicker. And the seepage continued, particularly in several specific spots. Seemed to me like maybe the seepage was not coming from the dam itself, but either from around the edges or maybe under the bottom of all that concrete.

I watched him and kind of chatted with him about it. "What are you gonna do now?"

He didn't answer. I suppose he expected me to look and learn. He drained the small amount of backed up water again and dug a trench in the mud about eighteen inches deep all along the water-side front of the dam where it met the ground. He then poured that channel full of concrete. Took him nearly all day. I didn't offer to haul any of those sixty-pound sacks of concrete from his shed down to the dam site. I did, at his kind request, hook up his long water hose to the faucet on the back of his house, however. He mixed and filled, mixed and filled. He sort of fumed a little when I left for home. I heard him muttering under his breath that I'd abandoned him and now he had to walk all the way back up to his house in order to turn off his water. It seems to me that he could have added a closing nozzle on the end of his hose. But he didn't, and I didn't suggest it.

When he finally closed the dam's water-control valve, water started accumulating and unfortunately, it rose once again to that same certain level, perhaps half way up to the top of the dam. And then, oh yes, water began to seep just like before. Sam cussed some more. Even Bobbie heard him all the way over to our back yard.

That continual seepage kept his projected pond from ever filling up more than five feet or so deep and running back up the gully a distance of maybe fifteen feet. Some pond! Boy, by this time Sam was getting seriously frustrated with his project. One day while I was sitting there overlooking it, he threw down his shovel. He stomped up the hill, barely glancing at me, and almost before I could get off the old log (still ant-free) where I was sitting, came back with a big sledge hammer. (I noticed that it was one he had borrowed from me two years ago.) Darned if I didn't think he was going to knock the whole thing down right then and there. But I guess by the time he got back down there he had cooled off a little and decided that he had gone this far so he might as well continue to try to plug up those leaks. He surely did want a pond for Clemmy real bad. I hoped along with him that it'd come to fruition. Maybe he had promised Clemmy she'd have her own fishing pond when she arrived. I didn't ask him about that.

His next step was to drain his small amount of accumulated water once again, take some big sheets of that four-millimeter-thick plastic, position it all along the front of the concrete, and stick that down with more cement. Boy, I will tell you one thing: my friend is persistent if nothing else. When he decides to do something, by George, he's gonna do it.

However, that last step didn't work either. His dam just kept on oozing and he still couldn't get himself a decent pond. I figured that about this time he'd give up on it, but he didn't. Boy, my good chum Sam sure is an optimist also. Even though he had not yet controlled the seepage, he went back and added another three feet (concrete) to the top of his dam anyway.

Sitting on his porch one evening, he said, "I think that eventually the dirt around the edges of all that cement will settle in and the leaking will stop. Then, I'll have a pond of a right decent size." He told me that he'd just leave it alone for a while and sooner or later there'd be a nice fishing pond.

No fish ever did start there that I know of, but he did grow a big bunch of frogs. In the evenings when Bobbie and I happened to be out in our yard, the sounds of the frogs coming from that pond of his sounded pretty good—at least to me. Bobbie doesn't care much for the sound of croaking frogs, though, so she spent very little time out there with me.

Now, almost a year later, that darn dam project of Sam's still seeps so much water that you can hardly call the backed up water a pond. Maybe you could call it a puddle. Well, sure, I guess you can call it a puddle now because it is gradually filling in with silt. No fish, just frogs, as I mentioned. I suppose pretty soon he will have no frogs, just mosquitoes. I strolled over there a few days ago and looked down there at his dam site. I must say, although he didn't have much regular water backed up, he did have a rather nice sort of swamp just down-stream from the dam. And a nice healthy-looking bunch of cattails was growing out of the down-stream mud. I actually spotted a couple of water oak saplings growing there also. Looked right pretty and sort of rustic if you ask me.

I will tell you a little later on what eventually happened to Sam's dam. The final result turned out reasonably well if you ask me, but he sure did have to go through a bunch of gyrations first. I've never heard how Clemmy responded to it.

CHAPTER 8

Clemmy

Ring!

Something startled me, but I didn't know what.

Ring!

Something beat against my leg. What was happening?

"Get the phone!" I felt Bobbie's foot against my leg again. I squinted at the shadowed ceiling.

Groggily, I opened my left eye, turned over and picked up the darn phone. Glancing at the clock as I did so, I noted that it was five-thirty in the morning.

"Hello," I mumbled.

"Hey Hank," said the voice. I knew instantly who it was.

"Yeah, Sam. What's up?"

"Hey buddy. I'm going to Nashville today to meet Clemmy. Since the accident with my roof, my ankle cramps up when I drive a long way and I thought you'd like to come with me and help with the driving. I'll share the expenses of course."

Well, what do you do when your best friend calls and asks for your help in something important to him? At this time of the morning I had to ask myself, *do I really want Sam to be my best friend?* But after all, he said he'd share expenses with me. Now I considered that real generous of him when he'd practically demanded that I accompany him. Yes sir—real generous. So, I said I would. I got up, showered, shaved, and gulped down a cup of instant coffee. Sweet Bobbie didn't seem too happy when I woke her again and told her what was happening. I tenderly laid a kiss on her forehead and headed on over to

Sam's house. Luckily it was a Friday and I had no pending work to hold me back from helping a friend.

I got over there after about forty-five minutes, all packed for an overnight trip and ready to roll. However, it seems that friend Sam had not yet gotten out of bed. He still hadn't repaired his doorbell, so I had to bang on the locked front door pretty loudly. That got him up and going and I fixed us a couple pieces of toast and started his coffeepot while he was getting himself ready. *Now, what on earth was he thinking—getting me up early and then going back to sleep himself?* After he finally came down and ate his breakfast, he needed to go spend a little time in the toilet, "concentrating, you know."

We finally left his house for Nashville about ten o'clock. By this time the clouds had gathered together and a slight drizzle had started. You know how far it is from our town to Nashville? A long darn way, I'll tell you. Anyway, we got there about nine hours later and let me say, that was some harrowing trip. I mean, particularly when Sam was driving. Now for me, I tend to keep right along with traffic speeds, regardless of what's posted, you know. I mean, it's typical to have a seventy-mile-per-hour speed limit on the Interstates, but the state patrol seems to allow most traffic to cruise along at maybe seventy-five. At least I have seen plenty of cars pass me, clearly going way above the posted limit while a patrolman on the other side, obviously with his radar on, lets 'em go. Boy, with my luck, I'll bet those patrolmen would sure as heck stop me if I were going that fast!

Well, it seems like Sam's ankle might have been bothering him or something, because whenever he was driving, he kept the car's speed up toward eighty-five or ninety. Now that is a little fast for my personal temperament, especially with wet pavement, but what's a guy to say when it is his buddy's car?

I did say, "Aren't you going a tad fast under these conditions?"

"Nope. It's okay," he responded. However, I did notice that he promptly tightened both hands on the steering wheel.

I must admit, though, that when Sam got stopped by the highway patrol just east of Asheville, I felt like maybe he'd finally be slowing things down a little bit. He seemed rather perturbed at being stopped, but he really didn't say anything other than "Damn."

The patrolman made Sam go back to his cruiser, where they sat together for several minutes. Finally Sam came back, with his face about as red as I have ever seen it. He came to my side of the car, opened the door and didn't say anything except, "You drive."

I didn't ask him anything and he just sat quietly there in the passenger seat for at least an hour—sulking, I guess you would call it. Happily, the sun had now forced its way between the cloud banks and the highway was dry. I punched on the radio and we listened to some country/western sounds. Anyway, we finally made it over to Nashville.

I was kind of excited to meet Sam's so-called fiancée. Would she be pleasant? Was she cultured? I wondered if perhaps she'd grown any eyebrows. I recalled from that old photo that she appeared somewhat overweight. My private curiosity was curious if she'd been dieting.

I also wondered what Sam was thinking and feeling at that moment. Would he like her as much in person as he apparently did over the Internet? Since Joyce and Carol (plus all the other ladies I'd ever seen him with) were slender, I wondered if he was at all concerned if she was chubby.

Sam said, "We've got to find the bus station. I told her we'd meet her there between four and five o'clock this afternoon." (It was now near seven in the evening.) After stopping several times for directions, we finally arrived at the bus station. We parked, went in and spotted her sitting half-asleep on a bench.

Golly gee, was she ever something? I don't know how Sam felt at that moment, but darned if I was not somewhat taken aback. Believe me, her picture that she sent Sam didn't half do her justice. Or else it was taken more than a couple of years ago. I mean to tell you, I could almost instantly recognize her because of her lack of eyebrows, and those ears of hers, but that was about all. It didn't show up in the snapshot Sam showed me back at his house those many months ago, but good Lord, she was FAT! I mean F-A-T! I bet she weighed nearly four hundred pounds if she weighed an ounce. Blubber was squirting out all over. Maybe it wouldn't have been so bad if she'd would worn some other outfit.

By the way, she didn't have those same earrings that she had worn for the photo, but the ones she had on were still really long things. Sort of Indian design, I guess. Looked like they must have weighed a ton, but I really suppose they weren't quite that much. They didn't seem to pull her earlobes down too far. But, now catch this, she had added another couple of holes in her right ear and each hole had a different color earring stuck in it. Same for her left ear, too. You know, in a way, it was sort of attractive. She had reds on top, then oranges, yellows, greens, and finally blues. Just about like a rainbow in her ears. The color of the stones in her dangly ones seemed to be sort of yellowish-green, maybe chartreuse, and they didn't exactly match up with any of the little ones higher up. But what do I know about color matching? Maybe they were supposed to go with that bright hair color of hers, but I really don't think so. Or, maybe she was color-blind or something. Speaking of color, she had the brightest shade of red hair that I have ever laid my eyes on. And, get this, two streaks of purple ran down both sides and kind of blended into two pony-tails. Well let me tell you, that was some interesting hair!

Now, I've never been one to care a whole lot about dress styles and what ladies wear and such, but this gal sure as heck didn't spend a lot of her time browsing through women's style magazines. The dress she had on was pretty wrinkled, but I guess she could be forgiven for that, having spent who-knows-how-many hours on a bus from Wichita Falls and then waiting on a hard bus station bench for a good long while. Anyway, her dress was sort of a flowered, bright-colored little thing. "Little thing" indeed; I'm talking about a big gunny sack! But if you want my opinion, it was nothing she should have picked out to meet a future husband for the first time. I guess the main problem was that it was way too short for somebody with her heft, and she seemed to only be about five-foot-one at best. I mean, it only came down to sort of halfway between her knees and her … well, where her legs began. Yeah, way too short. Maybe a little skinny fashion model might look okay in something like that, but not this gal, I'll tell you. If she ate a reasonably decent meal, I'd bet that dress would split right down. Now that'd be something. Anyway, let's just say I'd have picked out something bigger and longer if it'd been me.

"Hey, darlin'," she said brightly to Sam when she first saw us and got up off the bench. I guess she more or less knew what Sam looked like from some of their Internet chats.

"And who be's this here cute guy wit chu?" (I wondered what kind of education she had, to speak like that.) With that said, she immediately turned and hugged *me*, not Sam. (By the way, I couldn't help but notice that her morning deodorant's protection had worn off by this time.)

Sam at least smiled nicely at her and actually held out his hand to shake with her. She was continuing to hug me tightly, but stuck out one hand. He said, "He's Hank, my friend from home." I then separated myself from her hug and shook hands with her also since Sam had broken the ice with a manly shake. She did have a nice firm grip, not the flimsy, dead fish kind of shake I half-expected from her. But talk about a sweaty hand! I presumed it was because she was a little nervous. It didn't seem particularly hot to me there in the bus station. I guess it probably took me a couple of minutes of discretely wiping my hand on my pants to get my palm dried off decently. My shirt was a tad damp from her perspiration-loaded hug. A thought flashed, *Why didn't she give Sam a big hug like she did me?* Surely, that way the front of her dress would have been blotted somewhat dryer by the time she got to me.

Anyway, she and Sam chatted a little bit, while I politely wandered off to look around the station. I really felt somewhat out of place with them at that moment.

I found a magazine rack and thumbed through a motorcycle racing publication. Man, I had no idea of the intricate details that are involved in that sport. Since I know that NASCAR racing started with former bootleg whiskey runners, I had to wonder how it'd be to haul a dozen or so gallon whiskey jugs on a motorcycle at breakneck speed in the wee hours—maybe without a headlight—running from the revenuers.

After a few minutes, Sam chased me down. "Hank, I've decided that it's too late to try to head back home tonight." I'd already assumed we'd need to spend the night; that's why I packed my suitcase before leaving my house. "We'll find ourselves a motel and head out tomorrow morning." Since I'd done most of the driving and was a little tired, that sure did sound good to me.

So, anyway, we looked around and found ourselves a motel. Two rooms. Sure. Twin beds in Sam's and my room, thank goodness. Now I will admit that Sam's my good friend and all, but that doesn't give me any good feelings about sleeping in the same bed with him.

I had to do that one time with another friend, and he had some sort of rash on his arms and I lay awake all night long, just scared to death that I might accidentally touch his arm and catch whatever he had. Must have worked out okay, 'cause I never did get it, whatever it was.

Sam clasped me on the shoulder and, smiling, said, "Miss Clemmy and I are going to go over to that club across the street and party for a while." He winked at me while Clemmy stood somewhat away from us. She seemed to be studying the cracks on the old marble floor of the bus station.

"I'll see you back at the room later." I thought, *Well, thanks for nothing, Sam. Don't bother to invite me to go partying with you guys. I'm just your darn chauffeur.* I didn't really want to go out partying with them, but I'd have at least appreciated an invitation. I felt it was kind of rude of Sam to not ask me. Sort of hurt my feelings, don't you know. Maybe Clemmy could have invited me. I have to admit, however, that since I was actually a guest, and this was Sam and Clemmy's first real meeting, that by my tagging along would certainly be most inappropriate. I'd still have declined, but at least I'd have felt better about the whole situation.

Sam and Clemmy apparently stayed up most of the night. I don't know what time he got in, but it must have been pretty late (or should I say early in the morning?), because when I got up, it was all I could do to wake him. His is not a pretty face early in the morning, incidentally.

While he was shaving, he said, "That place we went to last night was a real high class cabaret. Sweet Clemmy and I had a great time. Hank, I mean to tell you, in spite of her being slightly overweight (Sam noticed!), that gal can really dance." Still obviously pretty hung over, he was not speaking clearly, so I had to have him repeat the entire sentence.

I replied, "Yeah?" I was thinking, *Who in their right mind would want to spend any amount of time with a dame like that, much less party?* But at this moment I didn't feel like saying anything about her. After all, Sam supposedly knew her a lot better than I did. Didn't seem to me to be the type of lady that I could ever imagine Sam getting involved with, though. This thought began to worry me.

He cut himself shaving and applied two small pieces of toilet paper to the wounds.

"And drink!" He grinned as broadly as his hangover would allow. "That lady can sure hold her booze. I tried to keep up with her, and almost couldn't walk back here. She was kind enough to help me. I think I kind of tripped once, but she grabbed me and we sat down on the curb for a minute or two. I don't believe we were there very long, but I honestly don't remember much."

Sam finally got his facial bleeding under control and finished dressing.

"You got in pretty late. I know that."

"'Spose so. Anyway, I'm hungry. Ready for some breakfast?" Without waiting for my response, he picked up the phone and called Clemmy's room. I heard him tell her to meet us at the motel's dining room. I wondered why he didn't offer to go to her room and escort her.

I thought Sam was pretty inconsiderate to his future wife, but kept my feelings to myself.

We did meet in the dining room about six-thirty. It was small, with only eight booths, two tables and an eating counter with six seats. Sam directed us to a booth where Clemmy occupied one entire side, Sam and myself on the other.

The lone waitress looked rather disheveled as if she had had a pretty bad night herself. She was at the pass-through from the kitchen and obviously engaged in a rather blustery argument with the cook. After we had seated ourselves, she finally strolled over and literally dumped three plastic-covered menus on our table. Sam grabbed the first one and I passed Clemmy hers.

This morning Clemmy had on a faded plaid shirt with a small ragged hole at the elbow in her left sleeve, faded jeans, and western-style, silver-toed boots. And goodness gracious, those jeans were so tight I figure that they must have been painted on her. I really don't know how she got in them, unless she oiled and greased herself down with something first.

Sam had brought his "uniform" from home and wore it this morning. I had to wonder what he felt about that. Meeting a bride-to-be for the first time, I'd certainly have dressed up more. Did he not respect her this early in their relationship? Of course, I soon saw that it sort of blended with her outfit—except that Sam's pants were quite adequately loose over his body—even his expanding waist. Maybe they had previously agreed to go casual.

The talk at our table that morning was rather subdued to say the least. It was apparent that neither Clemmy nor Sam were in the mood for any extended conversation. I didn't have any succinct verbiage either. The waitress fiddled with the juke box and got some loud unidentifiable music going. That helped ease the awkward situation at our table.

And let me say that I'm awfully glad I didn't have to pay for her breakfast. (Sam fumbled around sufficiently so that I had to pay for *my* own food.) But, let me tell you, that woman sure must've had a bad need for fueling that big body of hers. Or maybe she'd heard that old saying, "Eat a big breakfast and have a better day." Or something like that. This is what I saw her put away: two well-sugared grapefruit halves, one stack of (I think) eight pancakes, three waffles, four fried eggs ("over easy, with lots of runny"), six patties of sausage, a large order of grits, fried potatoes, four pieces of toast heavily slathered with butter, and four cups of coffee (three sugars, plenty of cream in each cup.) Now, that would have totally done me in. I'd not have been able to get it all down, and I'm a pretty good-sized guy.

I glanced at Sam while we were eating and saw that he also took note of what she was putting away. I'd have bet he was actually adding up the food bill for his future bride. Nah, he's a nice guy; maybe not.

By the way, funny that I'd not seen it last night, but this morning I finally noticed that her tooth space that I'd seen in the photo was gone. Here's what was there: a rather standard tooth, except darned if there wasn't a small solid gold heart right smack in the middle of that new tooth. Just as pretty a thing as you'll ever see, if you're into that sort of thing. Personally, I'm not, although obviously she was. I wondered if Sam liked it. I couldn't help but notice that

Clemmy grinned a lot, so I suppose she was right proud of her new tooth. I remembered that original picture that Sam got from her so many months ago, though. She was grinning even with that missing tooth. Maybe she just likes to grin.

Anyway, we finished our breakfast, and checked out of the motel. Sam was kind enough to split the cost of our room with me, even though I noticed that Sam allowed Clemmy to pay for her own. Then the three of us headed home to Aquaville, me driving the first lap. I was happy to note the day was beautiful, with a bunch of fluffy clouds playing tag with the sun. Things went pretty routinely until we got to the first rest stop. It seems as though Clemmy must have drunk a little too much coffee for breakfast, because our first stop was only forty miles down the road. Then, another after sixty, then another after one hundred thirty miles. I began to wonder if we'd ever get back home. But we did, finally, and Sam even drove some of the way. He dropped me by my house and the two of them zipped over to his place and unloaded their luggage.

I didn't hear from Sam, or even see him or Clemmy, for three days.

Incidentally, I don't want you to think that I spy on Sam or anything like that, because I don't. Let's just call it a "neighborhood watch" program that I have going. Whenever I don't have anything else occurring, I occasionally just happen to glance over at my friend's house. Sometimes I spot him, sometimes I don't.

On the side of my house facing away from Sam's is a big patch of woods, so there is rarely anything to see over there. Oh, on occasion I will spot a couple of deer, and certainly plenty of birds. And boy, let me tell you, although some are real pretty, I just don't like birds. I learned to hate birds when I used to work at a service station and had to clean off windshields. Golly, I really hate 'em! They're right nasty things, if you ask me. Observing Bobbie's bird feeders, I've noticed that they even go potty in their own food. Now, that's just not right.

Once a couple of weeks ago I had a real-live turkey buzzard swoop around my side yard a few times. Big old sucker too. I first noticed him by his shadow over the yard. I kept real quiet in my house and pretty soon he landed near my (or I should say, Bobbie's) landscaped garden, walked around a little bit and found a small dead field mouse. And that darned old scavenger just proceeded to enjoy it right then and there. He held that little animal's carcass with one claw and tore off little bite-sized pieces one by one until he finished him and then that old predator flew off. Ugliest red snout on that bird you ever saw.

You know, as I think about that event, I sort of wonder if that is not how I appear to old buddy Sam. Maybe I'm just a piece of meat to eat (use) whenever the buzzard (Sam) feels like it. Well, maybe I'm getting tired of such a deal. I think it is belittling to me. Sweet Bobbie and I have even talked about it, and she agrees with me. But after all, I still consider Sam about my best friend, and real friends accept the attitudes and foibles of their pals, don't they?

Nothing much ever seems to happen at the nursing home directly across the street from our house either. Except, of course, for the occasional ambulances and hearses coming and going. So, I simply spend time in my trusty rope hammock and peer over towards his place on occasion.

Anyway, I finally decided to stroll over to Sam's and pay a friendly call on my friend and his bride to be. I guess I should have phoned first, but Sam and I have been good buddies long enough to dispense with that little bit of courtesy. Seeing that he still had not repaired his doorbell, I knocked. Nothing. I knocked again, a little louder. (Sound like that rainy night trip over there?) Finally I tried the doorknob and, finding it unlocked, I stuck my head in the door and hollered, "Sam, you there?" I really was not certain that I should go in, not knowing what I would find. Or, should I say, what response I might get from Clemmy. I kind of felt okay walking in on Sam, of course, but how about Clemmy? Her presence there would surely change things.

And boy, did it ever? Clemmy was back in the kitchen cooking something that smelled like it was Mexican. At least, I smelled a lot of pretty-good smelling spices. I strolled into the kitchen and found Clemmy at the stove with nothing on but a *very* thin pale blue cotton nightgown and a kitchen apron. I was embarrassed as all get out! I was quickly backing out of the room when she turned to me and with a great big smile on her face, said, "Why, hi thar, Hank ol' buddy. C'mon in. You likes Tex-Mex cookin'?"

I didn't feel comfortable being there with her in her nightgown. (And barefooted.) (And without her gold tooth.)

"Maybe I'd better come back later," I uttered hesitantly. "Where's Sam?"

"Oh," she said as she sprinkled what looked to me like a double tablespoon of some kind of spice into the pot of stuff on the stove. "He's upstairs in the john, doin' his thing, ya know—'concentrating'."

Well, how's that for frankness? It made me feel even more awkward, so I said, "Tell you what. I'll come back over later on. Just tell Sam to call me when it's convenient." With that said, I backed out and left their house. Boy, it sure did look like my days of barging in on my buddy were behind me.

As I was walking by Sam's sitting room, I couldn't help but notice that it had been rearranged. Now the three sofas were back all along the walls, and the pretty Oriental rug that had been there in the center of the room was gone. Since I didn't see it over in the magazine-filled dining room, I wondered if Sam had rolled it up and tossed it down into the basement. Or, maybe he had Clemmy do that. No matter. Hmm. *Maybe they like dancing,* I thought. I told Bobbie about the incident when I got back home. She agreed with me that I didn't need to be hanging around Sam's house with Clemmy flaunting around like that.

After two weeks of Clemmy's being over at Sam's, Bobbie (mostly she) and I decided that maybe Sam had completely lost his mind after all. She was living with him, unmarried, and this just wasn't our taste. Not that Bobbie and I could or would ever dictate any of our morality to friend Sam, but his acceptance of this type of activity did surprise me. I cannot say what had happened in the past between my buddy and his various dates, but I do know none of them moved in with him. Well, maybe, overnight a time or two, but certainly not on a long-term basis such as we saw with him and Clemmy.

At my foolish insistence, I suggested that Bobbie and I should pay a "social call" on Clemmy and Sam one Sunday afternoon a few days following my unannounced intrusion. Bobbie phoned over to Sam's, and Clemmy had answered. After she hung up Bobbie repeated verbatim what she said. "Why shore. Y'all jest come rats on over. We's be glad ta see ya."

Well, let me tell you, it was crystal clear that her grammar didn't sit too well with Bobbie. I hadn't mentioned Clemmy's apparent lack of cultured speech to sweet wifey. She said to me with an exasperated look on her face as she hung up the phone, "Well, your friend Sam's really gone off the deep end this time."

I looked up at her from my chair. "What's wrong now?" I had a pretty good idea of what my sweet wifey was thinking. "Did she say we could come over there this afternoon?" I was trying to head off Bobbie's expected tirade about my buddy and his foibles.

Bobbie said, staring down at me. "She sounds just like a low-class, uneducated piece of trash straight out of a trailer park."

"Now darn it," I retorted. "It's none of our business who Sam picks to marry." I still couldn't believe in my own mind that my friend would pick somebody like her, but somehow I felt I needed to defend him. Good friends are supposed to support each other, aren't they? "Did she say we could come over there?"

"Yes," Bobbie said, with a shrug to her shoulders. "But now, after hearing her talk, I'm not so sure I want to go after all. You met her. Why didn't you tell me about her grammar?"

"Honey, like I said, it's not any of our business what she's like." I was getting pretty defensive about my buddy's decision by this time. "After all, it's Sam's choice. Now, let's go and be sociable. We don't have to stay long. Besides, since everybody living around here had at least a college education, maybe she'll improve. Remember, Professor Jenkins up the street, teaches English at the community college. Maybe they'll get together and he can straighten her out."

Arriving at top of the fourteen steps, this time Sam responded to the now-repaired door bell and opened the door for us. "Hey you two," he said with a huge grin. "Y'all jes come on in an' sit down fer a spell."

Oh boy! I immediately began to feel real bad. I was not particularly concerned about myself, but I knew Bobbie would immediately pick up on Sam's recently-acquired drawl. I could just hear Bobbie's comments when we got back home. Not only would my wife complain about Clemmy's speech patterns, but now Bobbie would have yet more ammunition against my having Sam as my closest pal.

We only stayed about thirty minutes. I would have been happy to remain longer and chat with Sam, but I could easily see that Bobbie was pretty uncomfortable with the social setting that she was enduring. Sam and Clemmy sat on one sofa against the far wall, while Bobbie and I sat on the one pushed against the wall on the right. Sitting this way and almost yelling across the room at each other was a little awkward, but after all, this was old Sam's house.

When Bobbie and I arrived back home, I immediately busied myself with a novel out in my hammock. I simply didn't want to listen to Bobbie spout off about Sam. Is that escapism on my part or what? I hoped my wife would cool off and let the entire subject ride.

CHAPTER 9

Clemmy's Relatives

Now let me tell you, it was only a week later that I spotted this caravan arrive in front of Sam's house. It consisted of a full-sized Chevy station wagon (with a great deal of the original paint faded away), a muddy jacked-up (I call 'em "high-risers") Ford F-150 pickup truck, and a big, black Buick Roadmaster sedan pulling a trailer that was loaded with an old rusty car of some sort. All those vehicles appeared to be weighed down with bags and luggage. In fact, the station wagon's rear sagged down so much that I would have bet that the lower edge of the rear bumper would scrape the roadway if the car hit any reasonable size bump.

I hollered into the house to Bobbie, who came outside, wiping her hands on her apron. "Hey honey," I said as she came up beside my hammock. "Just take a look over at Sam's." I suspected Bobbie's chin would drop. It did. She said, "Damn!" We counted fifteen people—nine adults and six kids—climb out of those overloaded vehicles and pile into Sam's house. From where I was positioned, it didn't look like anybody even tried knocking on his front door, or ringing his new doorbell—they just barged right in.

Bobbie recovered her composure, put her hands on her lovely hips and said, "You don't suppose ..."

I interrupted her speaking, "Yep. I'll bet they're all relatives of Clemmy. My gosh! You don't think they've all come to live over there, do you?"

She looked down at me. "Who knows just what that friend of yours would do? I guess you're just going to rush right over there and find out what's going on?"

"Well," (I could just feel the beginnings of a husband-wife confrontation coming on.) "Not right now," I said quietly. "I guess I'll just let things settle down for a while before I go over." I felt that maybe that response from me would head things off. Now I'm certainly aware that all marriages have disagreements from time to time, but I just didn't feel like getting into one about my buddy. Not right now, anyway. Plenty of time later for arguing (discussing?) with sweet wifey about my choice of Sam as a best friend.

The next day, one of his guests backed that trailer up in Sam's side yard and rolled that rusty vehicle off onto the grass. Then, three of the men and Sam came out of his back door and stood around that ancient auto frame. My curiosity about Sam's visitors was just about killing me by this time. I presumed that Bobbie's was too, but at that point she wasn't about to nudge me to get more information. Anyway, I left where I was watering some of Bobbie's flowers along the front walk of our house and casually ambled over to Sam's.

Walking up to the group around the pile of junk, I nodded to Sam and introduced myself to the various people there in his yard. None of them seemed too interested in carrying on a conversation with me, so I said to Sam, "Hey buddy. You guys going into the rusty car collecting business?" I had a rather deliberate smile on my face when I uttered that stupid remark. I felt like an intruder into some secret society's private meeting, but after all, I still considered myself to be Sam's friend and I felt that maybe he'd help smooth things over for me. He didn't respond for a moment, while the other guys there ignored me and began pushing that old car around beside Sam's garage. Friendly bunch.

I called Sam aside while this movement was going on and said quietly to him, "Sam, good buddy," I put my hand on his shoulder as if to demonstrate my friendship. "Can you tell me what the heck's going on? I know it's none of my business, but just who are these people? Friends of Clemmy?"

Sam looked furtively at the group that had once again gathered around the car. "Well, yeah, Hank. Sort of anyway. They're Clemmy's family—at least eleven of them are. The others are just friends of theirs." He didn't have a smile on his face. In fact, he had a deep frown.

He turned back to the group, as he and I noticed that the older man had placed himself on the exposed springs of the driver's seat of the old car, and gripped the steering wheel.

"You guys go ahead without me right now," Sam called to them. "I just want to talk with my friend here for a few minutes."

No answer came forth from his guests. They were busy talking among themselves.

"Walk with me, Sam," I said quietly as I turned toward my yard. Sam shrugged his shoulders, looked over at the men, then turned back toward me and began to stroll along with me out toward the street. The men continued to ignore us.

"Okay, buddy," I said momentarily, when I was certain we were out of ear-shot of the group. We kept walking slowly along the side of the highway toward my house. "Now tell me, what's going on? I can clearly see that you've got your hands full, and you don't particularly like the happenings."

"Don't want to talk about it," muttered Sam.

"Well, you'd darn sure better tell somebody, before you explode." I was looking at him when I said that and almost lost my footing as I stepped on a big rock. Funny that I'd never seen that old stone lying there before—as many times as I'd traversed this particular walkway between my house and Sam's. "Remember, I'm your friend and I can clearly see that this thing's got you all bottled up. Sam, you need to unload these problems to me."

Sam turned and looked back at his house and yard. "Don't want to talk about it," he muttered again.

We reached my yard, and I pulled up two green upright lawn chairs, motioned him into one and I sat in the other. "Okay, dammit now Sam," I said to him, looking him directly in the eye. "You just sit here and open up. You gotta tell somebody and I'm here. I'm your buddy, and I'm the guy you're going to talk to about it. So spit it out." Well, by golly, I was forceful. I felt that he'd have to open up to me now that I had put things to him that way. *Man*, I thought to myself, *this really* is *like trying to get blood out of a turnip.*

"All right," Sam began slowly. "Clemmy asked me if she could invite a cou-ple of cousins to come over from Pitt County to visit for a day or so. She said they'd never been in such a nice house as mine was and she wanted to 'show off' a little. That's what she said." He looked over the field toward his house. His face showed a lot of distress—big frown and huge wrinkles on his ever-expanding forehead.

"I told her, yes, of course. But then, this whole bunch showed up. I guess I'm lucky they didn't bring any more of their kids with them. But I couldn't just run them all off, could I?"

Sam proceeded to tell me why he felt like he just couldn't bring himself to insist that her relatives leave. After all, he pointed out, he did tell Clemmy that she could invite some family in. He told me he assumed that she meant just a couple, when she actually meant fifteen. "Just a minor point of miscommunication," Sam said, as he again glanced over at his yard. I looked over also, and noted that three of the men were beginning to do things with that rusty old hulk.

By the way, while I was over there I was able to take a pretty good look at the relic and determined that it was a 1949 Ford. I saw a couple of spots where the rust hadn't quite gotten all the way around it, and noted a little bit of a metallic blue color. I figured that was probably the original color of that old vehicle.

"What're you going to do about them all, Sam?" I inquired in earnest. Both Bobbie and I were a little concerned about the quality of the neighborhood being degraded. Certainly, as far as I knew, there was no city ordinance against having fifteen (seventeen, counting Clemmy and Sam) people living in a three bedroom house, but I wondered if the fire marshall might be concerned. Sam looked back at me and replied, "Well, Clemmy's really a pretty nice girl." He killed a couple of black ants with the toe of his shoe. "She's an excellent cook and makes me up some delicious meals." Sam smiled as he told me this. "She's real good on Tex-Mex eating, and gets up early to fix my breakfast for me."

I said, "Yeah, that may be true, Sam, but do you really think she's the gal for you?" I was aware I was pushing pretty hard, but felt that as long as he was in my yard and was willing to discuss his relationship with Clemmy, that I couldn't lose much by proceeding. Out of the corner of my eye, I watched a robin pecking the ground.

"Don't want to talk about it," responded my friend. "I'm going back on over now. Bye, Hank." Sam rose with a somewhat bewildered look on his face, turned toward the field between our houses and left.

Well, I thought, *how about that? Here I am, Sam's pal, and what do I get? Darn near a cold shoulder. How's a guy supposed to help a friend if that certain buddy won't let you help him?* Granted, he opened up more than he had ever before, but certainly not much.

Four days later, my curiosity about that car got the best of me. Once again I strolled over to where two of Sam's (Clemmy's) guests/relatives were out in Sam's backyard, tinkering around that rusty Ford. I just had to investigate.

I reintroduced myself and learned that the two guys were Billy and Bill. Now those names would be hard to remember. They had an acetylene torch and a bunch of tools and were piece-by-piece, taking that old thing apart. Several pieces that appeared to be fenders were already lying on the ground beside the car, and they were slowly working on the front bumper. Apparently the rust had just about ruined the metal and Billy and Bill were using the torch to cut through the metal wherever they couldn't unbolt pieces. What a job! I saw that Bill already had skinned the back of his left hand pretty bad—right across a tattoo of somebody's name—and it was bleeding. That didn't seem to bother him, though. It was obvious that they didn't need my help, so I said my good-byes and strolled on back home.

When I told Bobbie about what the guys were doing over at Sam's, she laughed and said, "That is the stupidest thing I ever heard of. Why don't they just go out and buy themselves a new car?"

I told her it was probably something like a hobby for them, and maybe just another guy thing. This must have soothed her feelings, because she didn't say anything else about it to me.

Well, those guys must have arranged a bunch of working shifts, because they continued to dismantle the car during the next four weeks, and I rarely saw the same two or three guys out there working. After the first week, I began to see that Sam was one of the workers, and that from where I could see, he was really getting into it. *Being around Clemmy all the time must have driven him to it,* I thought. *He must have needed a chance to escape from her for a while.*

Bobbie and I talked about Sam quite a lot during the time that his house was full of people. I didn't go over there much at all—felt like I was imposing. Once I did go over when Clemmy needed to borrow a "quart of sugar." Yep, that's how much she asked for—a quart. Luckily Bobbie had plenty, so I grabbed at the chance to go inside Sam's house once again. Boy, had it ever changed? This time, the sitting room was completely empty of furniture except for a floor lamp right smack in the center of the room—directly under the chandelier. A long, orange heavy-duty extension cord was trailed across the foyer from the dining room. All around the floor were sleeping bags, and quilt sleeping pallets of various colors. A couple of those quilts were right pretty. I decided right away that this was where most of the visitors slept at night. Walking by that sitting room on my way to the kitchen with the sugar, I couldn't help but notice a slight smell of stale body odor emanating from it. I had to wonder if any of them had washed their sleeping bags during their extended stay. I heard a bunch of talking coming from upstairs, so I gathered that most of the cousins were using Sam's master bedroom as their main meeting place.

Clemmy introduced me to the four other ladies there in the kitchen with her, but I'm not real good with names, and immediately forgot them. Two of them were right skinny, but the other two were obviously pretty close cousins to Clemmy—real heavyweights. One looked like her red hair was real, but the others had various and sundry mixtures of dyed hair. I guess you could call one of them fairly pretty. Not the others. I've never cared much for heavy facial hair on women, but maybe they can't help it.

Sam was in the yard with four of the fellows. They were working on the Ford, so I stopped by briefly before returning home. By now, they had taken that car frame completely apart, sanded out all the obvious rust spots and were reassembling it. Didn't have a motor in it. I had to admit that it did actually favor an original 1949 four-door Ford. I had one just like it once. Sold it when its odometer turned 100,000 miles. Somehow, I lost confidence in it at that point.

Sam seemed to be too busy piddling with one of the doors to spend any time with me, so I mumbled a quiet "so long" and went on back home. Sam didn't respond.

Bobbie didn't like it too much when she saw the bunch over at Sam's rig up two long clotheslines. They were in the field between our two houses. Actually, when I saw that, I said to myself, *By golly, maybe they're finally gonna wash some of their clothes and sleeping bags.* Yep. Both of those clotheslines got completely filled with washing. I just hate to see ragged ladies' underwear hanging on clotheslines. On the other hand, perhaps you could say that viewing that stuff was a very religious experience—very "hole-y." Unfortunately, this day was followed by six days of steady rain, so I guess those things got a good rinsing. I never did learn how the people over there handled their sleeping arrangements, what with all their sleeping bags and quilts soaking wet out on the line. It really didn't make much sense to me, because I know for a fact that Sam has a clothes dryer.

During these days I missed my chats with my friend Sam. I couldn't get him to come over and I didn't feel comfortable going over there. Phone calls didn't seem satisfactory, either, because Sam always acted as if there were others listening to his side of our conversations. *Why did he let them stay there so long? Three months and counting!*

CHAPTER 10

The Dinner

"Harry!" Bobbie called to me one morning. I was busy writing some checks in my study. She was out in the kitchen making us some chocolate chip cookies. Oh yes, my darling wife can really cook good. I mean, she hardly ever renders me a meal that I don't like. Of course, after being married for a bunch of pleasant (mostly, anyway—like most successful marriages) years, she has certainly learned what I like and don't like. And she tries real hard to stick with those things we both take pleasure in. I enjoy chocolate chip cookies. I don't particularly like the store-bought variety, though. They always seem to be sort of dry and not very tasty.

You know, they make these little packets of stuff that companies add in their packaging of new electronic equipment and such, that are supposed to keep the moisture level down to a minimum. Seems like somebody ought to invent a similar-type of gizmo that cookie manufacturers could add in their packages that would keep their products fresh-baked moist. Maybe someday.

Anyway, I answered, "Yes, honey. What do you want?"

"Didn't you hear the phone ring?" she said as she walked into the study.

Somewhat surprised, I turned from my desk and said, "No. Was it important?"

"Honey," sweet wifey said, with an interesting look in her eyes. "We, you and I, have been cordially invited over to Sam's for dinner tomorrow night. Clemmy did the calling. Now what do you think of that?"

My jaw dropped as I pondered this interesting turn of events. "What'd you tell her?"

"I felt like I had to say yes, but let me tell you, it took a lot of will power to keep from slamming the phone down," answered Bobbie. "I sure have no desire whatsoever to go over there tomorrow night and listen to all that poor-grammar chatter."

"Now, Bobbie," I replied as gently as I knew how, "we've talked about this, and you and I both realize that their education isn't quite up to our standards, but that we've already agreed to accept Sam's friends just as they are." I turned my head back to my papers. "Seems to me that also applies to his friend's family." I didn't particularly want to see her next expression.

"Yes, I know you're right, honey. But I still must tell you that I have no interest in going. I don't know anybody over there beside Sam and that Clemmy person, and if they're all like her, I don't think we'd find anything intelligent at all to talk about. And who knows just what they'll feed us?" Bobbie turned her head back to the kitchen, saying as she left the study, "I'll bet it'll be some of that Tex-Mex food that you said Sam told you he liked so much."

"We'll see," I said, as she left. I was curious also.

The next night, Bobbie and I donned our casual visiting clothes and strolled (albeit, somewhat hesitantly) over to Sam's place. We were met by four of the youngsters. None were very cute, in my humble opinion. At least none of this bunch would hold a candle to Bobbie's nephew, Jim. Now there's a real fine ten-year-old.

We went on into Sam's foyer and there were Sam and a couple of his visitors, sitting on his steps to upstairs. All conversation stopped. A moment later, Sam, still sitting there, introduced Bobbie to the bunch beside him, and then he got up and ushered Bobbie, followed by me, into the kitchen.

"Well, hey there, y'all," exclaimed Clemmy when she saw us. "Girls, this here be's Sam's buddy, Hank and his woman." She was at the sink washing some greens.

"His woman?" Oh ho! Did that statement ever make poor Bobbie stiffen? I don't think anybody else noticed Bobbie's reaction, but I sure did. I could just feel this party getting off on the wrong track.

Bobbie said a polite hello and nodded to the four other women there in the kitchen. All four of those ladies immediately stopped their food preparation and, one by one, shook her hand and gave dear Bobbie a bear hug. They apparently didn't feel it important to wash their hands first. Poor wifey wound up with grease and flour on her hands and a floured handprint on her back. The one with the bright red hair seemed to try to kiss Bobbie on the lips, until Bobbie discretely turned her head slightly. Friendly bunch.

Frankly, I have to admit that the kitchen sure did smell good to me. Since I was pretty used to being in and around Sam's house, I really felt pretty comfortable there. But poor Bobbie just hadn't been over there all that much.

"Smells mighty good in here," I said to Clemmy, as I nodded randomly at her cousins. "What all are you lovely ladies cooking up for us?" (Did I actually say, "lovely?")

Beatrice, one of the skinny ones, said, "I hopes ya likes country cooking, 'cause that is whut you's gonna get. And plenty of it too."

The cousin with the real (I think) red hair said, "I'm fixin' up you two a big scrumptious chocolate cake. Three layers, too. You two're gonna like it. Clemmy told us that Sam said you two were real good eaters, so we girls done planned on you having plenty to eat."

Bobbie just stood there nodding her sweet head. I noticed that she was clenching and unclenching her hands. I don't think anybody else saw her doing that.

Clemmy spoke up from the other side of the center console stove, "Y'all git on back to the other room. We'll git it going pretty soon."

So Bobbie and I strolled back into the foyer, where we found that the men had retreated back upstairs. We spotted one of Sam's sofas parked beside several stacks of smelly magazines in the unused dining room and sat ourselves down. Sam had disappeared. Nobody came to chat with us, so Bobbie and I simply sat there and watched the various children running in and out of the front door.

Shortly, Clemmy and the redhead came out with plates and forks for Bobbie and me and two big pots of steaming food.

The two ladies handed us our plates and, as we held them in our laps, plopped out heaping spoonfuls of food. What kind, you ask? Well, Clemmy's stuff kind of looked like some make of beans all covered with a reddish goo. I also spotted rice in there. Something green, too. The redhead plunked down several pieces of the greasiest-looking fried chicken I have ever seen. I mean, when I lifted a drumstick off my plate, you could see a big puddle of grease just staring up at me.

Now, neither lady left to go back to the kitchen. No, they just stood right there, waiting for us to try out their cooking. Bobbie and I stole a couple of quick glances at each other as we dove into those plates of food. Well, let me tell you something. That red stuff was spicy HOT! I mean, it started burning my mouth almost before it got to my lips. And it burned every bit of my being, too. Since I had nothing to drink, the only choice I could come up with to help temper the burning was the greasy fried chicken. It only helped a little bit. Poor Bobbie actually had tears running down her cheeks.

I asked "red" for a drink of water, so she turned her head and yelled out to one of the kids on the steps, "Hey youngun. Go gits these here folks a drink of water." But she didn't leave us. No sir. She seemed to want to insure herself that we'd eat every darn bit of the food on our plates, hot stuff, grease and all. I had no napkin, so pulled out a clean handkerchief from my back pocket and offered it to poor Bobbie. We shared it.

The kid got back with a single glass (half-full) of warm tap water for each of us to share and that helped a little. Both Bobbie and I graciously declined seconds on the food.

By this time all of the kiddies had lined themselves up at the doorway to the dining room. They stood there like little soldiers, in formation, silently, just watching us. None had any food.

Next, two of Clemmy's fat (Excuse me. I meant "full-bodied.) cousins brought us out more food. I couldn't spot anyone else eating—just us. This next batch of food was sweet potato soufflé, and frankly was real good. Then came the collard greens, seasoned with thick chunks of pork fat back. Real tasty too, once you got the grease floating on top out of the way. I will say one thing, my handkerchief was getting pretty soiled with grease by this time.

More water was requested and received—just like before—half a glass. The little five-year-old (I'm guessing) brown-haired girl never spoke to us. She just moved back in line and stared at Bobbie and me with those big brown eyes of hers. Kind of unnerving, in a way. I wondered if I would get anywhere asking for a nice clean napkin.

Well, I got my plate cleaned off pretty well, but noticed that poor Bobbie was beginning to struggle. Her bites were becoming smaller and smaller, and she seemed to be having difficulty getting each one down.

But still, the two heavy cousins stood there, pots and ladles in hand, ready to dish out more. Bobbie spoke up, saying to the stringy-haired one—the collards one, "I believe I have had all I want for now, thank you." Now, I would have thought that polite remark by my wife would have done it just fine, and no more food would be thrust upon us. But no … "Collards" and her associate said not one word, but abruptly turned and headed back to the kitchen. I looked over at Bobbie, wiped my fingers once again on the now-very-greasy handkerchief, and was about to suggest that it was time for us to leave and go home, when here came Clemmy and the one last girl from the kitchen. Uh-oh. More food! This time, even though Bobbie and I tried to decline, it was obvious that these gals simply had to know that we had eaten some more of their cooking. Black-eyed peas, stewed turnips, and scalloped oysters. (I hate stewed turnips!) The formation of children remained there, staring curiously.

What are you gonna do? We tried as politely as possible to decline, but we just couldn't convince those people. So, against all odds, poor Bobbie and I forced those full-sized helpings down. And the ladlers just stood there, saying not one thing, watching, so as to make sure we enjoyed every morsel. After all, apparently they determined that since they went to so much trouble to cook the stuff, the least we could do was to eat it—and enjoy it.

At long last Sam wandered into the dining room, eating a piece of chocolate cake. *Oh my gosh.* I thought through my over-stuffed fullness, *I hope he's not going to make us eat some of that cake.* Before he could get a word out of his grinning, chocolate-smeared mouth, I spoke up, "Sam, we've had a great time, but we've just got to go home now. Bobbie has an early appointment over at the nursing home tomorrow." I figured my sweet wifey certainly would not complain that I'd told a sort of lie to my buddy. "Sort of," nothing—it was a bald-faced lie. But after all, I was desperately trying to save our lives. One more bite forced down and I'm sure I would have exploded right there.

Sam finished swallowing his bite, and replied, "Hey, you guys. (Now my Bobbie's a "guy?") I'm shore glad you two done come over here tonight. Maybe we can do it again sometimes. Bye y'all." And, with that said, he and the dear ladies all left us and marched back into the kitchen. Thank God! I looked over at poor Bobbie, took her plate and put hers and mine on the floor in front of the couch, grabbed her arm and we quickly started to leave. We had to edge around the kiddie formation.

Just as we got to Sam's front porch, a voice called to us from back at the kitchen door. I turned hesitantly, and saw that it was the redhead. "I be's sorry you two gots to go home now. Here's each o' you a big piece o' my chocolate cake to take on home wit chu." She came to us and thrust two huge pieces of that heavily-frosted and sticky cake into our bare hands. We were to simply carry the cake home with us, bare-handed. Oh well.

Bobbie said, "Thank you for a delightful and entertaining evening."

Clemmy stuck her head around the kitchen door as we stepped down on the first step. "Let's do this agin rail soon."

That same non-speaking little girl had left her position in line and stood on the front porch. She was staring at us as we went out Sam's front door. Half-way down the path toward home, I turned, glanced back over at Sam's and saw the little girl still standing on his top step, watching us. Curious.

Luckily, Bobbie and I had plenty of Pepto at home, and finally struggled off to bed. I think we both drank at least a pint of that soothing liquid, and it seemed to help a little.

"Do it again, my foot," uttered Bobbie in her anguish. "I will never again set foot over in Sam's house. And did you catch his grammar? He's getting just like the rest of them."

I decided to ease myself on to sleep in my fullness. Didn't feel like defending my buddy at that moment.

Just as I was finally dozing off, I think I heard, "Damn!"

CHAPTER 11

The Departure

Thursday … Yes, I'm certain it was a Thursday. I remember it well. Clear day, kind of brisk outside. Bobbie called to me from the kitchen to get myself out of bed and look out the window over toward Sam's. Naturally, hearing my sweet wifey wanting me to see something over across the field toward Sam's, I immediately did what she asked. I peered through the window. Oh ho! "The group" had loaded that semi-restored (still no motor) Ford onto their trailer and were in the process of pulling out of Sam's yard. All three vehicles were set up in a sort of parade and were slowly proceeding down the street away from Sam's property. I could spot various and sundry arms sticking out the car windows waving their goodbyes to Clemmy. She was on Sam's front porch, some kind of towel in hand, waving to them as they left. She didn't appear too happy.

I expected a phone call from Sam later that day, but didn't get it. And Bobbie (mainly at her suggestion) and I decided to let things ride for a day or so before I called Sam.

So, Monday afternoon I made my move. I strolled over to Sam's and rang his front door bell. No response, but I could hear it ringing from back in the house. I knocked, but again, got no response. So, I bravely opened the door, fully expecting to spot Clemmy padding around in her bare feet and very thin nightgown. Nobody.

"Sam! Sam, you here?" I yelled loudly enough to awaken any sleeping body.

"Up here," came Sam's voice. He sounded gruff. "Come on up if you want to."

When I got to his room I could see right off, by the position of his body all hunched tightly over his computer keyboard and the expression on his face that something was somewhat awry.

"Where's Clemmy?" I asked. "What's happening, buddy?"

Sam was pecking away at his computer, and had a compact disk playing on his audio player. Nice, soft, relaxing music. He has a large collection of CDs from Readers' Digest or Time-Life or some outfit like that. I recognized something from Pachelbel's Canon.

Sam stopped typing, and turned toward me with a heavy frown and wrinkled forehead, actually sounding somewhat angry, but I don't think his pique was directed at me. I noticed that he had apparently not shaved for several days. "Gone," he said, "Things didn't work out between us. I took her to the bus station in Charlotte last night about nine o'clock." And then he abruptly turned back to his typing. It was pretty obvious to me that he really was not very interested in telling me any more about the situation just at that moment.

"Oh. Sorry, buddy," I said. "Well, I was just checking on you guys. I'm gone. See you later." He nodded, but didn't respond verbally. And I did leave, figuring that sooner or later Sam would probably break down and tell me what happened. Boy, let me tell you, I was sure curious. Of course, she'd never have been my type, what with no eyebrows and all—and all those relatives—but I was still surprised that my good friend would have somehow gotten hooked up with somebody like that over the Internet.

Actually, two weeks later, Sam had cooled off somewhat and we had buddied-up again. We were driving down to the coast to do some fishing and he got sort of talkative. He'd had himself a sherry just before we left, so I made sure that I drove. Sam doesn't usually do a lot of heavy drinking, but whenever he does, I make sure I'm not riding with him. He can probably hold his booze pretty well, but then, I'm just not all that sure how much a person can hold without getting too much for safety.

Anyway, Sam finally told me what happened between him and Clemmy. He said, "It seems like that first night Clemmy walked all over my house. It was obvious right off that she didn't like what she saw. Why, she criticized my furniture placement, and how I've laid out the different rooms." Sam said that he really didn't appreciate her attitude, because he is right proud of his house. "She even laughed at my coffee table."

Now Sam's a real good friend, but frankly I have found that he doesn't really take criticism too well. I guess it is because he's so smart and all, and when he sort of designs or invents a way to do something, I guess he feels that it's bound to be okay. So, you darn sure better not think bad of it. He takes it real personal. I've often wished that I could get him to change.

Anyway, that set him off that night, and he jumped all over her because of her laughing at his stuff, and complaining about his three-couch sitting room. I guess she didn't take too kindly to his reaction either, because he said she didn't apologize or anything. So, he told me that he got mad and stormed off to his bedroom and slammed his door behind him and locked it. "I left her to find her own bedroom, and do whatever she wanted to at that point. I was really angry." He told me that the next day was pretty bad. She didn't speak to him, wouldn't even cook his breakfast. "I was forced to cook my own and I'd already set up my taste buds for some of her cooking." I guess he figured that for a woman that large, she'd be a really great cook. She didn't speak to him at all that or the next entire day. Just sat around—away from wherever he was—and sort of sulked. Now Sam's not too bad in that sulking department himself. Must have been a fun couple of days for both of them.

But Sam told me he finally cooled off and figured that he'd better make peace with Clemmy. "It worked," he said, after he got all chummy and they cuddled for a while. "She got up and started cooking, and fed me the most scrumptious meal I'd ever had."

Lord help! I thought to myself, *there are certain things I just would not do for a good meal. No way would I ever want to spend any amount of time "cuddling" with that behemoth.* Of course, I realize that some people see beyond the heft of others, and accept them for their true "inner beauty," but not me. I just can't do that.

Sam told me he'd finally had enough of Clemmy's good food and, especially, had had it "up to here" with all her family, and the noisy kids, and the stinking clothes and sleeping bags all over his house. So after he ran her relatives off, he got on the phone and called the Charlotte bus station and found out that he could get her on a bus back to Wichita Falls that night. He said he told her it was all over. So, after she had tearfully fixed him a real fine meal (his words), he grabbed her bags and drove her over to Charlotte. He told me he did pay for her ticket, "out of the goodness of my heart." Sam said that she didn't speak a single word to him on the trip over to Charlotte, and she didn't even say goodbye when she got on the bus. Didn't even thank him for the bus ticket. Darn, what a mess. I don't know how her schedule worked out, but I'll just bet that turned into one long, and I mean long, bus trip back home to Texas for her.

I didn't push Sam for any more information about the incident, and certainly, as a friend, I'd never lecture him about his, shall I say, *faux pas.*

CHAPTER 12

The Plane! The Plane!

One day about eight weeks after Clemmy's departure, I went over to Sam's just to visit. Like most times, I didn't bother to call ahead, but just took a chance that he'd be there and would welcome me. As I've mentioned before, I sort of keep a casual eye turned toward my buddy's house, so I usually know if he's there and if he has got somebody there with him that maybe I'm not supposed to barge in on. Know what I mean?

Anyway, I found him in his backyard shop. Incidentally, for some reason, he never uses his garage for his car. He keeps some old cardboard boxes stored in there. He made his own concrete shop floor with these bags of self-mixing concrete that you buy at the big hardware stores; the kind he used on his dam. He'd bring home maybe eight of those sixty-pound bags and mix up two or three of them in his wheelbarrow with whatever amount of water he figured that he needed, and then just sort of splash the mixture over on the dirt where he wanted a concrete floor. After he got the blend on the floor poured as thick as he wanted, I'd guess about two to three inches, he'd stir up another batch and repeat the same process. But wouldn't you know it? He had problems.

Actually, I'd told Sam during one of our front porch chats that I read in a do-it-yourself book somewhere that for a large cement surface (like the one Sam did), you're supposed to put down steel rods crisscrossed first (for lateral strength, I think) so the concrete floor will not crack as bad later on. But before that, you're supposed to make up a wooden mold. For a floor the size of his shop, the book recommended that it be divided into equal sections. That would have called for maybe four sections about five feet square and then you would pour the floor about four inches thick. After the concrete gets to a certain degree of hardness, but is still pretty wet and soft, you're supposed to go back over it with a separate two-by-four or one-by-six board or something like that. Typically, there will be one person on each end, and they will sort of tap-tap-tap the top of the cement in the slightly overfilled mold until the face of the mixture is no longer showing the pebbles or rocks that were included in the bag. They just sort of sink down into the wet mix. This action generally smoothes down the wet concrete and gives you a level surface (if you first set up your wooden mold right).

Well, old buddy Sam didn't pay one bit of attention to my information. I suppose he figured that he'd skip that part and just freehandedly pour the cement on the floor. I presume he thought he'd be able to go back later and smooth things down pretty well. I watched him at that time for a while, then realizing that he didn't want my help or input, I went on home.

By the way, this particular incident that I'm talking about (cementing his shop floor) was about two years or so ago. Well, frankly, it didn't really work out the way I guess Sam would have wanted. I could have expected that. I mean, the final floor was not exactly either level or smooth, and it had the tops of lots of nice white pebbles in part of it sticking up through the surface. And in other areas there were gray, sharp stones showing. I gather he must have bought his bags at two different stores, or at least bought two different brands, because some brands use pebbles while others use gray gravel. Didn't look particularly good if you ask me, but then Sam didn't acknowledge minding it too much. It made a pretty rough floor to walk on. I didn't ever say anything about my friend's ignoring my suggestions about a concreting job of course.

Oh yes, one other thing. Apparently he must have run out of concrete one afternoon when he was doing his pouring and went out to a different store and bought some more. I guess that he bought whatever they had and didn't pay any attention to the label. This last stuff was the kind of "instant" quick-cure concrete that's used a lot in fence posts and holes for stabilizing kids' swing sets, and stuff like that. Anyway, it must have set up too fast for him, because not only was it yet a different color from the preponderance of the floor, but it seemed to kind of stick up in big hard clumps of cement and stones. I guess you could say this was kind of okay, because it was in a back corner where not much light would show on it. Also, it was hard to spot unless you knew it was there. The main problem was that once it hardened into those lumps, no matter what he did, he never could get it smoothed down anywhere near what you would find acceptable. Not anywhere as good as the rest of his floor, which as I said, sure was not an expert job. I'm aware that he used a hammer and chisel, trying to get that stuff leveled out. Didn't help much. Sam's a good man, but sometimes I wonder if his ego prevents him from studying up on something before he goes off half-cocked like he seems to do so often.

Oh. What I was going to tell you about was that Sam's brother out in California used to fly for some airline or another. A real four-striper captain and all. Well, his hobby, according to Sam, was flying small, single-engine planes on his time off. So, as an extension of this hobby, he sent off for a do-it-yourself kit for a special stunt flying airplane. He built it at his home out there and, according to Sam, subsequently flew it quite a bit. I never met his brother.

Sam mentioned to me late one afternoon (on his porch, of course), "A hobby of building and flying your own airplane might be a lot of fun." He turned toward me. "Don't you think so, Hank?"

I said, somewhat astonished, "Do you know how to fly a plane?"

Sam responded, "Well, no, not actually. But I doubt if it's hard to do. My brother does it all the time, and tells me he has a great time. I guess I'll take a couple of lessons after I get my plane built." Sam's shop is fairly well-equipped, so I figure he thought it'd be a reasonable place to put it together. But not even knowing how to fly? Hmm.

By happenstance, I was over there when the kit arrived on a big semi truck. Boy, you should have seen the look in Sam's eyes when he started opening the boxes and crates. Excited? You bet! Just like a small boy opening up presents on Christmas morning. Anyway, the kit was nothing like what I expected. Maybe Sam had discussed it with his brother enough so that he wasn't surprised. The home-built (Sam told me to never call something like this "home-made." It is always "home-built" or "kit-built.") kit consisted of what looked to me like maybe ten thousand pieces of specially shaped wood! I thought airplanes were made of aluminum, but Sam reassured me by pointing out that the first planes that were invented were made of wood and glue and fabric. Okay, I stood corrected. I still prefer to fly in metal airplanes, though. I don't know, they just seem safer to me.

Sam explained, as he was unpacking all that stuff, "What I'll be doing is to take these various pieces and, 'following specific directions' (Sam said that?), glue them together until I have the correct shapes. Then I'll cover the plane with the special fabric," he pointed over to a large bundle in a corner. "Then I'll paint the entire job."

"What about a motor?"

"Oh, the manual tells you what to buy and where to get it. Shouldn't be a problem."

I thought, *I hope it's a single-seater, because I don't think I'll ever want to go flying with him in it. What a lot of work!* But then, who counts hours with hobbies?

❧   ❧   ❧

Well, on this particular day he was out in his shop just fuming and snorting. I could hear him as I was half-way across his yard. Just as I was walking in the shop door, I think I heard him use some of those strange Vietnamese cuss words of his. Anyway, it seems as though he'd been building the frames for one of the wings, had sanded all the nice, contoured girders that give the wing its special shape, and then carefully mixed up the special glue and assembled the pieces together. He had about twenty or thirty of these shapes lying all around his shop. He had fabricated them all about a week before and was allowing the glue to completely set and harden to its maximum strength. Darn right, you sure as heck do want that stuff strong!

Anyway, Sam had just picked up a couple of these wing girders and the pieces just flat fell apart in his hands. Darn, what a mess. You know, I think I'd be pretty angry too, if I'd spent untold hours sorting out and sanding pieces and gluing them together, and then finding out that the glue didn't work. Phooey!

Thus ended Sam's excursion into home-built airplanes. He just quit right then and there. Later he said, "I never did learn what happened to the glue. I think it was an error made back at the factory."

I asked, "Did you call them about it?"

"Nope. I just decided I didn't want to build a plane after all." He just let things drop right there. He didn't seem to want to continue talking about that subject.

By the way, Bobbie and I saw several pretty big bonfires out behind his shop several days later. He's never again mentioned flying to me.

CHAPTER 13

The Band Practice

One night, Bobbie and I had finished a late supper and had put away the dishes. We were sitting on our screened-in back porch just chatting and enjoying the more or less peace and quiet of an early fall evening. The kids over the back fence had all been called in. We could still hear the numerous insect sounds, and a few frogs from Sam's fiasco—excuse me—pond, but the lightning bugs had disappeared for the season. Bobbie told me she heard an owl off in the distance, but, due to my slight hearing loss, I didn't hear it. We were planning to go on in to bed in a few minutes.

Suddenly, she said, "Do you hear that?" I did.

It was coming from over at Sam's house and it sounded like dance band music from the 1930s and 1940s. And you know, if I could hear it all the way over from Sam's house, you gotta know it was loud.

Bobbie said, "Somebody's playing stuff that Benny Goodman, Tommy Dorsey, and Johnny Mercer recorded on those old seventy-eight RPM records."

I listened for a couple moments. "This doesn't sound quite like those—the quality's nowhere near as good and smooth. Besides, it sounds like somebody over at Sam's is continually starting and stopping the record player."

My sweet wifey has an excellent ear for music and pointed out to me that parts of the music sounded almost like one of the orchestra members was playing off-key. Now, that didn't make any sense to me at all, because everybody knows that the music companies would never release a recording that was not perfect. Anyway, as I pointed out to Bobbie, it was basically pretty nice music, kind of enjoyable, and nostalgic.

"It's too loud," said Bobbie, even raising her voice toward me. She obviously wanted to make sure that I heard her. "We'll never be able to get to sleep with that racket going on this late at night." She stood up, walked to the edge of the porch to where she could look over at the nursing home across the street.

She continued, "I'll just bet that loud music is annoying some of those poor old people over there. It's probably especially bothersome to that sweet little old Miss Efird. You've heard me talk about her. Remember? She's almost ninety years old, and goes to bed at seven o'clock sharp. And her room's on the side facing Sam's house."

"Yeah," I responded. "You've spoken about her a lot of times. She's one of your favorites over there, isn't she?"

"Well, she certainly is. After all that racket, I expect that she's awake and sitting up in bed right now. Not only that, there's no doubt in my mind that she's calling for the attendants to go up and down the nursing home halls, turning off everybody's radios and televisions. She's sure to make a fuss, and tomorrow she'll be as cranky as all get out."

I said, "They can handle her, can't they? After all, that's why they have attendants, isn't it?" I knew full well that Bobbie would not accept my lame response. Don't know why I even uttered it.

"Well, Harold," she said to me with a fierce tone in her voice. I knew I'd had it this time. I just couldn't find it in my heart to sympathize with her concerns about Miss Efird, who I'd never even met. "You just march right on over to *your friend's* and tell him to stop that infernal noise right now. And you can tell him I said so, too." Clearly, my sweet Bobbie was getting more and more angry by the minute.

Whoo-ee, when dearest Barbara Ann says something to me in that tone of voice, I jump. I don't even have to ask how high. I move, now.

So, I hot-footed it over to Sam's to tell (ask?) him to knock off the loud music. Actually, as I was walking over there, I began to wonder why I didn't just phone him. But sweet wifey had rather insisted that I go in person, presumably, so it'd have a better effect. Besides, I was curious myself.

As I approached his house, I quickly learned that it was not a recording at all. I could see several cars parked in front of his house and I could spot through those big windows of Sam's first floor sitting room that he had six or seven guys in there with him. I got to his front door, and rang the bell. However, the guys were making so much racket in there that Sam couldn't hear it. So, I did the perfunctory knock, also not heard, pushed open the front door, and bravely strolled on in.

Sam and those guys all had musical instruments out and had sheet music all over the place. Sam was directing, and doing a pretty good job of it. In fact, the music really was not all that bad, if you ask me. When Sam saw me, he waved the group to a stop, turned to me and said, "Hey, Hank. I found a bunch of old sheet music up in my attic and thought it'd be fun to get a bunch of buddies together and go at it. Like it?" He grinned, automatically expecting me to say yes, I suppose. He turned back to the guys and said, "Hold it a minute fellows."

"Well, I'll tell you, Sam." I nodded at the other guys there. I didn't recognize any of them, which surprised me. I thought I knew nearly all of Sam's other friends. "You're making too much noise for us to sleep. How about stopping?" Well, darned if I was not pretty forceful with my buddy.

"Hey here now, Hank," Sam retorted. "Some of these guys have driven in from as far away as thirty miles, just for this band session. I can't stop this thing right now. It wouldn't be fair." In other words, Sam had just told me, "No, I'm not going to respond to your request."

I said, "Come out here into the foyer with me a minute, Sam." I didn't take him by the arm, but I was speaking with as much forcefulness as I could muster. And how about this? He did follow me out.

"Now look, Sam," I said to him. "I'm real sorry about your friends' problems, but you're making just entirely too much noise over here. Darn it, you've got to stop." Boy, I was really acting powerful now. I was not too sure how much more power I could show to convince my friend to obey my request.

"Just can't do that, buddy," Sam said to me as he glanced back into the three-couch sitting room. The six men in there were fiddling with their instruments, and examining their individual sheets of music. "I promised the fellows we'd make a full evening of it, and we're just getting started. Great sounds aren't they?"

I was up against it. Bobbie had insisted I get them to put a stop to the music, and now Sam was saying he wouldn't. *What the heck could I do?*

Suddenly a thought entered my head. "Okay, Sam. I'll tell you how you can fix this situation. You take those guys and all your music down in your basement. Play down there and then we probably can't hear you. That way, we'll both be satisfied. Will you do that?" I put my hands on my hips in order to show additional determination.

Sam again peered into the sitting room. He was thinking. Then he said, "Okay fellows. We've been ordered to quiet down." He turned his face back to me with a frown showing on his long forehead. "We're going to go down in my basement and continue there." Then, he said to me, "That suit you, your high-ness?" His face was getting red, and I felt that that was a rude response to me.

"Yep, Sam. That ought to make things better." I wasn't real sure what I'd do if his band music continued to be as loud as before. "Thanks. See you later."

On my way back home I saw the guys leaving the sitting room with their music and instruments. I was not sure how well the guys would be able to see their music down in his crummy old basement, but right then I didn't give a hoot. Maybe Sam'd break out that long extension cord of his again and take a floor lamp down there. Yeah, rude. Besides, Sam knows full well that I play both clarinet and saxophone, and he knew that I'd seen the music up in his attic that day when I was there. So why hadn't he invited me to sit in with the group? Well, darn his hide! He had really insulted me this time, and I sure as heck didn't like it. After all, I was supposedly one of his best friends. And he ignored me. Good friends just don't do things like that. I felt almost as if he'd slapped me in the face. The more I thought about it, the madder I got. *Well, by darn, if he is gonna treat me like that, maybe he can just find himself another friend.*

Arriving home, sweet Bobbie quickly saw the expression on my face. She's so smart. She figured out that I was real mad—just like that. My slamming the front door real hard had nothing do with it, I'm sure. She came up to me, mas-saged the base of my neck (I really like that) and said soothingly, "Honey, I'm glad you got that old music stopped. You did good. Now come, let's go on to bed."

There was not much more that I needed to say. I was still pretty mad at Sam, and yet I also felt that I really didn't want to lose his friendship. On the other hand, I was pretty proud of myself standing up to Sam and making him do something that *I* wanted for a change. Bobbie and I talked about it a couple days later and she made me feel real good about myself. It helped my ego a lot, too.

CHAPTER 14

His Yacht

As I mentioned before, Sam and I go down to the coast on occasion to spend a little relaxing time on his boat and maybe go fishing. And believe me, he does have a real nice boat that works very well as either a pleasure, or a fishing boat. I think he actually either stole it (not really, because I think Sam is a real honest guy) or won it playing poker, kind of like that fictional character, Travis McGee, invented by a real fine author, John D. McDonald. You may recall that I have said before that I don't know Sam's income or net worth, which is probably pretty high, but I really don't think he can afford to buy a new and expensive boat this nice. And I mean it is first class in every way. New, I bet it's worth in the high six figures. I really suspect that maybe he bought it at a bankruptcy auction or something like that. Sam's too smart a guy to pay full price for anything. He always seems to have the knack of persuading somebody to lower their asking price. I'll bet he's never paid full listed price for much in his whole life. How I do envy his abilities that way.

This boat has hot and cold running water, a flushing toilet, shower, galley, refrigerator, stove and oven, sinks, hanging lockers (closets), and it will sleep four people. (Well, only three if I'm there hogging the day bed. I will talk about that in a moment.) Now there's a yacht, not just a boat.

One thing I like about Sam is that he's such a good friend that he won't stay out on the ocean if I get seasick, which I have been known to do from time to time. It isn't like I get sick every time I go "outside," otherwise I would never go out on the ocean. But I don't, so I do. By the way, "outside" in North Carolina means out on the actual Atlantic Ocean, as compared with staying on the inland waterways and rivers, where it is usually much calmer and less likely to create motion sickness, otherwise known as *mal de mer*. And boy, if I haven't been pretty darn *mal* of *de mer* in my past. In fact, one time I was on another boat and I got oh-so-sick of all the rocking and rolling that I came very close to just ending it all right then and there and jumping overboard. Just joking, but man, I was one sick kiddo. Stayed sick and in bed for three days after I got home. Bobbie told me I deserved it, for being such a nut as to go out on the big, wide ocean.

Anyway, one time I went out with Sam and I did get sick and threw up on his boat. I couldn't help it—it just came on me too quick. Not only that, I had to be sacked out "recovering" when we returned to the dock, and I let him clean the boat and all the fish we caught. Just as he was finishing with those chores, I finally was able to struggle out of the bunk. I cleaned up my own personal mess for him. It was a little embarrassing for me, but he was good about it. Since that one time, he's always been a real good friend and will bring me back if I get to feeling bad. Hmm. I just happened to think. I wonder if he brings me back because he feels sorry for me or if he's afraid I'll mess up his nice boat again.

Actually, if he lets me "run" the boat from the flybridge, and keep wind in my face, I'm not as likely to get too sick to manage. I may feel somewhat poorly, and do a bunch of belching, and loosen my belt, but I can still manage. And Sam, who's never been seasick in his whole life, just sacks out down below in the cabin, enjoying life while I play "captain," steering us to where we anticipate fish to be.

❦   ❦   ❦

Now boating in general can be a very pleasurable thing. Or, it can be very unpleasant.

For example, if Sam decided that the weather was okay for us to venture out, it would be because the weather forecast was for mild seas. This means waves no more than, perhaps three feet or so. Also, maybe the winds would not be excessively high. Sometimes "out there" we'd find calmer water than on a lot of lakes. (I'll tell you about one of my "lake" experiences a little later.) Anyway, slow, easy waves. A lot of the time you could even peer straight down and actually see decent-sized fish, read: sharks and stingrays, under the vessel.

However, on some of those trips I made with my pal, we'd find that maybe the weather bureau should seek some new employees. For example, we'd suddenly find that the wind increased to maybe twenty miles per hour and it would whip up really big waves and white caps. Then, you (mostly Sam at that point) would have a busy time trying to keep the boat aligned properly. Otherwise, we may get in a trough, and tipped way over like a deeply-heeled sailboat. However, something like this is not very safe with a power boat. The hull design and free board just don't work well for such stuff. Yes, the deck is "self-draining," but who wants to take a chance on getting a cabin filled with sea water—or any other kind, for that matter. Sam wouldn't go out at all (especially with yours truly on board) if there was much hint of such heavy waves. It'd be too much work, and also very tiring, trying to keep the boat headed into the big waves and at the same time trying to keep your footing. Even with specially-designed "deck shoes" it's pretty slippery when you're standing in water.

I remember one time when the weather was supposed to be fine and while we were heading to our fishing location, a thunderstorm came up. Well, Sam decided it was time to take a nap, since we were still maybe thirty minutes from our destination. He left me up on the flybridge steering, even though thunder was banging loudly all around us. I yelled down to him that I was concerned ("afraid" would be a better word) about us getting struck by lightening. I think he was a tad upset that I disturbed his nap, but yelled back, "It's okay. The boat's grounded." I supposed he meant that made it safe from the storm. I still felt like quitting the helm, but the storm passed by soon—safely.

By the way, these days it's quite easy to find a good fishing spot and to return to it day after day. During the last century, the best thing out was the "Loran." That item used radio signals from two stations up and down the coasts. You used them to triangulate your position.

But these days, nearly everybody that wants to do serious off-shore fishing, owns GPS units. These things will bring you to within shouting distance of your chosen spot. Great invention, but I suspect the fish aren't too thrilled with it.

Sam sometimes might be called a "playboy." Yeah, sometimes. He always seems to have some lady around. Don't know where he finds 'em, but they're there. One night after he and I plus two other friends of his had been out fishing, he went out with some gal and left me back at the boat to do whatever I wanted. Luckily, TV was not too bad that night. Besides I learned to always take a novel with me on those fishing trips, just to keep from being bored after the fishing is over, mind you.

Anyway, Sam told me that he and this lady were going out to a local hotel bar and dance floor. I went on to bed at more or less my usual time.

Now, at this point, let me explain just how his boat was laid out. There was this day bed sitting to one side in the main cabin, just off the deck. This was my bed, that I mentioned earlier. Unfortunately, it was not as long as I happen to be, so my feet sort of dangled off one corner. I had to sleep catty-cornered. Then, his personal cabin was further forward, on the other side of the head (toilet) and galley (kitchen). Beside the galley was a dinette type alcove. Strictly first class. Well anyway, I was sleeping pretty soundly that particular night, and sometime in the early morning, maybe about two o'clock, here he came, soused to the gills. I suppose he was trying to not wake me, but as he was passing my dangling feet, he darn-near tripped over me. That's what woke me up, but I didn't say anything. Did you ever try to carry on a reasonable adult conversation with a drunk at two o'clock in the morning? Can't be done, believe me. Actually, I have never tried to do such, but I'd be willing to bet money that you just can't. So, anyway, I stayed quiet and let Sam stumble on by me. I'll tell you, I don't know what all went on earlier during his evening, but he was one happy drunk. Must've had a fine date. He was just humming and singing to himself. In a little while I heard him get into his bunk and I went on back to sleep.

However, the next morning he got up real angry and really got after me verbally.

"What's the matter?" I asked, thoroughly ignorant and curious about why he was so grouchy. "What're you mad at me for?" I figured he was just hung over.

"Because you opened the hatch right over my bunk while I was asleep last night and that big rain we had just soaked me and my bed." He rubbed his long forehead like he does when he's in one of his grouchy moods.

Now all I could do at this point was adamantly deny that I'd opened his hatch, because I knew that I wasn't guilty. (Actually, I kind of had to bite my lip a little bit in order to keep from laughing at him and that idea of his. But friends don't do things like laughing at other friends' goofs.) I know it was closed earlier, because whenever we came in from fishing offshore, we always washed the boat down. Certainly, it was shut at that point. Besides, there's rarely any reason for me to go down into his cabin in the first place. So, what I figure was that during the night, while he was still pretty drunk, he must have gotten hot and opened that deck hatch himself. Goes to show you, don't get drunk. You might wet yourself!

Well, I guess he got over it, because he continued to invite me to go fishing with him after that. Nonetheless, I seriously believe that he really thinks I opened that hatch.

❦   ❦   ❦

I must tell you that sometimes staying on that boat with Sam can be a little unnerving, though. As I've mentioned, he told me that he frequently had some gal hanging around down there in Wilmington. By the way, this was between his marriages, so it was okay for him to date. He never did bring any of these gals back to his boat while I was there. Since I'm married, perhaps he felt it might make me uncomfortable if he did so. So, I really don't know if they were lookers or skinny beanpoles or big fat slobs or whatever, but I suspect they were reasonably satisfactory-looking, judging by the few I saw him with around his house. I often wondered if he really didn't want me to know what kind of women he was dating. Not that I think my good friend would normally date anyone of unsavory character, because I think of him as being rather upstanding. How would I know? Maybe it is just that you sort of get to know your friends after spending some time with them. Although, to this day, I still don't understand about Sam's fascination with Clemmy. He must've been awfully lonesome.

Anyway, as I was saying, there was this one time down at the boat when I'd gone off to a movie (by myself, of course.) Sam does not care much for movies. For some reason that I cannot remember now, we both had our own cars down there for a change. I suppose it must have been because I arrived later than him and perhaps had to return home before he wanted.

Well, when I got back to the boat following the movie, the boat was empty, but I could sure tell that somebody had been there. I mean some lady friend. How could I know that? Well, I mean to tell you that lingering in that boat was the strongest smelling perfume that I have ever, ever smelled. Not just a little bit. She, the mystery woman, must have taken a bath in the stuff before her date with Sam. I could hardly breathe in that boat when I went in, and it was one of the cool months. I don't remember which one, but the weather was cold enough that you had to turn on the heat. That fact made the odor worse.

Incidentally, pretty good deal on that nice boat of Sam's. It even had a first-class heat pump, just like on a house. If you wanted heat, out it came. Same for air conditioning. Pretty snazzy. Although on some really cold days, that heat pump barely kept up. You could have some real fun trying to take a quick shower in a chilly head. I mean the boat's heat pump just couldn't quite make it work around corners into the toilet area. Of course, in freezing weather, all the water you had to work with was whatever was stored in the boat's own tanks, maybe seventy or eighty gallons. I mean, the water pipes from the marina would freeze, so the management shut the water off to the docks in the coldest weather. Sam always warned me relentlessly to take navy-type baths, where you wet down quickly, shut the water off, then soap up, then rinse down real quick. Otherwise you may not have enough water left in the boat's tanks to last the winter. Then, in that case, either you stayed dirty, or scooted along the exposed dock up to the marina's public showers.

So, the air was not even very humid that night, but that perfume was st-rong! I don't know how long they'd been gone when I got back, but if I had to guess I'd say not very long. And I know exactly where she'd been sitting, too. Where? Right smack on the couch that I was using for my bed. When I opened that thing up so I could lie down and go to bed that night, I could just barely catch my breath because of the lingering strength of her fragrance. I mean, that perfume of hers must have soaked down into the deep cushioning. It was something powerful, I mean to tell you. Finally I got to sleep, but woke up the next morning with a headache you wouldn't believe.

I'll have to admit, though, before I went to bed, I was so curious about where she'd been that I sniffed my way around the entire boat. I'm sure I looked pretty silly while I was doing that, but with nobody else around, I didn't care. I discovered that she'd been down in his cabin, and she'd been in the head in addition to my sofa-bed. I did try to clear out the place as best I could by opening all the windows and doors, but it didn't work very well. I just got cold. The next day I checked the T-shirt that I'd slept in and darned if even it didn't smell like her. I swear, I could still smell her scent two days later when I left the boat to come home. I sure hoped Sam would choose to date somebody else the next time I was down there. I will say that I was never aware of her being there again. I didn't smell her scent, at least. (Maybe I should use the word "fragrance.") But I do think that I got a hint of her odor off of Sam himself one other time while I was at the coast with him.

❦   ❦   ❦

Nevertheless, let me tell you that the fishing off his boat can be real enjoyable. We've been out on some nice days and really caught some fine-sized fish: amberjack, Spanish mackerel, king mackerel, and dolphin, just to mention a few.

We even brought on board a seven-foot shark one time, for some dumb reason. I thought, *maybe he just wants to prove to me that he can land a big fish like this.* Sam clubbed him senseless pretty good, and since his fish box was not quite big enough to hold him, he just left the beast lying there on the side of the cockpit deck. Well, I was just casually walking by that "dead" shark about a half-hour later, barefoot as usual, when that darn thing must have had a last gasp and snapped out at my foot. Either that or the smell of my feet gave him goose bumps or something. Talk about scaring a person. Sam was up on the flybridge driving the boat, and I will bet I darn near jumped all the way up that six-foot ladder to where he was. Talk about moving fast! Thank goodness those teeth of that old shark missed me, or I might be a hobbling guy right now.

Well, it sort of surprised Sam too, me suddenly bounding up to the flybridge that way. He was in the middle of gulping a beer and almost splashed it all over himself. When he found out what happened, he grinned and said, "Well, Hank, you just go back down there, grab the billy club and smack that 'mean old' shark again." I wondered, *Was he making fun of me—his friend?* I did whack the shark, but you better believe I kept pretty much away from him while I was yielding that shark-pounder. Seemed to do the job, though, because we didn't hear from that fish again. I was convinced that we should dump that dead shark overboard, but Sam said maybe we could sell him to some fish merchant when we got him back to the dock. Sam was always pretty good about getting a few bucks for the fish that we didn't keep for ourselves. Helped him keep his expenses under control I guess. By the time we finished our trolling, and got back to the dock, that shark was just beginning to produce a little smell. I wonder if "rank" would be a good word here. I don't think Sam ever did sell him. I was busy washing off the boat while he drug that old stinker off to the fish dealer's place. Sam didn't mention what happened to it. Probably just dumped him back into the water so that the crabs could have at him.

Incidentally, since we ran the boat almost all day, it took quite a lot of gasoline for the two engines. We usually divided the fish and then split the bill for the fuel, which would frequently run several hundred bucks. So you darn sure better hope you catch some fish for that kind of money. Nothing like going home to your wife with one fourteen-inch-long Spanish mackerel that cost you a couple hundred dollars. Some wives, I have heard, don't quite understand how something like that can be exciting for a guy.

One time Sam and a couple of his other buddies and I went out on the ocean early one summer morning. We stayed out all day, and I mean all day. It was almost totally dark when we got back in, maybe nine o'clock or so. And we caught not a single thing. Hardly even a real nibble. There was that one strike by some kind of unidentified fish, but the barracuda apparently wanted him worse than we did, and got to him and ate him right off the hook before we could bring him on board. Anyway, it was a l-o-n-g day. We split the gas bill four ways that time, which made it a little bit easier. I tell you, I was dragging that evening.

But after supper, Sam and the other two guys found some energy some-where and went off to a cabaret while I sacked out. Darn glad to have a chance for some peaceful rest too. Sleeping on a slightly swaying boat can really be nice. Especially if some drunk guy does not come rocking and rolling in on you in the middle of the night.

I recall one weekend when Sam had invited a couple of his other friends and me down to his boat for a (hopefully) great weekend of fishing.

On our way, he said, "I checked with the locals there and they told me the fish are really biting." He smiled broadly in anticipation. "I bet we come back loaded down with all kinds of fish."

I replied, "Hope so. Nothing much better than cooking your own self-caught fish."

"You don't know Howard or Benny, do you?"

"I don't think so. I've heard you speak of them, though."

"They were college friends of Terry and me. Benny flies his own plane and they're coming from Louisville. That's over in Kentucky, you know."

"Yeah."

The two were already at the dock when Sam and I arrived. Benny said they got up about three that morning and "zipped on down" to the Wilmington air-port. They had grabbed a cab to the marina, and were really anxious to hit the open seas.

We boarded, and began to untie the lines from the dock. We were all eager and anticipating a great day.

Suddenly, sirens were blasting loudly—breaking the silence. Looking over from our position several finger slips away, we saw a gas attendant and a fellow on his older boat appearing very agitated. The guy on the boat was rapidly climbing up the ladder to the top of the dock. It was at low tide and the dock platform was about seven feet above the water line. The gas jockey started dashing toward the marina's headquarters. I saw two other fellows that were waiting in line for fueling their own boats rapidly exiting theirs too. Clearly something dramatic was going on. We all stood on Sam's boat deck, wondering about the excitement. I didn't see any fires or anything.

In a moment, four guys exited the headquarters and began to yell at all of us boaters there in the marina. One guy in a uniform of some kind was using a bull horn. He said, "The marina is now closed. Nobody can leave or enter. Leave your vessel immediately and assemble here."

Stupefied, only a few boaters moved. What was happening? The four of us looked at each other. The uniformed man shouted into his bull horn once again. "I said for everybody to get up here. Now! Hurry! This is an order!" He pointed directly toward us on Sam's boat.

Sam finally said grudgingly, "I guess we've got to tie up again and do what he says." So, we finished tying up his boat, climbed out of the cockpit and walked down the slip toward the dock master. About this time we heard sirens coming toward the marina, and four police cars showed up, blue lights flashing, tires screeching.

The fellow with the bull horn blared out once more for the stragglers to get off their boats. We still didn't know what was going on.

About this time not one, not two, but seven fire trucks, plus three emergency responder vehicles arrived. There were two boats out on the Cape Fear river, obviously wanting to come in and either load back onto their trailers, or perhaps gas up. The bull horn guy blared at them that they couldn't enter the confines of the marina. "This marina is closed!"

We were baffled. Were we under a terrorist threat? Did some fool shoot somebody? What was happening?

In a couple of moments it all began to become clear. A fireman climbed down onto the older boat and raised its hatches—slowly and obviously, gingerly. Four of his fellow companions stood up on the dock above him with hoses. (We later learned they had a special foam for the dangerous situation.)

I was standing beside the dock master—with his bull horn—and asked what was going on.

He turned to me and said, "That old boat was refueling and something inside his fueling pipe must have broken. He was squiring raw gasoline into his bilge instead of his tank."

I said, "My gosh. That's pretty dangerous, isn't it?"

By this time I could see that the one fireman had climbed down under the boat's deck. I couldn't see what he was doing.

Sam spoke up, "I know that boat. It's about twenty years old, and the owner rebuilt it last year. Must've missed something."

I finally noted the name tag on the dock master's chest: "Doug Spurney." He said, "The owner just returned from a pleasure trip up to Wilmington and back again."

I naively said, "So?"

Spurney snapped his head at me. He declared resolutely, "It means that his engines are very hot."

At this moment, hearing our conversation, Sam interjected, "Hank, he means that that boat could blow up at any moment. It could take those other boats down there with it. That's why he closed the marina, and moved everybody up here out of danger."

"Good gosh!" I said.

Then Sam added, "I'll bet that poor fireman is cutting the wires to his automatic bilge pump. One tiny spark and the whole thing will blow."

"Whoo-ee," I muttered. "That fellow sure is brave. I'd hate to be the one that had to do that."

Sam said, "I suspect he has special metal in his wire cutters, so a spark wouldn't likely happen."

Several more emergency and Hazmat trucks had arrived by this time. Clearly, this was a potential disaster. It was easy to see why all the attendants became so alarmed and frantic.

I saw a couple more boats arrive out on the river, wanting to enter the marina. Once more, the bull horn announced that the marina was closed to all traffic—in or out. I hoped none of the outside boaters were anxious to use the marina's toilets.

A couple of dozen of us remained on the porch of the dock house for the rest of the day. No explosion occurred—no doubt because of the careful attention of the fire department. A special company had needed to be called in because of the environmental concerns and it took them until midway through the afternoon to arrive and go to work on that guy's boat.

Finally, about four thirty, Sam said to us, "Fellows, I'm real sorry about all this. But as you can understand, there wasn't anything I could do about it. That poor guy could've lost his life, boat, as well as maybe all of us here. You don't ever mess with explosive gas pouring onto hot engines. If he'd had diesels in his boat, the danger might not have been as bad, but he doesn't. I have to admit that Spurney did the correct thing."

The fire engines remained there in the parking lot beside the marina for the remainder of the afternoon, with numerous firefighters continuing to keep wary eyes peeled. By this time several dozen land-based spectators had worked themselves into viewing locations. Having assumed that the road to the marina was closed during the emergency, I was surprised at the number. Lots of folks do like to chase fire trucks, though. I noticed that Sam pretty much kept his eyes on his own yacht.

Sam said to Benny and Howard, "Boys, I'm sorry about all this. I realize you've been through a long day and all, but the weather report calls for heavy wind and storms out there tomorrow. That means we can't go out tomorrow, and I'm going home on Monday."

Benny and Howard looked off at the affected boat, the firemen still on the dock. Benny shrugged sadly. He said, "Come on, Howard. Let's go get our stuff and head back to the airport. If we can't fish tomorrow either, we might as well go back home." Benny turned to Spurney and asked if he and Howard could go down to Sam's boat and collect their things.

Spurney looked at them intensively, saying nothing.

Benny said to him, "We're from Louisville and need to go back home. I have my plane out at ILM.

Spurney handed his bull horn to a fellow officer and said, "Okay. Follow me." He pointed to Benny.

Sam and I started after him. He turned his head and snapped at us, "Not you two. You guys stay put." He then walked Benny down to Sam's boat. Sam's face reddened.

When they returned with the two fellows' overnight bags, Howard said he'd go call a cab.

I felt as though Sam could have at least offered to drive them back to the airport, but he didn't.

They finally reopened the marina around nine that night. Spurney, after some discussion with Sam, said that it was okay if Sam and I spent the night on the boat as long as Sam didn't start his engines.

I had to feel sorry for Benny and Howard, though. They had gotten up real early, flown all the way from Louisville, couldn't fish, and then had to fly all the way back home. What a way to spend money. I wondered how much aviation gas costs.

Of course Sam spent a lot more time on his boat than I did, and as a result, he kept a set or two of regular clothes down there. I remember one time when there was some kind of party going on over at the marina's main facilities. I think it was concerning the finale of a fishing tournament of some kind. We didn't participate in the competition, but Sam was going over to the function anyway. He showered, and put on his nice shirt and trousers and then pulled out his navy blazer that he kept there in the hanging locker. Apparently, that locker didn't get a whole lot of air circulation. Well, Sam put on his blazer and looked real sharp—pressed gray slacks, dress shirt, tie and reasonably decent-looking deck shoes. Then, however, he and I both noticed that something was not quite right. It seems as though his nice wool jacket had picked up a real fine dose of mildew. It had gray mold nearly all over it. Well, Sam's not one to be too distressed about something like that, and he was determined to get to that cocktail party (probably to check out the unattached women, if there were any there), so he got busy and took a dampened cloth and started wiping that mildew off. I guess it was working okay for a while, but pretty soon it became apparent, at least to me, and maybe I should have spoken up about it, that he was not really removing the mildew so much as the dampness was sort of making it invisible. Anyway, he apparently thought that it'd be okay, so he put it back on and took off for the party. By the way, have you ever smelled an expensive wool blazer full of mildew?

He got back later on that night and didn't say much about the party, except that he met several single ladies there but couldn't get any of them to go out with him. He's a personable guy. I wonder why nobody would go out with him that evening? You don't suppose it could have been the odor or appearance of that blazer he wore, do you?

As usual, I enjoyed a quiet evening on the boat with TV and a good book. Incidentally, I have long since learned that to do things properly, you sit with a

TV controller in your hand. Then, whenever a commercial comes on, you turn off the sound and read your book until you spot that the show is starting again. Then you stop reading, turn the sound up and watch the television until that next commercial. Very efficient, I think.

CHAPTER 15

The Waterway Adversity

At this point I want to mention that Sam's what I call a very good boatman. I mean, he served in the Coast Guard during the stuff in Vietnam. And after that, for a short while, he worked chasing drug smugglers out from Florida. So, he's a pretty experienced guy on a boat. As a result, you get to feel real comfortable going around with a fellow like him piloting the boat you're on. Yet, unexpected things happen from time to time in everybody's life, don't they? I mean, sometimes things happen to folks that you'd never dream would happen. Understand what I mean?

Well, anyway, there was this one time when Sam and I were just out for a joyride. It was one of those absolutely gorgeous balmy Sunday afternoons in the spring with a few puffy clouds slowly floating by and the gulls and pelicans having a delightful time. Over at the beach some swimmers were frolicking and watching the occasional surfer. Like they say, it was the best of times. That's what boating's all about. There were just the two of us, and here we were tooling along up the Intracoastal Waterway (locally known as "the ICW"), not making much speed—just buzzing along real comfortable-like. That usually means about maybe ten miles per hour or so. That way you can create a little wind in your face, and that's good, but it's still slow enough to have a chance to sight-see. And also you're not burning up too many gallons of gasoline. Boy, if you really opened that boat of his up, I would bet it'd burn maybe fifty gallons of gas each and every hour. Now that's what I call real boating: using up money as fast as you can. Maybe you've heard that old saying, probably originated by the wife of some boater, "A boat is a hole in the water into which you pour money." That's not too far from the truth. You may also have heard, "The two best days of a man's life are when he buys a boat and when he sells it." Yeah, right.

Anyway, here we were, just casually cruising along up the Waterway. I wasn't paying much attention to where we were going, had my back to the breeze, while Sam steered, as he usually did when we were in close quarters. He and I were casually chatting. Maybe we were yakking about some house or estate we were passing. There are a lot of very elaborate and expensive homes beside the Waterway. Most of them have their own private docks and will often have their pricey yacht parked there. I had a soda and he had a beer. Sam likes to sip on a beer or two when we're boating, but usually does the hard stuff only after we dock. I just happened to be looking astern (that is toward the rear, incidentally) and suddenly there was this big, slow noisy crunch and abruptly the boat came to a complete stop. We had run aground! I darn near toppled forward right over the front railing on the flybridge. Well I mean to tell you, I'm not sure I have ever seen Sam so red-faced and upset. Now, he's usually a real cool and calm guy, and real careful about keeping mother nature happy and our environment clean, but I saw him rare back and throw that half-full beer bottle right over the edge of the boat way out into the marsh that was now right beside us. I expect there are a lot of NFL quarterbacks that cannot throw that far. I guarantee you that bottle will never again be seen by human beings. And cussing! I won't pass on to you what words I heard him use that nice sunny afternoon, but trust me, he proved he had been in the Coast Guard. I guess the Coast Guard must use even more profanity than the Navy.

Sam was yelling at nobody in particular, just screaming all the profane words I have ever heard as fast as he could—and adding in those peculiar Vietnamese words of his—for emphasis, I suppose. I'd heard him cuss like that only a couple of times before. I guess he reserves those words for his worst rages.

All I could do was to stand there dumbstruck. I just looked at him, wondering what might come next. He didn't even look back at me. He had this glazed look in his eyes and just stared off into the marsh. He sat back down in the captain's chair and replaced his hands on the steering wheel. He squeezed that thing for all it was worth. Maybe his subconscious was trying to replay the incident and steer the boat back into the proper channel. I began to worry for an instant that his fingers might break.

It appeared that Sam, for some dumb reason, hadn't been really watching where he was going as carefully as I'd thought he was and ran that big yacht of his smack into a shallow spot just off the channel.

You see, the ICW is carefully marked and maintained by the Coast Guard; in fact, it has red and green markers all along it to show you where the deep areas are that you're supposed to stay in. You just don't vary from this marked channel unless you're in a small flat-bottomed fishing boat of some sort. Then, you might slip over to the shallows, anchor and do some bottom fishing for some flounder or trout. Or, some folks go out of the channel and drive their small craft onto the dry land on the edge of a marsh wherever there might be a small sandy beach. A lot of times, these people may set out a grill and picnic stuff, sunbathe and maybe grab some charcoaled burgers while they're there. These places are usually pretty private, because fishermen won't bother them, and everybody else would be in a big enough boat to not be able to get over there. Actually, once I watched one couple get out of their small boat in a place like that and walk hand in hand through the marsh grass until they were out of sight. Now that's privacy, you know. Hmm.

Anyway, getting back to my tale of woe for old Sam that afternoon. Once he sort of half-way recovered his temper, he still didn't look at me or even speak a single word to me, but just put the boat in reverse and tried to back out of the sand. I suppose he figured his ego and expert knowledge would come into play during his obvious embarrassment and he'd just easily slip that boat right back into deeper water. No good. Next, he juiced both of his engines up to what must have been full power. It made a heck of a roar, and water just churned out from behind us. I thought at one time that he might ruin them, as hard as he was gunning them. Still no good. Then he sent me down to the stern of the cockpit and told me (no, naturally he didn't ask, he told me) to try to rock the boat back and forth sideways. Now, his boat is a pretty wide one, so I guess I must have looked pretty silly, sort of jogging back and forth from one side to the other, as he gunned the motors. Again, no good. A few more of those unidentifiable profane words escaped his mouth. I said nothing. And I sure as heck didn't grin at him. I'm his friend and all, but Sam really doesn't take criticism or teasing too well and he sure as heck wasn't going to get any from me at that point. I did ask Sam what he thought we ought to do. He didn't answer. He turned his face toward me and just glared.

Finally, he said with a tone of resignation in his voice, "Well, the tide's going out now, so we're going to get stuck even more pretty soon."

"Are we going to spend the night here, until the tide rises again?" I asked. I hoped not, but really didn't know what he had in mind. I'd wanted to go on back home that night, so I had no desire at all to have his boat stuck on that sandbar all night long with me on it. I suppose now, in hindsight, that maybe I could've climbed off the boat, since it was obviously pretty shallow, and walked back to the dock and my car. But that'd be like abandoning a friend, so I ruled that out.

Crews in a couple of nearby boats saw our predicament and stopped by to offer their help. Boy, I could see that really made Sam seethe because I know he considered himself one of the better boaters around. And to have to publicly acknowledge to the other boat owners (otherwise known as "captains") that he'd made such a stupid (my word, not his) mistake, just couldn't be accepted by his ego. Anyway, none of the passing boats were as big as Sam's and so couldn't even begin to try to pull him off. We were wedged on that sand pretty darn far, not just a little bit. And of course, with the tide going out we were settling deeper and deeper into the sandy bottom, making things worse by the minute.

Sam, still quite angry, yelled at the captain of one of the larger nearby boats to try to pull us off sort of sideways, kind of like he had me jostling back and forth, trying to rock the boat. The captain agreed to try. So, we tied a line ("rope," to use a less nautical term) from the back cleat of Sam's boat to a cleat on the other boat. Then, as the other boat pulled Sam's boat sideways, Sam again tried running his engines in reverse. Didn't quite work out, though.

The other boat was driven by a great big two hundred-horsepower outboard, and with all the pulling power the captain was using (I mean, he was really trying to help Sam out), the sheer pin on the helpful captain's motor broke.

Now maybe I'd better explain something here. Inboard motors, like on Sam's yacht have the drive shaft bolted directly to the transmission, so that when you push the throttle, the drive shaft and propeller turn, and as fast as you want within the limits of the motor. With an outboard, for protection of the motor, the manufacturers have set up a safety device called a "sheer pin," since lots of times, for some silly reason, captains with outboard motors have a tendency to run their boat into more shallow water. If you drive into a shallow spot and your propeller bumps the bottom, instead of putting too much strain on the motor, this soft-metal sheer pin will break in two. Thus, the main workings of your engine are not harmed. Your propeller will spin freely, but the motor will no longer turn it. But then you do have the lousy inconvenience of having to raise that part of the outboard motor up out of the water where you can work on it and replace your broken sheer pin. Now, if you have a boat as big as the one that stopped to help, the motor is a pretty heavy one, and to try to get to the sheer pin is a real major operation. It just couldn't be done in the water. The captain would have to somehow get his boat hauled out of the water before he could get to the broken pin. Of course he'd first have to get somebody to pull his boat back to a marina or his trailer. And, as I said, the propeller won't turn without a new pin. Moreover, the boat will not go without it, either.

Well now, here's the situation. We have Sam's big yacht over here stuck on a sandbar at the edge of the waterway. The tide's still going out, so we're seeing more and more sand all around the bottom of Sam's boat. (The boat's rear end is still floating in the water at this point.) There are now about a dozen other boats that have been lured over to see the unpleasant and embarrassing (for Sam, anyway) situation.

Let me digress here just a little bit. Every boat captain thinks (hopes?) he's fully capable of running a safe and efficient operation. So all these guys out there watching us are inwardly gloating at "those crazy fools" on the big yacht getting themselves into such a stupid situation. They're all theoretically laughing (inside) at him, but then, I'm part of the crew, so I suppose they were laughing at me too—just because I was on the boat. However, they're also thinking to themselves: *Thank goodness it's not my problem.* Now those are what can be called "mixed emotions." Naturally they all offered verbal help; they shouted words of advice and encouragement to poor old Sam, who by this time was beginning to show a really serious drop in his ego and confidence. (Now, maybe I shouldn't tell this, but Sam went down to the head while we were stuck there and I would swear that he had tears in his eyes when he came back out.) But the more unrequested advice he heard, the madder and more red-faced he got. Here he is, the former Coast Guardsman, plenty of experience, owner of a great big expensive yacht, and these peons in the little boats have the audacity to tell him how to fix the situation. And now we had the other boat, out of commission right beside us, with another furious captain. And it appeared to me that this other guy had probably been hoisting more than a few beers during the afternoon and was almost ready to fight. Now that his own boat was disabled, I had to quickly jump over to the side of Sam's boat and repeatedly stick my foot out to fend him off, so his boat would not bang up against Sam's beautiful yacht and damage either one. Lovely afternoon.

Finally, I guess Sam figured he'd about had it. He picked up his radio microphone and made a call. I presumed at the time it was to the Coast Guard, but found out later it was to a commercial boat-towing company. It seems as though there are these companies out there that specialize in helping boats in casual trouble. The Coast Guard will help somebody if they declare a life-threatening emergency, but not just for inconvenient or embarrassing things like this.

About an hour later, up the waterway came this other boat. It was obviously the one Sam called, because it was quickly evident that he was here to help us. I gave a hard shove and pushed the disabled outboard boat away from us. I thought the captain was going to throw his beer at me. The other boats that had gathered around us, now numbering I would guess about fifteen, sort of separated and let the big one maneuver adjacent to us. It was more like a tug-boat, and it looked like he'd be able to pull us off with no trouble at all. The captain talked with Sam a little bit, but I didn't hear the conversation. I was down in the cabin getting myself a soda at this point. Anyway, when I got back up to the deck, the tug captain and Sam had finished their conversation, and I could see that Sam was pretty darn unhappy with whatever had transpired. Of course he wasn't happy to begin with at this point on this beautiful afternoon. At any rate, we again tied the heavy lines to each boat, and with Sam running his engines and the tug pulling us straight back, finally Sam's boat slid off the sand into deep water. You should have heard all the people on the surrounding boats just whooping and hollering and clapping joyfully. What a party for them, except for the guy with the broken motor, and he still didn't look happy at all. He just sat on his boat with another beer in his hand and a disconcerted and angry look on his face.

I finally learned what Sam and the tug captain had discussed that made Sam so angry, even though he was getting his boat off the sandbar. Sam had to fork over a pretty big bunch of cash to the tug captain for doing the job. I even had to loan Sam a hundred bucks. I think he had to pay the man round-trip mileage from his own home port marina wherever that was, and then apparently a specific amount for his pulling job once he got there. Boy! And Sam has never been one to like to part with his money unless it was something that he specifically wanted. And he specifically didn't want to spend money this way.

Well, we got going again and went straight on back to his dock at the marina. I grabbed my stuff, said my goodbyes, and left. Sam barely spoke a word to me. Just said he'd see me at home sometime. Not wanting to be around an angry Sam particularly, I was glad to leave. He has never spoken to me about the incident, except to pay me back the hundred bucks. I really don't think he ever will. Of course, since I'm his friend, I certainly won't bring it up.

CHAPTER 16

Sam's Sail Boat

Well now, you remember I mentioned that lot between Sam's and our house. Bobbie was reasonably happy just to have it re-grow a bunch of weeds, and not be filled with clotheslines holding Clemmy's relatives' stuff. Maybe she felt it a real shame that Sam had no interest in horticulture. If he had, then maybe he'd do some real decent planting over there. Maybe he just liked growing plain old weeds. Or, he simply didn't care how it looked.

But let me tell you about something that did indeed blossom on that piece of ground between our two houses. Now, in all honesty, I guess I need to mention here that I actually became aware of my buddy's intentions several weeks before sweet Bobbie knew about his plans.

As is quite frequent Sam and I were sitting in our rocking chairs on his front porch, just chatting away, and listening to birds, car sounds, and in one short moment, a train horn pretty far off. I guessed it was that freight train that goes to the feed mill on the other side of town.

Anyway, Sam suddenly said, "Even though I have the 'Foxy Lady' (name of his yacht) and all, I'm also kind of fascinated with sailing."

I casually said, "Yeah?"

He glanced over at me and continued, "Like, sailing provides you with hours and hours of quiet solitude, interrupted on occasion with a few moments of stark terror." He grinned at his joke.

I knew what he meant. That's when a sudden big gust of wind whips up from an unexpected direction and surprises you by tipping the boat further over in an alarming fashion.

Happened to me several years ago. I was out on a big lake on this small rented sailboat trying to learn how to sail all by myself. I'd read a bunch of books about sailing, and it looked pretty simple. For instance, all you do, I thought, was to spread out your sails and the wind would fill them and off you'd go. But, boy, that lovely fall afternoon, the leaves on the trees lining the shore line were just crammed with yellows, oranges, reds. Life was good. It is a nice sound to hear the hull swishing through the water when you're sailing. Until that darn unexpected gust of wind hit me. Well, I learned real quick why sailors seem to have the reputation of cussing. Although I don't cuss in Vietnamese, I feel pretty confident that I did make a few sounds that might be considered unintelligible at that point. Quite loudly, too. Well fortunately, the boat didn't tip quite all the way over and dump me out of the cockpit where I'd been sitting, so I was able to hang on. Nevertheless, it sure wasn't much fun. Lost a paper bag with my lunch in it. Darn bag got soaked when water ran over the low edge of the boat. Frankly, at that point, lunch really wasn't on my mind. Anyway, I recovered and decided not to sail any more that day. Lowered the sails, started the outboard motor and drove myself straight back to the dock, still cussing to myself. At least, at that point I was not yelling at the top of my voice like I had been. The dock guy asked me why I'd quit so soon when I had rented the boat for the day. I just told him I remembered that I had to be somewhere else that afternoon. Yeah, somewhere away from sailing!

Well, back to my buddy and his plans. Old Sam decided that he wanted to have an interesting experience in building his own boat. So he wrote off to a boat design company and bought himself some plans for building a thirty-five-foot long sailboat. He showed me the blue prints, and about fifteen single-spaced pages of directions. They also sent him a bunch of full sized sheets of paper for outlining the size and shape of the ribs. Maybe I'd better say he had half-sized plans. No, that is not right. He had full size plans for one side of the boat only. He was supposed to make one rib for say, the right side, then turn the plans over and do the left side. I think there were about twenty of those.

He decided to build that boat out of fiberglass. He told me during one of our front porch discussions, "You know Hank. Lots of boats are made out of wood, and some out of metal."

I acknowledged that obvious bit of information.

He continued with his unasked-for lecture. "And a few are even made out of concrete, if you can imagine such a thing."

When I heard that I decided right then and there that after watching my friend's cement work, I'd never ever get in a cement boat that *he* made.

I didn't really know much about fiberglass at the time, but, boy, I sure do now. I said, "I thought fiberglass boats were just sort of poured into a mold and that was that."

"Oh no, no, no. It's more involved than that. I've been reading up on it. Let me tell you how I'm going to do it."

Turns out it's a lot more involved, especially the way Sam was building this one. I found out later that he didn't really know much about the stuff either—how to work with it and such. However, as I said, he bought himself a bunch of books that were supposed to educate one about it. I told you he was smart.

He continued, "Seems like what you do if you're not a commercial builder of fiberglass boats is to do what's called "one off." I've learned that manufacturers make themselves a "positive" mold this same way that I'm planning to do, and then use this to make a "negative." Then they can build a whole bunch of boat hulls from this latter mold."

"Yeah?" I wondered what might happen next. He didn't tell me.

Anyway, one day a couple of weeks later Sam had a bunch of cheap pine boards delivered and he started building this wooden frame over in the lot between our two houses.

Anyway, what he was to do was to use those patterns I mentioned and draw the necessary shapes out on some wide boards or plywood. Then, turn the patterns over and make the opposite sides to match up with the first ones he had sketched out. Then, you start cutting your frames. He invited me over to help cut them out, and I did help a little. I'm sure you were supposed to label each piece as you cut it out, but I guess my buddy figured he didn't need to waste his time doing that. I soon saw that he got several rights joined up with the wrong lefts. I have no idea why he didn't notice his goof right away. I discretely chose to say nothing. He doesn't favor being corrected.

Oh yes, I almost forgot to mention that he first had to build a strong platform onto which he was to attach those ribs. Anyway, he started putting those cut-out rights and lefts together on his construction platform, and somehow, got a few mixed up. I guess he put some number three right-side frames with number four lefts and stuff like that. At any rate, when he was finished you were supposed to have a neat-looking shape of a boat, but it didn't work out quite that way at all. If you got down in front and sort of "eyeballed" down the side of the frame, it was pretty obvious that darn boat would never "fly," if you know what I mean.

Luckily he had only nailed these shapes in place and not glued them permanently, because after a while, and a few Vietnamese words later, he fussed and fumed and finally got the correct numbers matched up. Kind of windy that day and several sheets of his paper plans got blown out of his hands, but since they blew over to my yard, I easily picked them up and carried them back over there for him. Seems to me he should have thanked me, but I suppose his mind was elsewhere at that moment. But, I try to help friends whenever I can.

Once he finally had all of those big wooden shapes aligned correctly, he ran a bunch of wooden strips all the way from the tip of the front to the stern. Now the thing really did begin to look like maybe it'd be a boat after all. Kind of neat looking if you used your imagination a little bit. It was similar to those balsa wood models from my youth. Except it was great big and he was doing it upside down. While I was over there he had me walk with him while he verbally admired what he had done. I simply acknowledged that it looked pretty nice and went on back home to my well-aligned hammock.

Boy, you should have heard Bobbie take on when she saw him over there banging away on that wooden frame. "Sam's Folly," she called it. My sweet wifey had that boat of his named before he even got it built.

A couple of days later I was again positioned properly in my trusty hammock, just watching a couple of bluebirds zipping back and forth across the street. Never could figure out where their nest was. Or, maybe it should be "nests." As for myself I have never been able to determine the boy from the girl bluebirds. I can do pretty well with cardinals, finches, chickadees, and maybe blue jays, but I have never learned about bluebirds. Not that it matters.

Okay, I was laying there comfortably and noticed Sam exiting his shed with a big white roll of something. Knowing in my heart that my good friend would want me to know what he was doing, I raised myself off the comfort zone and ambled through the weeds over to his boat frame.

Maybe I should also mention here that by this time it kind of looked like the wooden framework for one of those Polaris submarines. I mean, since he was building the thing upside down, he had added a big projection up on the top (Should I say "bottom"?) of the frame for the impending keel. I thought keels on sailboats were these big heavy things that hung down from the bottom about five or six feet. Not this one. It was only about eighteen inches tall, and about four feet long. Kind of stubby-like. I could only wonder at that point if Sam had misread the plans again, but he didn't cuss about it and he left it alone, so I guessed it was what he wanted.

I picked off a few cockleburs from my jean pants, then asked Sam about the white stuff. On closer examination it was a huge roll of loosely-woven cloth. He started cutting that stuff into smaller pieces and laying it onto his wooden boat frame. Funny looking stuff and I just couldn't imagine him making a boat out of that material. Why, it'd leak like a sieve.

Anyway, I strolled back over to my yard and happily found that my hammock was still comfortable. That made me feel good. Didn't see those blue birds again, but I did hear a crow somewhere off in Sam's deep back yard.

After my nap, (Hammocks'll sneak up on you that way sometimes.) I glanced over toward my buddy's yard and he'd just about covered the entire frame with that cloth. I also found a darn twig and couple of leaves on my chest. Don't know how those got there. Maybe a squirrel or something was working up on a limb above me and dropped them. Sloppy things!

Seeing that boat all covered with cloth reminded me of when I used to build all those model airplanes upstairs in my room at my parents home when I was a youngster. (I wonder if this dates me.) The kits I'd buy would usually have tissue paper included with which you were supposed to cover the balsa wood frame. You'd carefully wrap the paper around the model and glue it on securely. It was during this drying time when I would start peeling the dried glue off my fingers where I'd smeared it all over myself. Kind of fun if I remember correctly. I could use my childhood imagination and pretend that I was really peeling my skin off. Momma got pretty mad at me, though, when I smeared the wet glue on my pants. It didn't come out of the material and that bothered her to no end. I remember she especially got upset when I built those models in the winter and was prone to wearing corduroy pants. Darn, that corduroy stuff would really work good to help get the glue off your fingers, but then I'd have to apologize to her again. It is a wonder she ever let me buy more models.

Anyway, after the glued paper set firmly, you were supposed to slightly dampen the tissue with water and when that dried it'd shrink and be real nice and tight over the stringers and frames. After all that stuff dried completely, you could use airplane dope and paint the model some fancy colors.

❦   ❦   ❦

Anyway, Sam got that thing covered with the stuff and quit for the day. The next day was when Bobbie started ranting and raving and darn near screaming about something that old Sam was doing over there. Seems as though I'd been to town to the store for something and when I got back and got out of my car I smelled something emanating from Sam's direction. Smelled sort of like mineral spirits or paint thinner or something. Didn't bother me, but boy, did it disturb my sweet wifey! So, after hearing Bobbie's standard tirade about "my friend," I put my purchase away and strolled over there. Sam was applying "resin" all over that cloth covering. And boy, did that stuff smell strong! Good thing it was outdoors, because if it had been inside, Sam might have asphyxiated himself. He was using a standard six-inch paint roller to apply the stuff, and pretty soon he (as did yours truly) noticed that the nap was becoming loose from the roller and making a rather big mess. I think he wanted it to go on smooth, but now lots of little pieces of fluff were sticking out all over the place. His boat hull was beginning to look like a wool-covered sheep.

It seems you have to mix up the resin which comes in two parts—A and B.

I asked Sam, "How do you know how much B to add to A?"

He said "There are some general guidelines, but I'm just sort of winging it."

I shook my head in astonishment, and wondered if maybe I shouldn't be ambling on home before some sort of difficulty developed with his "winging." However, I stayed a little longer anyway, and soon learned more about how much A and B to mix. Sam put about five gallons of the stuff together and as soon as those paint rollers started to dissolve from the strong-smelling resin, he had to stop and slip a new roller on. This apparently delayed him from his projected progress because I watched him dip his fresh roller into that big bucket and suddenly, he couldn't pull it out. Seems as though the resin hardened on him when he was only about a third of the way down into his mix. So, out came his cuss words, and he looked kind of weird as he picked up that bucket with the roller handle sticking out and gave it one of his big, long-distance tosses. I didn't bother to pace it off but I think it probably traveled at least forty feet before it landed. He didn't look very closely to where he was tossing that thing because it crashed against his garage/shed and broke out a window pane. Just one though. The other three panes in the window frame survived. I left.

Later on the next day I saw my buddy leave his home, to return after a couple of hours with several more of those five-gallon buckets of resin. I figured that he had cooled off and was about ready to begin again. By this time I'd had my hammock nap and lunch and had listened to Bobbie go on and on about the smells emanating from over at Sam's. I also listened to her happily cackle about his misfortune with the bucket of resin.

❦   ❦   ❦

I was now reading a Clive Cussler Dirk Pitt novel in one of my lawn chairs and with a nice frosty glass of real Bobbie-made lemonade on the small table beside me. Darn she's a good wife. Cooks good too. Maybe it shows because of the beginning spare tire that I've started wearing around my waist. Had to buy myself a new belt. Bigger.

Perhaps she learned her cooking from her mom, because let me tell you, in spite of her mother's terrible temper, she was a real fine cook. I think fried chicken for Sunday dinners was probably her best stuff. Hey, a thought just popped into my mind. Maybe she got her bad temper from messing up a lot of food before I came on the scene courting Bobbie. Mess up enough chickens and I guess you finally learn what not to do.

I tried to fry some chicken by myself one time and didn't realize that you've really got to give it time to cook all the way through. (I was still a bachelor at the time.) Darn stuff tasted pretty good on the outside, nice and crisp, even if I'd put a tad too much salt in the flour I rolled it in, but when I got to the inside, it still had raw parts. Not too tasty at that point. I suppose I'm lucky it didn't make me sick.

Hmm. Just got my taste buds watering—thinking about good old Southern-style fried chicken, nice and hot (not overly greasy), crisp, with steaming mashed potatoes, hot and sweet English peas, fresh-baked scratch biscuits, plenty of tasty brown gravy and spicy chicken dressing. Follow that with chocolate pie, crisp crust and lots of fluffy meringue, washed down with cool ice tea. Scrumptious! A thousand-fold better than Clemmy's family's cooking.

❦   ❦   ❦

Getting back to Sam's project, I saw him start putting that resin on the cloth covering again and I guess he'd learned from his previous errors. Things seemed to go along pretty well this time. Besides the wind had shifted and we could no longer smell the resin from our yard. About dusk he finished and went over to his shed and replaced the broken window.

It rained the next day, so Sam didn't work on his boat.

Two days later a truck from the local lumber yard backed into the side yard and deposited a bunch of one-by-fours boards beside the boat. I thought, *What the heck does that Sam have in mind now?*

Bobbie and I were having a coffee break at our breakfast table. She had a blueberry muffin, while I nuked myself a glazed donut. Darn, those glazed things are tasty. When I was a kid, almost every Sunday we'd stop by the donut shop on our way home from church and pick up a dozen of those delights. What nice memories! I don't remember any of the preacher's sermons, but those hot, round ecstasies are certainly etched in my memory banks.

Well anyway, the next thing I noticed was that Sam was building some frames of some sort out on the ground beside his boat hull. Naturally, since I enjoy building things, as I think I mentioned, I finished my snack and strolled over. This time I took the dirt walkway out in front and didn't wind up with so many cockleburs on my pants. Got one mosquito biting at me, but he was doomed as soon as I heard him on my ear. Kind of strange to have a mosquito nip at me during the bright sunny day, but maybe he was mentally retarded. His genes will no longer stay in the mosquito gene pool, I'll tell you that.

Well my buddy was building a bunch of wooden frames from those one-by-fours and I was quite happy to help him with them.

I asked him, "What are we building? And why?"

He looked up at me with his sweaty face, glasses slipping down on his nose, and said, "You'll see."

Guess I was simply supposed to do my work and not ask questions at that point. So, I sawed and helped put together some of those big frames for him. They were pretty flimsy by themselves. For the roof parts he wanted them made of two eight-foot lengths nailed with sort of a point at the middle, so that when we finished each frame, you would have the shape of a building with a pitched roof. He'd told me by this time (at his leisure) that we were going to assemble a shelter over the boat. I acknowledged this, not really understanding how that was going to be possible, since these frames were so terribly fragile.

Anyhow, we did all twenty-four of them and then he had me support two of them at a time while he began bracing the side frames together with some more one-by-fours. He nailed the uprights with *carefully-measured* two-feet spacing. Still pretty flimsy. When he and I finished these things, it actually did look like the shape of a building over the hull, but with nothing but open walls and roof. I could only wonder what was coming next from his fertile mind. Eureka! He went into his shed and brought out a couple rolls of that four-millimeter-thick clear plastic sheeting. And a staple gun. Yep, you probably guessed it. He covered that entire "building" with clear plastic. Darned if it didn't look like it'd actually work okay—if you ignored it's appearance—and as long as a big windstorm didn't happen by. Bobbie didn't ignore the appearance of it. She sort of mentioned it to me when I got home that evening. Yeah, you can believe she mentioned it—a cheap-looking plastic house next door to us … and in the preservation district.

Well, Sam wired up some electric lights and a big exhaust fan in that thing, and made a sort of door on both ends. Rigged up a work bench and all. Pretty neat if you ask me. I guess he figured the boat construction might take him a few weeks. It actually took seventeen months, four days, three hours. But who bothered to count how long his toy stayed over there? Bobbie, that's who. I didn't question her counting, of course.

Apparently, in building this sailboat of his the instructions told you to keep on adding layer after layer of that cloth and resin until you got to a certain thickness. He did. I didn't notice how many layers he used, but it seemed like a bunch. He'd apply one, let it sit overnight and then another one the next day and so on. I noticed that my friend had started using one of those old cheap plastic raincoats, turned around backwards, and rubber gloves. This was supposed to keep the resin off his clothes and hands.

One day while I was visiting him and before he put on his raincoat and gloves I noticed him scratching his arms pretty vigorously. I queried, "What's the matter? Did you have a bad reaction to some kind of medicine or something?"

He curtly informed me, "The fiberglass cloth imbedded tiny unseen particles of fiber in my arms. They itch like crazy until they finally work themselves out. Takes a few days."

I replied, "I'm glad it's you and not me."

"Just comes with the territory," he said. Watching him scratch, I decided not to offer my help with that detail of his boat building. Of course I'd already decided to be an observer rather than a doer at this point. I'm telling you that resin odor was really strong—especially when you were enclosed in that plastic building of his. He'd turn on his exhaust fan, but that only seemed to move the stench around a little bit. What it actually did was blow it over towards our house where it turned Bobbie on to griping some more. I didn't blame her, as I was getting pretty tired of Sam's stuff by this time myself. I expect if you didn't have some way to move the air around it might really overcome you and that wouldn't do at all. Pretty strong stuff.

After a couple weeks of this kind of action I guess Sam figured he'd had enough thickness and the boat actually had begun to look like something. Except it's surface was almost like one of those old washboards—corrugated, with mounds and gullies. It would never slip gracefully through the waters that way. Sam of course had a fix for that. He bought a big bunch of some brown filler stuff and after mixing it all up with resin, just trowelled it smoothly on top of all those hardened fiberglass cloth layers.

Oh no! Something didn't work out very well here. Sam had obviously been sweating pretty much on that particular day, and I'll admit it was kind of hot outside and with that backward raincoat and those big plastic gloves of his, it's no wonder. And something I learned a little later was that you just never—I mean, never, never, never—let any moisture get in your resin mix. If you do, you can be sure that it will not ever harden—not ever! Well, this was apparently what happened that day. Sam must have dropped a tiny little bead of sweat into the mix because it just stayed gooey on that entire boat surface. And I do mean, the whole boat. Didn't harden like it was supposed to do. Sam was not too horribly upset at first. Just thought it'd need a little longer to "kick" due to the addition of that brown stuff. So he waited. And waited. And waited.

Bobbie and I went on a nice trip to the mountains of North Carolina about this time. I figured it'd be good for us to breathe some fresh mountain air instead of Sam's resin for a while. When we returned two weeks later I saw him over there with a metal paint scraper. He was scraping and digging every bit of that stuff out of all those gullies and depressions and curves and all. Talk about nasty work! And it was real sticky, and clogged up his multiple scrapers. Left such a mess on the ground around that hull that I wouldn't even think about walking into his shelter. I could hear his cussing with every breath without even leaving my yard. I didn't venture over to his house for a few days afterward. He told me later that he had inadvertently tracked a bunch of that smelly stickum into his house one morning and what a chore he had cleaning up his kitchen floor. Said he had to use acetone and almost ruined the appearance of the grout in his tile floors.

Sam finally finished that fiberglassing and filling chore. Then the sanding began. Yuck! Apparently he had to sand that entire hull until it was top-drawer smooth. He used his electric rotary sander for several days and then finished the tedious chore with something that I found out later was professionally named "foam glass insulation." However, and you can check with Bobbie about this, even though I'm not positive she has ever had the real experience. It's smell, when Sam was smoothing down the fiberglass hull with it, was very similar to one you might detect if walking behind a mule on a hot summer day and it had been eating a lot of green corn shucks. Not a very fragrant odor. Do you like soured, rotten eggs? And of course, Sam's venting fan was blowing this delightful fragrance over towards our house. Whoo-ee, did Bobbie raise a lot of Cain? Can't say that I could blame her, because a lot of that smelly dust landed on some stuff she had on the clothesline. I'm kind of glad Bobbie doesn't know any Vietnamese cuss words. By the way, we do own a clothes dryer, but Bobbie likes to hang some items out on a small line we have—things that the dryer might damage, she says. The clothesline, I might add, is placed discretely behind our house, where it can't be seen from the street. Besides, she owns no religious (hole-y) underwear.

Well, my buddy finally finished all that nasty stuff and painted his hull. I must admit it looked just great. He actually did a good job for a change. Of course it was still upside down. Now its appearance really did favor a light beige-colored Polaris submarine.

Since I'd not had many front porch chats with Sam lately, I wondered what was coming next. Incidentally, by this time the original plastic sheeting over his building had long ago deteriorated, turned opaque-gray and ripped to pieces, so he had just added more on top of the original. And then more. He didn't bother removing the old stuff, just wrapped on more. Now his building looked like a haunted house, what with shreds of opaque plastic sheets stringing all down around it. Would have been real spooky looking in the moonlight to some kids, I'll bet. Would have made a great "Haunted House" at Disneyland.

Okay, there I was one quiet morning, lying comfortably in my trusty hammock, listening to a train horn in the distance and trying desperately to decide if I had any chores that I felt like I wanted to tackle that day. Couldn't come up with any.

About that time, dear Bobbie came to the door. She said, "Guess who demands your presence next door?" And she added, "He said ASAP, too." I went of course. I really didn't have anything else to do, so I was available to help him if he needed me. I'd already decided that if I did have any home chores to do, he could just get along without me for a change.

It was "tear down day." He handed me his spare hammer. "Here," he said. "Now let's tear off all the plastic sheeting." We did. Then he said, "Now we're going to carefully take these frames apart. Gotta be real careful, though, because we're going to reassemble my shelter later on."

So, we carefully moved all those individual frames over to the back of the site and lay them down on the ground. I was then released to return to my own abode. Nice of my buddy to have consideration for me and my time.

Boat turning time! Well let me tell you that was some day—for Sam at least. He had finished all the hull and now it was time to turn it over. When I learned how he planned to do this I just about quit breathing. What he did was take some big two-by-sixes and build a frame over the bottom of his hull, which at this point was still upside down on its original construction frame. Now he had a topside frame as well as the original lower one on that boat. Then, I watched him as he sawed out a couple of one-inch-thick sheets of plywood into big curves and attached these to his topside frame. Looked sort of weird if you ask me. But then, as I studied what he had done, it began to make a little sense. Old buddy Sam wouldn't tell me what he had in mind. He just sort of gave me something between a sly smile and a smirk and said I'd see. I saw. He'd made that outside frame into a rocking chair kind of thing! He intended to literally roll the entire gizmo over—by hand. I'll bet it now weighed close to a ton. Personally I would have expected that he'd have to hire a big construction crane to come out and do it, but as I said, Sam's always been pretty shrewd with conserving his money.

For lunch that day Bobbie fixed me a very nice BLT, slightly toasted, and a glass of mint tea. Then I went back on over to watch the big event.

I always have liked iced tea with a sprig or two of real mint in it. All stirred up real good so that you get an honest flavor of the mint leaves. Nice and cold. I'm not much of a gardener, but I do try to keep a patch of mint growing somewhere in our garden.

Anyway, my buddy Sam's usually pretty smart about staying safe at whatever he does. Not always, like the roofing fiasco, but usually. This was not one of those times when he put his own safety on the top of the heap. He went to his shed and got out one of those old fashioned car jacks that we had to use where it hooked onto the metal bumper—when cars had such. You know the type? Where the vertical rod is about two feet long and you literally jack the car up. As compared to the "wind up" type used so much today. Well, he set that jack on a concrete block at about the center of his boat, hooked the lifting piece under one of his two-by-sixes and started jacking. Every so often he'd reach the extent of his jack and take three or four shortened two-by-fours and climb *under* the elevated hull and support it to where he'd jacked it. Then, he'd pile up another stack of concrete blocks, re-position his jack on top of these and start jacking again. Well darned if his idea didn't seem to be working. That hull and frame were actually turning over on those curved rockers he made. Remarkable. But let me tell you that I'd never have done it that way. Because whenever he had to stop and position those interim bracing props of his, he'd be under the darn hull with nothing keeping it up except his flimsy-looking jack, which by this time was sitting perilously on several tilting concrete blocks.

I said, "Sam, I'm really concerned about this. What you're doing doesn't look safe at all. What if it should slip and fall on you?"

"Not gonna happen," he retorted as he continued to prop as before.

"Why not call for a big crane to come do this for you? Wouldn't that be a lot safer?"

He didn't respond.

"Sam?"

He didn't even look over at me. I said, "I'm seriously concerned for your safety." And I really was. One little-bitty slip of that jack on one of those blocks and that whole thing would have fallen on him and I'd have to find myself a new best friend. Really, it'd have crushed him right then and there.

He still didn't even look toward me. He finally said, rather tersely, in my humble opinion, "I know what I'm doing. It'll be okay."

Well, amazingly, it was. He finally got that hull turned completely over in that manner, and without incident too. Thank goodness.

I almost forgot to mention that I'd also carried my cellular phone over there and kind of kept my finger on the nine-one-one emergency memory button; just in case, you see.

Well, after he finally got that hull safely turned, he climbed up on top at the bow of that thing and made like George Washington on that boat crossing the Delaware River that frigid night. Even stuck his right hand in his shirt like Napoleon did so famously. Of course he didn't quite look the same as either of those great men—what with his filthy and grimy shirt and jeans.

Sam was one proud man, let me tell you. Or maybe just relieved that his plan worked out okay. Anyway, I was real proud of my buddy's accomplishment too. He'd actually planned his work and worked his plan—successfully—for once. He subsequently spent the next couple of days removing the original inner frames.

Early one morning after he finished cleaning out the hull, I got "the call" to run right over and help him reassemble his shelter over the boat. He wanted to rush through with it this time because heavy rains had been predicted for the upcoming week. Poor Sam had a slight problem though. We got the shelter frames put back together okay, and nailed the two-foot-long cross braces and all, but then Sam realized that he'd forgotten to buy some new rolls of the four-millimeter plastic for the covering. The old stuff had deteriorated too badly to use again. So, we had to stop while my friend ran to the hardware store in town for the plastic. Problem. The store didn't have enough, so Sam had to drive the forty miles over to the next town where they had it. And the rains came earlier than expected. And Sam didn't get that hull covered in time. And so, he had a nice boat-shaped fiberglass swimming pool when he got back. By this time Bobbie and I were sort of watching from our window and just visualizing how much water might be accumulating in the hull.

The next two days it continued to rain. I was casually sitting in front of our television, watching Oprah Winfrey discuss some inane stuff with Barbara Walters, when Bobbie called to me from the kitchen. She was laughing so hard that I could barely understand a word she was saying. Besides, Oprah and Barbara couldn't seem to decide who had the greater television rating. So, I turned off the TV and strolled into the kitchen so as to learn what in the world Bobbie was finding so very humorous.

"Look … over … there at Sam's," Bobbie stuttered, as she covered her mouth with her hand to try to stifle her belly laughs. I swear, she was almost dropping to the floor with her laughter. Turning to my left, I went to the window.

"My gosh!" I could hardly believe my eyes. I quickly saw what had stirred my wife's emotions so much. Oh boy! As a matter of fact, it was so downright funny that I pulled up a chair and simply sat myself down to enjoy the sight myself. We spent the next little while punching each other on the shoulder with merriment.

A flock of geese had taken up residence in Sam's flooded boat. No kidding! I looked over at Bobbie and we looked at each other almost in disbelief. Who'd have ever thought something like this might happen? An entire family of Canadian geese, living right next door to us. I counted eleven, and they all looked like they were adults, but I'm not really sure I could tell an adult goose from a baby, excepting maybe for the size. They were right pretty things, too. As a matter of fact, they all looked to me like they might be related. At least, I could hardly tell one from another. There didn't seem to be enough room for them all to swim around in Sam's boat-shaped pool, so a couple would perch on the fiberglass edge, while the others would casually stroll around on the ground beside the boat hull. Looking for something to nibble on, I suppose. After a little while, the swimmers would apparently figure out that there was no food in the water, so they would jump down and others would soon take their place. I'll tell you one thing; it was a pretty interesting study of nature right there in Sam's side yard. I was tempted to look up the number for the Discovery Channel and call them so they could come out and video the whole thing. Like I said, real interesting. I will admit, though, that their incessant honking throughout the day did begin to become a tad tiresome. I suppose they were pretty happy. But, the next afternoon, as the rain was easing up, that flock of geese just up and flew away. Couldn't find enough food, I guess. Bobbie and I were kind of sorry to see them leave. I had a brief thought of running into town to the feed store and buying a big bag of corn to feed those hungry geese. But Bobbie told me she figured that might make the birds stay longer and that my buddy Sam would probably get real mad at us for aiding and abetting. Seems like Bobbie wanted to stay a good neighbor with Sam almost as much as I did, maybe more. I'm not sure why.

I chose not to go over there for the next few days, as I saw Sam bailing water out with a bucket. I could also see him wearing a big pair of thick yellow rubber gloves, and using a great big rag of some sort, cleaning off the edges of his fiberglass. Apparently those geese weren't potty trained very well. (Of course not … they were birds!) How rude of them. Then he tried to use his water hose as a siphon. Finally I saw him using a sponge and some big bath towels down deep inside of his hull. He'd disappear for a moment or two, then raise up to the edge and wring the sponge or towels out. Then he'd disappear again. This went on for at least two hours that I'm aware of. I got kind of tired of watching after a few minutes, and would just check on his progress from my window whenever I'd have an occasion to pass by.

Of course, it rained again before he got the complete shelter covering on and he started bailing all over again. I couldn't hear him, but I would have bet he was using some of his special cuss words again. Didn't see any more of the geese. I presume they ventured on to their original intended destination.

CHAPTER 17

The Final Touches

I naively presumed that maybe once he'd built the hull, that was the biggest part of sailboat building. Not so. For the next several months, Sam continued to build the interior, deck and then superstructure of that sailboat of his. I helped a little bit on occasion.

I learned from Sam that while building the hull he'd been making quite a few trips going around to local tire companies. Naturally, I had to ask why.

He said, "I'm collecting old tire balancing weights. For ballast." Seems like he could buy these dirty old things for practically nothing. Later, when he was ready, he rented a plumber's lead heating pot, made some wooden molds, and melted all those things down into ingots, which he then inserted into the bottom of his hull. Sam told me he had accumulated about a ton of ballast. Lots of work, and needless to say, Bobbie didn't care much for the smell of that melting lead drifting over toward our house either.

We began to wish that the prevailing winds blew from our house over toward Sam's. I don't think one can change nature, though.

Would you believe that old buddy Sam finally finished that sailboat? And it was darn gorgeous if you ask a novice like me. It looked as nice as any boat I have ever seen. Really. I was so proud of Sam's work! Of course I'd helped a little bit with the inside carpentry, so I had some reason to exude a little proudness myself. He installed a small diesel engine, and assembled a tall mast, and everything. Inside were nice cushions, a dinette table, a head, a hot water heater, galley, shower, small refrigerator, and even a propane stove. I can't think of what it didn't have. Sure was first class.

We took his nasty-looking shelter down and he had a nice Bobbie-hating bonfire of his old frames and pieces of plastic. He started the fire about dusk and it looked real pretty until the ashes and cinders started drifting over towards our house. Then, I had to go out in my PJ's and squirt water on a pile of dead weeds in our back yard. His breeze-blown embers had started a small fire. That didn't give me great thrills.

❦   ❦   ❦

Moving day! Sam had contracted a boat-moving company to haul the boat down to the North Carolina coast for him. He hired a big crane to come and lift it off the construction stand and place it on a special boat-hauling trailer. The entire procedure went like clockwork. I guess that's what usually happens when professionals do a job. I still don't understand why Sam didn't hire a crane when he turned the boat over. Sam invited Bobbie and me to go down to the coast with him to view the launching. Bobbie hesitated a little, but I coaxed her into going with us. Kind of glad I did. She's such a sweet thing.

Oh boy! The big day had finally arrived. The moving truck had parked the boat on some props at the marina and then a big boat-lifting apparatus moved over it, lifted it off the props and gently eased it out over the water. Now was the big moment! The culmination of a couple of years' efforts would finally pay off. Sam's baby at last would be lowered into the water. A big bunch of people had gathered around to watch the event. It is not every day a homemade boat is launched and lots of amateur mariners just had to observe. Several had their cameras ready for the magic moment when Sam's boat touched the water for the first time. You could easily see that old Sam was very proud and excited. He was grinning like the famed Cheshire cat from *Alice in Wonderland*. After all, he'd put in lots of hours and a fair amount of his money towards this intense moment.

Things went quite well as the professionals at the marina did their job nicely. They erected the mast and began lowering the boat. It went right into the water and the workers released the restraining straps. Then we saw it! Sam's darn boat tilted about twenty degrees! It didn't sit straight up vertically as it was designed to do. In fact if you've ever seen a sailboat at work, with its sail full of wind and all, it's real pretty with the tilt or "heel" as it slices cleanly through the waves. Things like that make a beautiful site for paintings and photographs. But unfortunately, Sam's boat had developed a built-in list—even though he didn't even have any sails up and there was practically no wind there in the marina. Mostly, you could hear gasps, and a few guffaws from the bystanders. But from Sam—nothing. I looked over at him and really thought he was going to cry. I couldn't tell if he was angry or chagrinned or embarrassed or what. I felt real sorry for my good friend. All this time, effort, money and then to have a defective boat for all to see. Poor guy. I looked at Bobbie and could see that it was all she could do to keep from bursting out laughing at Sam's dilemma. But she did manage to maintain control.

Well, to finish this tale of woe, Sam determined that he'd have to add more ballast in certain areas in the bottom of that boat in order to balance it better and let the mast stick up vertical, like it was supposed to do. So, he docked the tilting boat there and we traveled back home. He was real quite during our drive.

He started collecting tire weights again. When he figured he had enough ingots, he and I went back down to the marina so he could play with the balancing act. Bobbie didn't bother with going this time. After several attempts, and lots of unwanted input from bystanders, Sam finally got the boat properly vertical. Great! The only thing now was that the additional weight had pulled the boat down to where the original, planned waterline was now about twelve inches below where it was scheduled to be placed. Looked kind of funny to me, but I said nothing to Sam about it. A couple of other guys there pointed that out to Sam and got some rather interesting words thrown at them. Since I'd heard Sam's Vietnamese cussing, I understood it, but those guys were really taken aback. They walked away muttering to themselves.

I never did sail on Sam's boat, but he told me that he re-marked and re-painted the waterline and that it sailed "okay." I never really knew what he meant by that.

I learned later that shortly thereafter my buddy tried to sell that homebuilt sailboat of his. He found out that he couldn't even get an appraisal for as much money as he had put in it in materials alone, much less his time. I'll bet that made him mad. Some time later he sort of smiled at his own shrewdness and told me that he donated the boat to a charitable organization down there at the North Carolina coast. He got a much bigger appraisal this way, he said, and wrote the whole thing off his income tax. I told you he was smart.

CHAPTER 18

The Old Cars And Trucks

I guess Sam's experience with helping to rebuild that old Ford while Clemmy's people were living over there with him, sort of got to him. Because, since he had watched them and talked rather extensively with her male cousins about the reconstruction of old vehicles, he decided that he just might try his hand at such an activity.

So, a few weeks after he dumped his sailboat, Bobbie yelled at me to come to the kitchen window and look over at Sam's house. There was a big flatbed truck delivering two old rusty vehicles to his side yard, right beside his garage/ shop. One looked like it might have been one of those old "woody" station wagons, Fords I think, where they used real wood on the sides. There was not any wood left on the old rusty carcass at this point, though. The other one looked like it might have been an old pickup truck of some make or another.

And the next day, darned if another truck didn't deliver two more cars. These seemed to be much closer to our modern types, though. Not as rusty, and both still had some chrome bumpers and stuff on them. I think one was an old DeSota and I immediately recognized the other one as a Nash.

That old Nash instantly brought back memories from when I was a kid. My dad owned many cars, mostly Plymouths, but for some reason or another, one time he bought a used four-door Nash sedan. Now I'll have to tell you that my dad was what you might call frugal. Nah, in truth, he was a serious tightwad. He could really hold on to a dollar and was always seeing how much of whatever he could get for his money. For instance, he was right proud of how much mileage per gallon he could squeeze out on an automobile trip somewhere. He only bought stick-shift cars so he could control the engine speed. The one trip of which he was so proud, and told about to anybody that would listen, was when he drove from our home here in Aquaville to Atlanta. This was a distance of almost exactly three hundred miles, before Interstate highways were built. Gasoline sold for about twenty-five cents per gallon (except for when gas wars started up. Then you could buy a gallon of regular gas for about a dime.) Cars of that era averaged about twelve to thirteen miles per gallon, but who cared much in those days? Well, Dad bragged about driving that Nash those three hundred miles with only ten gallons of gasoline. No kidding. He told me (and I remember seeing him do this lots of times) he'd get to the top of a hill or rise and then throw the car's gear into neutral and turn the ignition off. He'd coast down the hill, using no gas. Then, just as his car started slowing down at the bottom, he'd turn on the car ignition, and put it in gear and the engine would catch again for the climb up the next slope. Boy, what an effort! I've never really understood why Dad went to all that trouble. It used to get my goat, because you sure as heck didn't make much headway in that manner.

One time while I was out cruising with a bunch of my teenaged pals, while going down this long hill I tried Dad's stunt. But I must have done something slightly wrong, because when I turned on the ignition switch again, the darn car backfired loudly and blew a hole in the muffler. Boy, my friends really split their sides laughing over that one! Since I was driving Terry's car, he didn't.

Well, needless to say, Bobbie was something pretty close to incensed when she saw all those old cars arrive next door to us. Granted, Sam's yard isn't exactly that close to us, at least in my opinion, but for something like this, even a quarter mile is too darn close for my lovely wifey. But what could I do? Sweet wifey said, as she has said quite a number of times, "That boy needs a wife to straighten him out. He has entirely too much free time on his hands. Why don't you run over there and talk to him?"

Sure, I could change him. He listens to me and my suggestions just about like an Eskimo listens to a freezer salesman. That'd be just about like trying to stop a hurricane by blowing your own breath at it.

Anyway, there they sat, grass and weeds growing pretty high around them for several weeks. Finally, one day I saw that Sam had ordered a bunch of lumber delivered and he started on a shed for those rusty relics. And boy, was this one a biggie? It was similar to a great big five-car garage, except that it was sort of added on to the side of his previous garage/shop. Frankly, I was mostly hoping that my good friend Sam would roof that thing with something that Bobbie could or would tolerate. I really didn't want to have to listen to her harping about my buddy. Sam called me over with my tools and I helped him build the new shelter. It was right much fun because I enjoy helping Sam and I also like to build things with hand tools. Never did build a real house or anything like that, but Sam has had a lot of experience and sort of directed me on what to do. Except a couple of times, I accidentally got some numbers wrong and sawed a few boards too short. Didn't mess up too many, but Sam gave me a sort of perturbed look for it.

He roofed the thing himself and I actually think that he did a pretty darn good job. Also, I think the color was reasonably acceptable to Bobbie. One thing was nice: This shed was hooked onto the old one and extended *away* from our house, not toward it. That made it somewhat less noticeable from our view. Bobbie liked that. She told me so. That made me happy. She doesn't have to like Sam the way I do, but I feel much more comfortable and at ease when she doesn't express as much criticism about him or things he does. I guess it kind of bothers me when somebody criticizes something one of my friends does. It's because I take it as a personal affront to me, that maybe I don't know how to choose friends wisely.

Into each of those bays went one of those old rusting vehicles. I was a little concerned to note the fact that there was one open bay left. Did this indicate that another old car was coming? Little did I know at that moment that within three months that bay would be filled with a nasty, rusty (of course) eighteen-wheeler "semi" cab. I suppose Sam's ego must have been working overtime, because he'd obviously decided that since he was trying to become such an expert rebuilder, engines and all, he'd try a big diesel-powered vehicle for a change. I opened the nasty old door, peered in, and let me tell you, that old truck cab really stunk. I'll be darned if I don't think it was previously used as a chicken coop. If odors had colors, I wonder what color of dingy brown that foul odor would have been. Oh, and his new toy was a lot taller then a regular car, so he had to raise the roof on that part of his shed and kind of rebuild that end. I thought my friend's construction looked pretty stupid at that point, but naturally I didn't mention that to him. He didn't bother to paint this part.

Boy, let me tell you that Sam didn't do as much fishing or traveling for almost a year. He seemed to spend just about all his spare time working on one or another of those old vehicles. Ah, so what, you say? The "so what" turned into one of the biggest messes you ever saw. I mean Bobbie darn near went wild; poor dear thing. There were old rusty parts strewn all over his yard, and not just on the far side of his sheds, either. In addition, he had several big fifty-five gallon drums of oil, gasoline, diesel fuel, cleaning solutions, and smelly stuff like that all over the place. At least he didn't have any fiberglass resin sitting around over there anymore. His place was just about like an automobile junk yard. That didn't look too neat.

The Preservation Society tried to get him to at least build a shielding fence around his mess. As usual he ignored them.

I don't guess I have to tell you that one of those barrels caught fire one day, do I? Don't know how it started, but you should have seen the heavy black smoke rising from that flaming barrel. Luckily it was far away enough from everything so it did not endanger anything. Sweet Bobbie made a few disparaging remarks about my buddy after the soot from that fire drifted down on her wet laundry out on the clothes line. But, after all, it was just an unfortunate accident. Sam apologized to me and I relayed his feelings to Bobbie. Lotta good that did. Bobbie wouldn't even utter his name for a few weeks. I will bet Sam didn't even notice though, because she never did spend much time with him anyway.

It seems that, after a while, Sam must have joined some kind of automobile restoration organization, because gradually more and more out-of-town folks started coming by his house. I thought at first that Clemmy's family had returned. On some weekends you'd have thought he was having a party, because he might have as many as ten or fifteen cars parked in his yard and out on the street. And you should have seen the caliber of people that showed up over there. Now, I don't want you to think that I'm from real high stock or am stuck up and stuffy, but some of those people sure didn't look like they'd been out of the grease pits very long. I mean, the beer guts, and hairy faces and tattoos and all, and that was just the womenfolk! The men looked much worse.

Oh, Bobbie and I had a great time sneering at these people from our own house and behind closed windows. They may have been the salt of the earth but frankly, they weren't the type I would choose to buddy up with. And I really don't think that Sam would have invited many of them to be his guests at our country club. I guess that he shared a lot of ideas with these people, and that they had similar hobbies. Whenever I did go over there, he'd fill me up with all kinds of ideas on how to restore the old vehicles. I never did bother to tell him that was one hobby I had no intention whatsoever of starting. He'd tell me where to get parts for no-longer-manufactured vehicles. (I really needed to know that.) And how to track down an old car or truck for which you might have a hankering. Important information to Sam, I guess. Not me.

Anyway, Sam's hobby continued off and on for who knows how many months. He had no more serious accidents that I'm aware of, although he just may have been too embarrassed to tell me about them and handled them privately. At least when he could. It is pretty hard to keep oil fires and diesel stink private from your next-door neighbor when that neighbor lives downwind.

But, one by one Sam finished whatever it was that he wanted to do on each of those steel chariots. I must say, they did look almost like new when he'd finally roll 'em out of their individual garages. I mean, really. Well, I have to admit that I didn't go over and inspect the final results. I guess he sold them, because they disappeared fairly soon in each case. By the way, the Nash was the last car to go. Maybe there simply was not as much demand for it. The neighborhood talked about throwing a block party when all of Sam's rebuilt vehicles were finally gone. I don't think Sam would have been invited, though.

Sweet Bobbie said to me that night as we were preparing for bed, "Honey, do you think Sam will ever straighten out? I mean, will his crazy stuff next door to us go on forever?"

What could I say?

CHAPTER 19

The Command Car

I guess it was while he was in the Coast Guard that Sam sort of became infatuated with the old type of command cars—like the ones used by General Patton in World War II. Either that or he saw the movie *Patton* starring George C. Scott, and liked the way he looked standing up in that thing during a vigorous and intense battle. I will admit, Mr. Scott did cut a striking figure doing that sort of stuff. Anyway, I really don't know exactly what it was about those command cars that fascinated Sam so much, but there it was.

He and I were sitting on his front porch one day, just chatting about various and sundry things. We weren't gossiping, of course, because it's our firm conviction that men never gossip. No way. Women gossip—men chat and discuss.

Anyway, in the course of the conversation, his feelings about command cars came up. He said, "Hank, let me tell you about command cars and their history."

Then of course, as is his way, I got a complete and very detailed rundown about the inner workings of the engine, tires, gears, power train and about twenty other things that I really didn't have any serious desire to stuff into my brain. I got it anyway, because I'm Sam's friend and certainly would not ever want to cut his conversation off in mid-subject.

"I think I'll find one and fix it up. I think it'd be a lot of fun to own one and drive it around town. I've been on the Internet, (I thought to myself, *uh-oh, not another Clemmy*) and corresponding with a bunch of rebuilding experts all around the country."

I snuck in a friendly, "Yeah?"

"I finally located one. Of course it's not running and the photo I received showed that it was pretty beat up and real rusty. However, I think I'll get it, and restore it. What do you think?"

I thought, *He's asking me for my opinion?* I said, "Sam, I can't wait to see it." Sure ...

I really don't think Sam knew much about cars and their maintenance and such before the Clemmy incident. I mean, I'd never seen him working on his regular car at all, but then he usually buys a new car about every three years anyway. Sometimes he'd buy one of those expensive luxury cars, and then other years he'd buy just an average priced one. He told me once that it'd been his experience that expensive cars wear out just like the cheaper ones, and won't go any faster either, at least not legally. Sam mentioned that he had no desire to go from zero to sixty in three seconds. All you get is perhaps a slightly more comfortable ride, and maybe a little quieter one. But just have a small fender-bender sometime and see how you like the bills. Whew!

After a long dissertation from Sam to me about upscale automobiles, Bobbie and I bought a "luxury" German car one time and was I ever disappointed in it? Its trunk latch was plastic and broke within two weeks of owning the darn car. Then lo and behold, if a month or so later both the rear power window motors gave out. Finally, after about two years, the leather or plastic covering the dashboard cracked, and the car started looking just as run down as any old cheapy. Of course, there is no such thing as a cheap car these days, is there?

Anyway, a couple of weeks later, here came this big truck hauling a monstrosity of an old beat-up command car. At least, having seen *Patton*, I could recognize it as a "once-upon-a-time" command car. The man unloaded it in Sam's backyard, left, and after a few minutes, I received the expected phone call: "Hank, come over here." Although I really have very little interest in cars and absolutely no interest in command cars, I am, after all, Sam's friend, so I didn't try to find an excuse, but went on over.

Boy, was he beaming? Just giddy with excitement! And that darn thing looked like it had been bombed and buried under the dirt for ages. Yet, apparently Sam thought that he could rebuild and restore it. He proceeded to tell me (of course) just exactly how he was going to go about the restoration, what parts he'd need, where he'd get a new motor for it and everything. Boy, he was excited. I just acknowledged all that he was saying, smiled politely, "yessed" him, and finally left and went on home.

I told Bobbie all about it, and boy, she really laid back with some good belly laughs. For some reason she has never gained much confidence in Sam and his abilities and decisions. I guess I'll have to say once again, he's not really her friend like he is mine.

Well anyway, I just knew that this was going to be fun to watch, as Sam began to work on that car. Actually, I would have called that thing a small truck, but what do I know? The car sat untouched out there by itself for about five weeks. I just couldn't figure out why Sam didn't go ahead and move the darn thing into one of those sheds he made while he was rebuilding all those other vehicles. After all, they were just standing there empty, with their doors wide open, almost like a bunch of hungry cows, standing around with their tongues hanging out, waiting to be fed. The grass and weeds were growing up all around that command car by this time, whereas the rest of Sam's yard was cut to more or less its normal height. Sam just couldn't get his lawn mower close enough to the command car to cut that section of the grass really short, I guess. He doesn't have one of those "weed eaters," but borrows mine from time to time. I don't know why he didn't use it this time. Maybe things like irregular grass and tall weeds just don't bother him.

I'll tell you something funny. I went over there once and actually saw a little sprig of a tree growing between the front bumper and the main chassis. I figured that if he didn't do something pretty soon, he'd have to borrow my chain saw or axe and cut that developing tree down. It also had a bunch of pretty daisies growing beside it. I was tempted to pick some and take them home to Bobbie. I thought it might embarrass Sam, though, so left them alone. As I was looking at that relic that day, I also noted that it had completely rusted all the way through the sheet metal in several spots. I don't know where the darn thing had been stored for lo these many years, but it must have been behind a barn, or someplace maybe down near the coast to have so much reddish-brown rust. I never did ask Sam how much he paid for it, either, but I hope it wasn't more than fifty bucks or so. I respect Sam's financial decisions, as I may have mentioned, but if he paid more than that, I will tell you, he really got snookered.

At long last, I spotted my old buddy working around that truck. Sort of. I just had to go over and see, because what I saw really picked at my curiosity. When I got over there, Sam seemed somewhat relieved. I guess he had been thinking about calling me over and was happy that I came of my own volition this time. You don't suppose he'd have been embarrassed to call me, do you?

Nah. But it seems as though Sam had decided to move that rusty command car into one of his filthy, spider web-filled sheds.

"This will be a simple little thing," he told me as he brought six four-inch-round fence posts out from one of the sheds. These things were eight feet long. I doubt if he wanted the Preservation Society to know he had them. Next, he got out a jack (the one he used with his sailboat) and proceeded to elevate one side of the truck up high enough to where he could then slide a twelve-foot-long two-by-six board under the vehicle. Then he repeated the same action on the other side of his car. He gave me one of the round posts and instructed me to lay it under the two-by-sixes, just under the motor area. I began to gather that he intended to roll that sucker right into the shed. Yep, that's what we did. Old Sam had figured it all out. We made like Egyptian slaves moving big blocks of stone toward a pyramid. The only thing we lacked was dressing in short skirts like those poor souls. My task was to keep putting those multiple rollers under the heavy-duty boards while Sam used an eight-foot two-by-six to wedge and pry against the rear of the car. Slowly, and laboriously, we got the darn thing moved into one of Sam's sheds. Believe me, it was heavier than I'd have thought and was a tough job, but we did it. Sam went into his house and brought me out a soda. What a nice guy, my buddy!

The next morning, I saw him walk out from his back door with his tool box. He was going to begin work on that command car of his at long last. I strolled over, carrying my second cup of coffee, so I could casually watch him as he got started on his truck rebuilding. (Oh yeah, as Sam reminded me on several occasions, it wasn't a truck, it was a car—a command car, nothing less.)

Sam started working around the edges of the car with a couple of wrenches, trying to take some fenders off. I think that today they weld those things on, but these had bolts. Or what you might call heavily rusted bolts. Well, he couldn't budge them even with several badly scraped knuckles and four or five well-thought-out cuss words. I tried to turn a couple. Neither of us could get any of them to move. Sam squirted some oil on them and finally we got a couple loosened, but not enough to get a single fender off. Talk about hard work. After that, I told him I had some work to do at home and politely left him to play with his own toy.

The next day I glanced over there and darned if Sam didn't have a local welder, cutting fenders and other parts off the car. Bet Sam had to pay a buck or two for that service. But at any rate, what Sam wound up with was a main rusty chassis sitting up on some concrete blocks (no tires of course, just rims) with a couple dozen assorted pieces lying all around. His shed was not big enough to hold all those pieces, so a lot of the parts wound up outside, just lying there in the dirt and weeds. What a mess.

When I got back home that first day and was trying to get the dirt and grease off my hands, Bobbie said, "And just how long is that idiot friend of yours going to have that junk in his yard for me to have to look at?"

"I dunno," I said, "but I suppose he'll have it finished in a couple of months."

All she said then was a resounding, "Humph!"

What do I know? It took him ten months.

I fully expected the Preservation Society to raise Cain once again. Didn't hear from them, though. Maybe they'd just resigned themselves to his messes. Bobbie told me she was so embarrassed to live next to him that she even considered dropping her membership. I told her I didn't think that would solve anything. After a little thought, she agreed with me.

The rebuilding procedure almost became like a race. Cut the grass around where the various parts had been laid, find a part, put it on, trim the grass where that part had been lying, find another part, trim the grass, et cetera. Kind of funny to see him going through all those shenanigans, but at least he was reasonably steady with it.

Now this is how he went about his reconstruction: He'd take say, a rusty fender and sand and grind it all down through the rust until he hit good solid metal. Nasty work, if you ask me. Lots of times he ran out of solid metal and then he had big holes in the piece. At that point he had to take some sheet metal of about the same thickness and weld it over the hole. Then he had to grind and sand that section down to where it looked like it matched. On occasion he had to shape the sheet metal with his hammer. Kind of a noisy procedure, if you ask me (or Bobbie.)

Oh by the way, by this time Sam had figured out that his smartest move would be to do his own welding. Lots cheaper and more convenient that way. So, he went off to the local community college and took a short course in welding.

He told me, "I learned enough to do the job and got bored with it, so I quit before the classes were completed. I figured I could sort of extrapolate where the remainder of the training would be heading."

I don't know how much that cost him, but I did see that during the course he wound up with a bandage around his left arm. Something to do with a torch burn, I think. That slowed him down a week or so. Didn't leave much of a scar. Ruined a nice Rolex watch that he had, though.

At any rate, I could gradually see some progress being made on that command car. Actually, though, I began wondering about the name, "command car." Seems to me its original use was as a vehicle from which an officer in the service issued commands. But at this stage of its existence, the old rusty thing seemed to be *giving* commands to Sam. Nonetheless, I guess he was enjoying it. Bobbie and I could be in bed at night and see the lights from the shed over there where Sam was just welding and working away. My hearing isn't too good, but I swear, on a couple of occasions I heard him let out a few more of those strange cuss words of his. Bobbie didn't make any comments about that. She's so polite.

I remember one day when I was visiting with my pal in his shed. He had welded on a pretty important brace for holding a piece and then attached the part to it. The entire new part fell off. Meaning: His weld didn't hold. Start over. Or should I say, cuss a while, then start over. I will say one thing about my good friend, he has a lot of patience. Or persistence, or something.

Another time while I was over there, I noticed a little problem that I pointed out to Sam. He had painted on a coat of base paint after he finished some of his reassembling. And then he had moved on to another section of his car. What I noticed was that he already had some rust showing through the new paint job. Now, when I pointed that out to him, he gave me a look you wouldn't believe. As if it were my pointing it out that messed things up. He didn't say anything, but that look … I'm real glad I'm his buddy and not an enemy.

Late one night, Bobbie and I were just laying in bed reading when she heard a fire truck siren just blaring. It seemed to be coming out our way, so we got up and went out on the front stoop and looked around. Sam's car sheds were on fire—all of them. We could see him out in his yard with his garden hose, but it didn't look like he was making much headway. Lots of old, dried and oily timbers, making a real firetrap. Once the firemen arrived, about a minute later, it only took them about five minutes to douse the flames. After they left, all that we could see standing were the four corner posts and a couple of roof timbers. Of course, his command car was covered with burnt wood from the caved-in roof. I decided not to hassle Sam with my company for the next few days.

If Sam has any deep, inner thoughts and so-called "gut" feelings at all, I guess it is determination. He cleaned up all that mess from the fire and promptly built a new shed just like the old one, except with only one stall instead of five. I later learned that he was using his welding torch and a mosquito snagged him, and when he swatted at it, he accidentally dropped the torch into a pile of old rags.

For some reason, he didn't bother painting this new shed at all. Bobbie wasn't very pleased with that, as you might imagine. And I guess he'd about used up all his original shingles from his house job, because it looked like he had to go down to the store and get several more packets. Now these weren't anywhere near the same color as the others; they even had a weird kind of circular pattern in them. But he stuck 'em up anyway. Bobbie 'bout blew a gasket. Guess he didn't realize Bobbie's feelings, because I'm sure he'd have considered her perspective if he'd have known. Sure, he would've.

Well finally there came that glorious day when Sam had completed the restoration of his command car. He had bought and installed a brand-new truck motor (probably just killed Sam to put a truck power plant into his "car"—probably damaged his wallet too, don't you know). I'm not sure, but I think it took a sort of special engine to run that thing and that he had to search all across the country to find one that would fit. But he did. And he actually did a pretty good job painting his vehicle up just like it might have been when he was in the Coast Guard—you know, kind of a blend between battleship gray and white.

Of course, when you got up real close you could see all the little drips and runs where his spray painting inexperience showed through. Frankly, after all the time spent rebuilding that darn thing I'd have hired a real honest-to-goodness professional automobile painter to do it right. Maybe Sam should've enrolled in another short course in auto painting at the community college.

He even stenciled some special numbers and lettering on the thing, just like a real Coast Guard vehicle. Well, I guess in fact, it was a real command car, because after all, it started its life as a real one. Sure didn't look like much when he first got it, though. I'll admit, I really didn't think he'd actually ever get it done.

Sam phoned me and naturally, I went right on over. He was going to give his car its first trial run out on the highway. And he offered me a chance to ride along with him. Was I ever honored, or what? Anyway, he cranked that machine up and you could just hear the motor purring. I mean, it really sounded great—real smooth. Sam slipped the car into gear and off we went. For about half a mile, at least. We were traveling at about twenty miles per hour when Sam decided to try out the brakes. Uh-oh. The darn left side brakes caught and stuck, while the right side didn't work at all. The command car swerved violently to the left and almost threw me out. No seat belts, of course. Luckily, though, Sam quickly recovered, said a few interesting words, and he immediately nudged the command car around and back to his house.

"Just needs a few adjustments," Sam said when we got out of the vehicle. "But it sure did ride smooth there, didn't it?" Sam exuded confidence and was obviously very proud of his accomplishment.

I walked on home from his shed. Told Bobbie about my harrowing experience. Not sure I should have, because she ranted on about it for the rest of the day. "*Your* friend this ..." "*Your* friend that ..." Finally she said, "Harold, please tell me that he will change. Please say he will." Ah well, such is married life, I suppose. I quickly determined that my best bet was to retreat to my trusty old hammock, and think happy thoughts.

CHAPTER 20

The Parade

My good buddy Sam finished his repairs on that command car on July first, and since we were scheduled to have a big Fourth of July parade in town that year, Sam had worked it out that he and the car would lead the parade. He told me that he convinced the parade leaders to allow his "unit" to be first because it was a Coast Guard command car, and it was sort of patriotic and all that. It was to be one of the largest parades we'd had for several years, with eighteen big floats, ten marching bands, and a bunch of other marching groups—teeny twirlers, Cub Scouts, stuff like that. And of course, a bunch of horses and riders bringing up the rear—thankfully!

I saw a parade one year when the people managing the procession arranged to have the horses way up in the middle of the parade. Not a good decision. Kinda funny, though, watching all the poor high school marching bands trying to step around the manure piles those horses had laid down. Unfortunately, a few kids didn't see what they were coming to in time, and for the rest of the parade you could see these "afflicted" kids sort of hobbling along, dragging the bottoms and sides of their shoes, trying to get "the stuff" cleaned off. And, of course, they were still trying to stay in step with the music and the rest of the band members marching along. Actually, it was kind of sad.

Anyway, the actual finale of our parade would have the town's new hook and ladder truck, of which we're so proud. That same night after the big parade, they had planned a big picnic and professional fireworks display over at the high school football stadium. I'm telling you, the whole town was awfully excited, and with due cause.

Well, comes the morning of July fourth, and I saw Sam up about the crack of dawn. (Bobbie and I usually get up early anyway.) I couldn't help but glance over there to see if he was up yet, and as I said, he was. I saw him go into his shed, and crank up that engine and drive the car straight on out to the edge of his driveway. And, he started polishing that vehicle with some kind of soft cloth. Boy, I could sure tell he was one proud man.

As Bobbie and I were finishing our breakfast, the phone rang and, as suspected, it was Sam. "Hey Hank," said the bright and ebullient voice. "Come on over here and ride with me in the parade. It starts in a couple of hours and I've got to go on down to Main Street and start forming up."

"Hey, I'd love to," I replied seriously. Actually, I'd kind of been hoping he'd let me ride in that thing again. After all, I'd actually helped him do some real work on it over the months, and I was kind of happy with it too. He told me he'd fixed the brakes. I have to admit, I was pretty pleased with my friend's accomplishment and his restoration of that command car. I felt confident that his repairs had been successful.

So I put on a white shirt and white pants, and got down out of my attic an old red, white and blue "Uncle Sam" type hat that I'd worn to a holiday party several years earlier. Bobbie said I looked kind of tacky, but since it was the Fourth of July and I'd be in the lead vehicle, she guessed it'd be okay. Oh, I also got out some old white bucks that I hadn't worn in about fifteen years, and with some thin white socks, squeezed into them. Those shoes were pretty tight, but since I didn't figure on walking in them anywhere much, I thought they'd do. I'll tell you, I honestly felt like I looked pretty snazzy.

Talk about looking snazzy, when I got over to his house, my pal walked out on his porch wearing that old World War I Second Lieutenant's uniform I told you about. He'd gotten it out of that box that I spotted up in his attic that time. Really! I was somewhat taken aback, but Sam's broad grin quickly tempered down my feelings. Boy, was he ever excited? I could hardly believe that he could fit himself in that old thing. I wondered if he had to grease himself down like I suspected of Clemmy and her overly-tight jeans. It appeared a little snug, but not so much as to hinder his appearance. He had his cap perched over at a slight angle, and I seriously thought that he looked pretty good. Of course, a First World War "soldier" in a Second World War Coast Guard Command Car in a modern-day parade is somewhat of an incongruity, but at this point, I doubted if anybody'd care.

"Okay, Hank, here we go." Sam grinned as we both got in. He drove slowly and I noticed that he carefully tapped his brakes periodically, just testing them, I suppose. They worked fine.

The parade organizers had done a real good job, so we got started off right on schedule. They'd told Sam not to drive so fast that the rest of the floats and marchers couldn't keep up.

That remark by the parade president reminded me of a time when I was in school over in Durham. Our technical school had a marching band (never heard of any other such institutions having bands) and we were ninety strong—all snappy young men, I might add. I'm not sure why they didn't let women into the marching band in those halcyon days, but it may have been because our uniforms made us all look like toy soldiers. I guess the girls probably just couldn't fit into them—at least the better proportioned of them. We were quite proud of our marching abilities. We had a real great snare drum corps and always used a very fast cadence. I mean it was fast, and we would typically use pretty short steps, so it looked and sounded like we were really going fast, real sharp-like. However, in actuality, we were traveling at a reasonably routine speed. We were invited to play over at the Duke University football games on occasion and our cadence really looked great out on the football field during our half-time maneuvers. We didn't get any awards, but we all felt that our classy marching band could hold its own against any other.

Well to get on with my story, off our school band went that one year, leading the city's annual Christmas parade. We began with our fast-paced cadence as usual, but for some reason we all marched with a more traditional, longer stride. Now you just don't do that with fast-pace cadence, but we did that time. I'm telling you, the Christmas parade in Durham that year finished in record time. I mean, we simply flew down that street. Although they had a big bunch of floats, and other units, I expect they had a heck of a time in the back keeping up with us. I'll bet the entire parade didn't last ten minutes from start to finish, with Santa at the end, up on the usual siren-blaring, lights-flashing big red fire truck, throwing out candy to all the kids lining the street. Bet he had plenty of candy treats left over, finishing that fast. We were never asked to march in their Christmas parade again. I'm not sure why.

Anyway, here goes Sam, in that army uniform, so darn proud of his newly-restored command car, leading the parade and all that. Sam had a sort of stern, dignified look on his face and kept his hands on the steering wheel at the ten and two o'clock positions, apparently like he was taught while he was in the Coast Guard. As for myself, I couldn't help but grin broadly, there in my

"Uncle Sam" uniform. I was so happy and felt real proud, being one of the leaders in the parade. Lots of spectators seemed to admire my getup as we passed, too. Things went along just great for a little while, and I could just see all the former service people admiring that spiffy command car. Sam told me the parade people wanted him to decorate his car with red, white, and blue bunting, but he wouldn't do it. Told them it'd be like desecrating a monument.

There was a real big high school band with maybe two hundred members right behind us, playing "Stars & Stripes Forever" just over and over and over. I guess it was the only tune they had a chance to practice, here in the middle of summer. It's a nice lively tune and all that, but to hear it ten or fifteen times in a row can get a little old.

Now, our town of Aquaville isn't poor by any means. I mean we have a reasonable amount of tax collection and all that, but maybe there are times when a little more ought to be spent on street maintenance. Anyway, here we went, just breezing along at the head of that spectacular parade, and just ahead of us was a pretty good-sized muddy trench right there across the middle of Main Street. A new water line was being installed. The trench had been amply filled with dirt by the street folks I guess, but due to the heavy rain the day before, the cut across the street had sort of sagged down at least two or three inches. Now, Sam saw this spot coming up and I guess he sort of figured that he and his new command car ought to speed up just a little, so as to sort of jump over the sunken spot. Bad decision, if I can allow myself to say so.

The front wheels moved over the pothole pretty easily, but by the time the rear wheels hit it we were going faster and we really took quite a jolt. That is when it happened. I'm telling you, the center of that magnificent restored command car just bent and sagged down right in the middle, about five inches. I mean in half. It just stopped moving right then and there. I guess Sam had missed some really thin and weak spots in the main chassis when he was doing his rebuilding, and his command car must have had more severely rusted areas than he'd found. And I also suspect that big swerve with the brakes the other day may have initiated the separation. He certainly wouldn't have intentionally painted over a bunch of rust without first inspecting it. I don't think he would've, anyway.

Oh Lord, what a mess! Here Sam and I are in the very front of the best parade we've had scheduled in years, and all of a sudden we've literally broken down. In the middle of the street. In front of hundreds of spectators. Talk about humiliation. I guess Sam wished he could die right there on the spot. So did I. It was so public that he would not dare use his strange cuss words; not out loud anyway. He just got red.

Well, it happened so fast, that the band behind us must not've noticed that we weren't moving forward any more. I suppose they had their eyes on their music. Those kids just flat walked right into us. Couple of 'em fell down and got stepped on by the next row. Just about like a stack of dominoes, you know. It was downright pitiful, seeing those kids there getting back up and fumbling around with their uncertainty. The ones in the back didn't seem to note what had happened up front and just kept on marching and playing "Stars & Stripes Forever" until they began to realize that they were almost playing solo. Then the music sort of slowly died down and the kids just stopped marching and stood around our car, looking. Not saying anything. Just looking in wonderment.

Behind the band was a beautiful float, nice dark blue thing, silver trim waving splendidly in the slight breeze with three pretty girls perched up on top and the whole thing sponsored by the First Bank of Aquaville.

I don't know how many people realize it, but they build these parade floats for beauty and not particularly for drivability. In other words, the driver might have a little peephole to see where he's going, but not much more. I've heard somewhere that in parades as large and important as that one they hold out in Pasadena, California, on New Years day, the drivers and floats all are controlled by radioed directions, but our town's too small to have something like that.

I suppose you can guess what happened. The driver of that really beautiful float didn't see what was happening to the band, and especially what had gone wrong with us and didn't stop moving forward. The kids in the back of the band fortunately saw the float's nonstop approach and scrambled out of the way in time to keep from getting hit and possibly run over. But the float still kept on coming. The pretties up on top of the float saw us, screamed, and began to clamber down off their high perch, safely, thank goodness. But here we were, Sam and I, already exasperated with our predicament, when we look behind us and see this big float bearing down on us. There seemed nothing we could do short of jumping out of the car, (which we managed to do promptly) and then it hit. Well, that pretty well did in that beautiful, bent-in-half, command car. I mean it just broke into right there. There was the front half, and then there was the back half.

I never really thought about something like this, but I guess cars have a center of gravity of sorts. The front part of the command car had the heavy motor, and it was now kind of cocked down on the front bumper. Where we'd been sitting sort of stuck up in the air. And the rear section just sort of collapsed forward. The drive shaft came completely loose and slowly rolled down on the pavement toward the curb. I guess maybe it had some rusted bolts left in it too. Funny that Sam didn't spot 'em during his rebuilding process. I'll have to admit that in spite of my concern for my good friend Sam, it was almost the funniest sight I have ever seen. Maybe if we'd had some people sitting in the rear seats, the balance might have been better and this catastrophe might not have happened. But on the other hand, more passengers there could have weighed the back down so much that they might have toppled right back into the band or on top of the formerly nice blue float. But anyway, there weren't any passengers, and so they didn't, thank goodness.

Well, there we were on this sunny and balmy day, with all these folks lining the street expecting to see a magnificent and dazzling parade, and Sam and I stopped the whole darn thing right there in the middle of Main Street. No marchers were working themselves around us to continue the parade, because everybody seemed to want to just stop and gape. Maybe I'd seen Sam's face this red before, but I'm not sure. I was afraid my buddy was going to have a stroke right then and there. We didn't even get far enough down the parade route to where Bobbie could see us leading the procession.

Finally, the director for the band got his troops organized and started again in front of us, so that the parade could more or less continue. I suppose things went along fairly well after they and all the other bands got around us, but of course none of the floats or any other motorized rides could pass us. So that part of the parade just fizzled. Luckily, the horses left no calling cards as they walked by us.

Soon after the breakdown, Sam left me there with the wrecked command car and went over to the phone booth on the corner to call for a wrecker. Since it was a holiday, apparently most of the wreckers weren't available. Finally though, he did make contact with one who subsequently got on the way to help us. In the meantime, of course, here I was, just standing beside that front half of the car, like a dunce. I thought about leaving the car, Sam and all, and walking on up the street to find Bobbie, but then I remembered I'd put on those old tight white shoes. It'd have half-killed my feet to voluntarily walk much in them. So I stayed where I was. Dressed up pretty much like Uncle Sam. Quite a few onlookers grinned at me, almost as if we had planned for the stupid car to split into two pieces in the first place. You know, like in circuses with real, honest-to-goodness clowns. A group of little kids had an absolutely great time pointing at me and my outfit and the car and just laughing and laughing to beat all.

And of course, all the subsequent band members that had been way back in the parade and hadn't known what had happened, had to sort of peer at us on their way by. It finally got so that I could tell without even looking that the next band was almost upon us. Their music sort of faltered, as the students just had to stop playing long enough to move around me and the car and take enough time to look at what had happened. The floats sort of edged forward and bunched up behind our—no, Sam's car—no, command car. They certainly couldn't get around us. Most of the float drivers just climbed up on top of their pretty decorated vehicles so as to be able to see us. I guess there were a dozen or so immediately behind us, just sitting there enjoying watching the happenings, or should I say, lack of happenings.

Well at long last, and maybe twenty minutes after the last marching unit and horses had gone on past us, the wrecker arrived. Only problem was, that the other floats now had to crank up and sort of wriggle forward and backward and sideways, one after another, until the wrecker could slip by them and up to us. All this action took almost an hour and by that time the parade was over and still more folks drifted back down Main Street to see our predicament.

Sam still hadn't said anything to me about the incident. He just sort of looked under the car at the damage. When he was doing that, of course, as you might have guessed, those old wool uniform pants he was wearing split right up the back. I suppose the material just felt like it had served its time. Poor Sam. I guess his embarrassment must have just about killed him. He's my friend and I really felt sorry for him. Of course I sort of felt a little embarrassed for myself, being all dressed up for the parade and everything, and just having to sit and stand around there like an idiot all afternoon. Bobbie never did see me in that pitiful predicament, because she was way up further on the parade route. But she'd certainly find out what had happened and we'd chat about it later. Boy, would we ever chat about that incident!

Anyway, the wrecker finally got each piece of Sam's fine command car taken to his backyard again. For some unknown reason Sam couldn't work it out to have the pieces stuck put back in his homemade shelter so he could go about repairing it, so he tore down the old shed and built an entirely new one over the two biggest parts.

"Maybe this time, he will use better color roofing," Bobbie said later. He did, but not much better, if you ask me.

Surprisingly, Sam did repair and rebuild that command car all over again. This time his work went faster, I guess because he had already done it once (for practice?) and he kind of knew what to do. Actually, I think he simply welded the broken frame back together this time, because I used to see the lights from his welding torch a lot of nights over there. No fires this time, I guess because once Sam learns how to do something, he does it right. He's pretty smart that way.

By the way, the pictures in the newspaper the next day, along with the article, were pretty good, considering. I mean, the photos of me came out pretty clear and Bobbie said she was actually quite proud of how I looked in my white "uniform" and all. She told me it really wasn't all that tacky after all. They had one of me still sitting up in the slanted perch of the front section of the command car after the big breakdown and then one of me sort of standing at attention, military-style you know, right beside the vehicle. Sam refused to allow his photo to be taken. I think he was pretty mad, but not just because of his embarrassment at what happened to his uniform pants as well as to his beautiful command car. When he got back from calling for a tow truck, he told me that a bunch of old-timers sitting on the bench on front of the drug store actually stood up and saluted him in that old soldier's uniform. He said they were making fun of him.

Unfortunately, I blistered my left foot pretty bad while walking home in those tight old white bucks of mine.

Bobbie glanced over towards Sam's a few days later, and then informed me that his command car had disappeared. I never asked Sam where it went.

CHAPTER 21

The Trailer

Time went by and the old empty shed in Sam's backyard gradually became a storage facility for whatever junk or objects that he found that he wanted to keep. Seems funny sometimes; maybe there is some old adage that sort of goes like this: The more room for junk that you have, the more junk you'll accumulate. Or maybe I just invented that. Anyway, gradually we saw that shed deteriorate, which by now had no doors because time and storm winds had broken them off their hinges. Frankly, the entire back yard over there didn't look too good to us, but after all, it was Sam's place, even if he didn't seem to realize how trashy it was beginning to look.

Maybe if you look at "ugly" long enough, you get used to it and it begins to grow on you. At least it seems that way to me after observing some of the couples I have seen in my short life. I just can't understand how some of these folk ever got together with their spouses, as ugly as they happened to be. Probably real nice people under the skin, don't you know. Thank goodness Bobbie is a beautiful lady. I guess I'm not all that bad either, if I can say so myself.

You know, speaking of "ugly," I think that Bobbie and I did pretty well choosing our parents and genes. You see, my dad's folks were (as seen from their old photographs) a big bunch of fairly ugly people—skinny, angular, drawn looking. Whereas my mom's ancestors were fairly attractive—good facial and body symmetry. And with Bobbie, her mother's folks were ugly (kind of like my dad's) and her father's people were reasonably attractive (like mom's side). Well, I kind of think that I got most of my better looks from my mother's side of the family and Bobbie got her good looks from her father's side. The net result is that we're certainly not considered in any way unattractive. But if you look at some cousins on each side that picked up too many of the wrong genes, they didn't fare too well. Glad we lucked out. I will bet that if we'd ever had any kids, they would have been real good-looking winners: movie stars, political leaders, and people like that.

❧   ❧   ❧

Anyway, things had been rather quiet for quite a while over at Sam's. I'd go over on occasion and spend some late afternoons sitting with him on his front porch, him with a sherry or beer and me with my soda. And we'd have some real interesting conversations. Sometimes he'd tell me all about the details of how to invest in the stock market or which mutual fund to buy into, stuff like that. I somehow failed to mention to him that Bobbie and I were already working with a brokerage firm and were letting it handle all of our investment stuff for us. Sam's information was interesting anyway. Sometimes he'd go into more detail about how to set your lines for trolling for king mackerel, how deep to run your planers, how much leader to use, what size reel to work through … stuff like that. Sam likes to go into a lot of detail when he explains things to somebody. I don't always feel the need for so much information, but it does make for interesting chats with my friend. At this point Bobbie was not as actively mad at him anymore, but she never did have much interest in going over there with me. Lots of things that Sam and I liked to talk about sort of bored her.

"Too much guy talk," she'd say.

Sometimes we'd have Sam over for a steak. I guess Bobbie doesn't care much for "man talk" because after dinner she'd usually find some excuse to leave us alone.

Oh boy, did it ever hit the fan one day, though? I mean, the sky just about fell down for sweet wifey and yours truly. Bobbie and I were sitting there at our breakfast table one morning, enjoying our second cups of coffee, you know. It was a Wednesday, I think; cloudy, but not raining, for a change. It had been rather dreary weather, I guess for maybe over a week. I mean, rain at least for a little while every day. Our yard was pretty squashy on the grass and there were a bunch of never-drying-up mud puddles where we had no grass growing. The weather person on TV said that we'd have to expect rainy weather at least until the weekend, when she thought a new weather front would pass through. Maybe then we could get some of the mildew under control.

❧   ❧   ❧

Oh, by the way, Bobbie does make the best coffee anywhere around. I'll tell you, it is second to none. She didn't start out our marriage making great coffee, though. I remember the first time she made coffee. We were still on our honeymoon, having been married maybe five days, and we were staying at my folks' old house. Nobody had lived in it for a long time, and we had it for our own use for a couple of weeks.

It seems that Bobbie had never made coffee at all. She somehow failed to mention that during our three-year courtship. I'm not sure why, because we drank quite a few cups of coffee together on dates.

When I'm off on a trip someplace I sort of wish I could enjoy it just black. Lots more convenient that way, when you wouldn't have to mess around with finding some sugar or sweetener, perhaps having to guess at how much you're adding when there is no teaspoon available. It'd also be pretty nice to not mess with milk or creamers, either. Funny, though. I drink my decaffeinated coffee straight black, and my caffeinated stuff with sugar. They say they both taste the same, but not to me. Bobbie only drinks decaf. Black.

Anyway, on our honeymoon Bobbie was anxious to show me just how good she could cook breakfast for me.

Bobbie did try hard to put the coffee together that morning, I will give that to her. But apparently that coffee had been sitting in the cupboard for a long time. When we (Bobbie and I) looked at it more closely a little later, we found quite a bit of mold growing in it. I really didn't know coffee would mildew. Actually, darn near everything in the house was mildewed. The house hadn't been lived in, or opened up for a long time and we'd had a fairly wet spring. Mom's old percolator didn't have any measurements with it, so I guess Bobbie figured it needed a full amount of coffee to make the right flavor. Wrong! Now, I love Bobbie, and after all, we were on our honeymoon and she was perhaps a little nervous, but you just don't serve somebody coffee that is so thick that you can barely get it to pour out of the pot, moldy or not.

But, being the dutiful and gracious newlywed husband that I was, I gave it a good try. I mean to tell you, that was just about the worst stuff I have ever tried to get in my mouth and keep down. Darn, it was foul; worse than Sam's. I've seen people in the movies and on TV complaining that their coffee tasted like kerosene, but believe me, that stuff was not anything like a petroleum-based liquid. No sir!

Now what do you do in such a circumstance? Tell the truth and listen to your bride cry the rest of the day? Drink it and stay sick the rest of the day? And when she asks you what's wrong, explain fifteen different times that no, it's not her, and you still love her, and you're real, real glad you married her? You guessed it. And we're still happily married. That sweet Bobbie of mine has since learned how to make a pot of really great coffee.

By the way, if Sam ever offers you a cup of his "fresh-made" coffee, try as politely as you can to decline. Man, it's got to be the worst stuff in this country. I'll drink his elixir in the name of "friendship," but that sure as heck doesn't mean I have to like it. I know he goes to the store and picks out two or three different brands, then brings 'em all home and blends them together. And oh yes, he won't use regular tap water in his coffee so he buys these gallon jugs of distilled water solely for that purpose. So, with all that kind of effort you would think it'd turn out okay, but gawd! Anyway, take it from me, don't drink his coffee. No amount of sugar or cream has ever made it okay for my taste buds to endure. Whew!

Now, let me say here and now that I think that the smell of fresh-ground coffee is one of the world's great aromas. Boy, I can recall the first time I smelled it. It's like it was only yesterday. It was in an old-fashioned grocery store in my home town. Oh Lord, did that place ever smell good with the fragrance of that fresh-ground coffee wafting through.

But then, I also remember my very first taste of coffee. Hey, talk about being disillusioned! I had the real naive idea that coffee would actually taste as good as it smelled. I was at the technical college trying to stay awake in those boring eight o'clock classes and finally forced myself to learn to handle the taste of coffee just for the caffeine. Bet I put ten teaspoons of sugar and who knows how much cream in it just to get it down.

Finally I worked it to where I could handle it better. It's more manly, you know, to drink coffee when you're eighteen-going-on-twenty-eight years old and a college student. You can act real grown up and philosophical sitting around a small table in a dingy coffee-house with other "intellectual" chums. If you don't have a coffee cup in front of you, you're just not "with it."

❧   ❧   ❧

As I was saying, there we were at our breakfast table when we saw this huge extra-long and extra-wide house trailer being backed into the side yard between our place and Sam's. A standard semi-tractor was doing the work. I swear, it was one of the biggest mobile homes I have ever seen. Purple, too! No kidding, the darn thing was painted purple. Well, sort of, anyway. I guess it was faded to more like a light lavender. Now, who in their right mind would ever buy a purple home? And boy, was that thing real beat-up? And the roof looked like it had been sitting under about a thousand birds for years. Nasty, I want to tell you! Looked like maybe a small tree had fallen onto the edge of the roof and bent it in one spot. The resultant gully was filled with washed-down bird droppings. The sides were beat up pretty badly too, and it had at least one pushed-out screen and broken window pane on the side that I could see.

Bobbie got so upset that she blew just about a mouthful of coffee all over me, sitting right there across the table from her. After I wiped off my face and cleaned up the breakfast table, I called Sam on the phone.

"Hey Sam, what the heck's happening, buddy? What's with the trailer?"

"Well, morning, Hank. Shake you guys up? Here's the deal: As you know, I have owned the Elegant Life Mobile Home Estates for several years. Remember?"

"Oh yeah, now I remember. I'd sort of forgotten."

Sam continued, almost without letting me finish my last statement. "I also own several of the mobile homes out there and this is one of them. My last renter just cut out on me, busting his lease and all. I've got a new guy that wants to move onto the property, Lot Number 4-B, out in the front by Highway 751. You may remember it. I took you out by there a couple of years back. This is the one where the tenant planted a big bunch of bamboo cane out in front and it really took off growing and spreading." He didn't stop for any of my response. "Hank, did you know that bamboo will grow in our local soil quite well? And it does have a nice tendency to spread. Bamboo will not take in just any kind of soil."

"Anyway, Hank," he continued. "I needed to remove the old trailer from the property because the new renter is furnishing his own. Bought it brand-new and it's gonna be delivered to the lot tomorrow. Too bad though, we had to cut down all that nice bamboo in order to get the old trailer moved off the lot. I did have the roots left there, so I think the stuff'll grow back up in a pretty short while."

While I thought he was catching his breath, I started to say something dumb like, "Yeah?"

However, I wasn't quite fast enough, and he continued, "Did you know that bamboo will grow several inches a year?" Sam was off on one of his lectures. I wondered if he was saying all this in order to change the subject away from his confounded trailer now parked next to our house. "And in addition, if you fertilize it with a little 8-10-10 twice a year, say, once in the spring and once in the fall, its root system will spread horizontally quite rapidly. I have seen it spread as much as three feet laterally under the turf and then start popping up its sprouts real quick."

I thought to myself, *Yeah, Sam. That's something I've always had a yearning to know.* But of course, I didn't want to cut him down. Friends just don't do that to each other.

Sam continued on, "I'll find some other place to park that old trailer. Right now, though, I don't have anywhere else. There aren't any more lots available over at the mobile home park. So there it is. I expect I'll get something done with it in a few days."

Apparently, though, Sam must have had a little trouble finding somewhere else to park that monstrosity, because it just sat there and sat there. Didn't seem to be bothering anybody else, but boy, you should have heard Bobbie ranting and carrying on every morning when she looked over at Sam's yard and it was still there.

The Preservation Society had the town's Board of Commissioners come *en masse* and look at the trailer. They didn't do anything, though.

"Harold Robert," she said one morning (she usually calls me "Harry," or "honey," or sometimes things even more endearing, but when things aren't particularly going well, it is "Harold Robert"), "Why don't you go over there and demand that your friend move that god-awful thing?"

Now let me get you to understand my sweet wifey, Bobbie. She's one of the most genteel, sweet, and tender women that I've ever known. She just doesn't use profanity. Not as a general rule at least. Maybe I have heard her swear half a dozen times since I have known her. She's just a very controlled individual.

Of course, there was that one time when we unknowingly had a family of field mice living in our house, and one came scampering across our bedroom floor one night when Bobbie was on her way to the toilet. She told me the darn thing ran right over her left foot. And in the near-dark, too. We have a little night light in our bedroom. It helps us a lot, so we don't really have to turn on a big light if one of us gets up in the middle of the night.

Anyway, there I was, sleeping pretty soundly. I don't remember now if I was having a dream or not. But all of a sudden, even with my lousy hearing, I heard this really blood-curdling scream of "Damn, damn, damn!" I really don't know how many times she yelled it, but I woke up to hear at least three of those "damns."

And then, "Harry, get up! Now!" Well, in the middle of the night when Bobbie says "get up," by golly, I get up. I mean right now. What else does a loving husband do? I was immediately afraid the house was on fire. I, of course, jumped right up and popped on the overhead light. There she was, Bobbie I mean, standing on top of the foot of the bed, holding her nightgown up to her knees! I mean, she usually doesn't do a lot of vigorous exercise like running and jumping, but apparently this sweet wifey of mine must have popped right smack up on the bed. I'm not sure I knew she could hop up real high like that.

Okay, I got up and tried to locate that fool mouse. Couldn't. I could only console Bobbie and try to get her to realize that the mouse was probably more frightened than she was. Didn't work. I guess she didn't sleep any more that night, because she put on her shoes (not her usual bedroom slippers, but real, hard-soled shoes) and went into the kitchen and got a broom. Bobbie brought it back, and stood it right beside our bed. She also (real thoughtful of her to consider my own sleeping) turned on the ceiling light in her closet. Well, maybe you can say its light didn't shine into our bedroom all that much, but it took a pillow over my head before I could get back to sleep. Bobbie apparently just sat up on her side of the bed the rest of the night, just in case that darn mouse returned. She said it didn't.

First thing the next day, I drove down to the hardware store and bought several mouse traps and some rat poison. We caught one little mouse the following day, and I found that just about all of the poison had disappeared from the boxes, so I guess that consoled Bobbie satisfactorily. We never did have any more evidence of mice in our house.

Okay, so the day Bobbie wanted "that god-awful thing" moved, I went over to Sam's and politely suggested that it might be a good idea if he found someplace else to park the trailer. I pointed out that "neighbors" were beginning to complain about it, and that the city officials might get him for breaking some ordinance or another. Now that was about as polite as I could figure out a way to talk to Sam about it. I didn't really lie, because Bobbie and I are his neighbors, aren't we? You just don't lie to your friends. Do you? Anyway, he said he'd do the best he could to get it moved away. "And real soon, too," he said. But frankly, I think that Sam figured that if the city officials didn't get on him for all those ugly sheds, oil drums, and rusted car parts, they'd not bother him because of his nasty-looking mobile home monstrosity. I began to believe that he'd had some behind-the-scenes conversations with several of them.

Two days later I heard this ruckus out in front and lo and behold if the ladies of the Preservation Society weren't out in the street with their loud-speaker, just ranting and raving. This time they were shouting, "Hey, hey hey, ho, ho, ho. The ugly trailer's got to go!" I glanced over at Bobbie, who had also seen the ruckus. "I didn't know they were gonna do that," she said, with her hand to her face. "I thought they were just going to send a delegation to see him personally."

I looked at her. "Yeah. Some delegation. This is embarrassing."

She said, "Damn!"

❧   ❧   ❧

A couple of weeks later the trailer was still there, but Sam invited me to go down to his boat at the coast to do some off-shore fishing. The weather was very nice, sunny, almost balmy, no wind to speak of, and I was really looking forward to it, so we did go and all went well. We went trolling and we caught us a big bunch of pretty good-sized king mackerel, and some Spanish mackerel. We also landed one good-sized barracuda, which we threw back. We did some bottom fishing one day and landed some black bass, trout and several real nice red snapper. I really like red snapper filets. I have this special way of fixing them; Sam gave me the recipe.

Now as I've said before, Sam has a real well-equipped boat, with all the proper electronic gear on board to keep us safe and help us find fish and stuff like that. He also has a cigarette lighter plug, like on cars, where you can plug in a cellular phone without having to use up its battery. This enables you to talk to home folk or anyone else, if you're not too far off shore and out of range. It's better than using the ship-to-shore radio if you are just talking to friends.

We'd been down at the coast for about three days, and like I said, things were going pretty well. I mean, the fish were really hitting. There we were, reel-ing in what looked to be a nice-sized king, when Sam's cellular phone started ringing. Well Sam and I were pretty busy down on the deck, bringing in this nice fish, and frankly, both of us were pretty messy, what with the fish slime on our hands. I mean, you can wipe it off with a rag or towel, but you're still going to be pretty slimy. That's part of fishing, you know. But at that moment friend Sam turned over the landing of the fish solely to me, quickly wiped his hands on a fish rag hanging from my belt, and dashed up the ladder to the flybridge where the phone was.

I got a little perturbed that he left me to tend to that fish all by myself, because it felt like it weighed at least twenty-five or thirty pounds, and a fish that size gives you a darn heavy pull on your rod. Sam was obviously a little upset too, at having to stop what he was doing just to answer a phone call. Frankly, I would've let it ring and whoever it was could call back later.

Anyway, when I glanced up at the flybridge where he was, I saw that he got it answered, listened a moment, made a weird face, said something I couldn't hear and slapped the cover back over the phone.

Sam came back down after just standing almost like a zombie up there on the flybridge for a minute or two. By this time of course, I'd already gaffed that big king and brought him on board. Let me tell you that holding a rod up out of the way and using the gaffing hook on that big king all by myself was a real chore. But, being tough, I managed to get it done. Into the fish box he went, to flop around and bang against the lid for a while until he expired.

After a little while Sam told me that the phone call was the Aquaville city police and that his trailer had burned up. I've no idea where they got his cellular phone number. They wanted him to return home immediately and go about arranging for the disposal of its remains. He didn't sound upset at all. Maybe the fire just solved his problem of what to do with it.

So, we brought all six rigs in and returned to the marina. Then of course, we had to do the usual refueling, boat washing, fish cleaning, stowing the fishing gear. Sam didn't seem to be in much of a hurry. After we freshened ourselves up, we headed home.

I must admit that since Bobbie doesn't care much for fish, and as a result I'm the only one at our home to eat it, I've been accumulating a fairly good amount of fish in our freezer. Maybe I ought to have a big fish fry. Maybe I'd invite all the residents from the nursing home across the street. That'd clean that freezer out pretty quick.

Well anyway, Sam drove us back home, didn't exceed the speed limit a single time, and so we didn't get stopped by the highway patrol this time.

I remember one time when I was riding with a car full of guys heading down toward the beach on another fishing trip. We were all excited and looking forward to a great weekend. However, the driver was drinking a series of beers as we were tooling along. Now I don't have any particular concerns if a friend wants to drink a beer or two while he's partying, but I do hate to be in a car with somebody who's sipping the suds while driving. I guess I could've said something about it, and maybe he'd have stopped his boozing. But I didn't want to make a big thing of it, so I didn't say anything. Neither did the two guys in the back seat. I just sat there in the front passenger seat and sort of cringed. And the guy was doing about eighty most of the time, too. And it wasn't an Interstate either, just a two-lane country road. Well, finally I felt that my salvation had come. As Tom, the driver, was doing close to the eighty miles per hour that I mentioned, and he had maybe his fifth beer right up at his lips, we zipped past a highway patrol car that was backed up on a side road. I said to myself, *Hot damn! He's gonna get it now, and maybe he'll slow down and we'll all arrive safely.* But—and here's the big "but"—that highway patrolman was doing some kind of paperwork and was looking down into his lap when we passed him. Didn't even have his radar going. Darn! End of story, except that we did indeed arrive safely and had a great weekend fishing. I rode back with some guys in the other car. To my knowledge, Tom never has been caught driving drunk, and I'm rather surprised.

❦   ❦   ❦

But anyway, Sam and I arrived back in Aquaville, reached our street, and there it was—the burned out hulk. If you've ever seen a burned-out mobile home, I'll completely understand why you'd never buy one to live in. I mean to tell you, that darn thing was all but completely leveled, with nothing left standing except for a few corner pieces of melted aluminum. A little of the original furniture could be seen, badly burned and charred. Even the paint on the washing machine had been scorched off. And of course, everything left in that trailer of Sam's was just nasty due to the charring and water damage from the firefighters. Actually, I don't think the poor firemen had much of a chance to quench the fire, because I understand that it was going pretty good by the time they were called. I heard later that old Miss Efird in the retirement home across the street saw the reflection of the flames in her room and had the authorities notified. Bobbie might well have seen it, except she'd taken the opportunity to go visit her sister in Siler City while Sam and I were off fishing.

Well, Sam and I just stood there, saying nothing for a little while. Finally he said, "I was going to sell it for a nice profit!" That's it; that's all he said. I was pretty well expecting some of his Vietnamese swear words, but none came forth.

The next day I was over at Sam's. He told me, "The fire marshal figured out what caused the fire. It seems as though my empty house trailer looked awfully enticing to a rowdy bunch of teenagers."

I said, "Hey, I'll bet it did. But how'd they get in without somebody seeing 'em?"

Sam continued, almost cutting me off in mid sentence. "The marshal supposed that, seeing nobody real close by to stop them, they'd simply move in."

I interjected, "I guess that's about right, what with you and me gone and Bobbie off to Siler City."

He didn't acknowledge my words.

"Of course there was no water, power, or sewer hooked up to it. I think that's how the marshal figured things out. Told me he found a bunch of broken booze and beer bottles lying in the rubbish on the floor. Also a couple of piles of human waste out behind the trailer. He reckoned the kids broke in with little difficulty and used candles for lighting." He spoke as if I wasn't even there and he was speaking to some distant stranger. "Maybe one of the candles got knocked over and the cheap paneling or some curtains caught on fire. The tire tracks around it indicated that the kids got scared and scattered in their cars as soon as they saw things beginning to flare up."

I thought, *Too bad my personal "neighborhood watch" wasn't in effect while I was away from my hammock.*

Well, Sam hired a trash guy to come with his front-end loader and big truck and they finally got that thing scraped up and moved away. It left a pretty blank area in the yard where it had been, but I guessed it'd fill in with the usual weeds pretty soon. Unless Sam needed to move another of his investments onto the lot. Heaven forbid!

You know, when Bobbie got back from her visit, that now-vacant lot was the very first thing she saw, and I'll swear, was she ever excited? She didn't just give me the usual sweet hug and kiss when she came into the house and saw me, but darned if she didn't scream, "It's gone! It's gone!" It's been a long time since I have seen that woman so happy. Made me real happy too, if you want to know the truth.

CHAPTER 22

Victoria

Well, darned if I didn't get another one of "those calls" from Sam, and as luck would have it, it was again on another one of those dark and stormy nights.

He said, "Come over here. I want to show you something." That was it. No polite request, just a flat-out demand. It didn't seem to matter to my good friend that it was dark and rainy; he just wanted me to get over to his house immediately.

I said, "Are you kidding, Sam? You actually want me to come over there on a night like this?"

"Yeah, good buddy," Sam said, his voice softened somewhat. "I think you'll find it real nice when you see what I have to show you."

I said, "For crying out loud. Can't it wait until tomorrow? It's a horrible night." I looked over at Bobbie with a shrug of my shoulders. "Naw, Sam. I'm not coming over tonight. Maybe tomorrow."

"You'll not be sorry if you come over tonight, I promise you," Sam retorted in a friendly fashion. "Come on, Hank. Come on over here. I'll turn the porch light on for you."

I thought, *Well, whoop-ti-doo! You'll turn the porch light on for me. What a real nice guy.* But I said back to him, "Why can't you come over here, if it's so darned important to you?" By golly, I was getting real tough by now.

"Well, I can't find my raincoat. And my umbrella's all beat up and don't give me much protection from the rain." (I couldn't believe my ears, hearing Sam say *don't* in such fashion.) Then, now catch this: he said, "Aw, Hank, please come on over here. Please." He was pleading by now. Amazing, simply amazing. My buddy Sam, actually pleading with me to do something he wanted. Unbelievable!

So, once again, I got on my raincoat, boots, got out my over-sized umbrella, told Bobbie I'd be back shortly, and went on over. Sam actually almost begging me to come over to his house. Wow! Man, there was no way that I wouldn't go when he was beseeching me in this manner. I could hardly believe it. He did have his front porch light turned on and met me at the door this time. He even handed me a paper towel to dry myself off before I entered his foyer. Now that's a real good host, thinking of me that way. No wonder he's my best friend.

Standing there in his doorway, Sam said to me with a pleasant smile on his face, "Hank, I think I've really found the girl for me this time. Here, I want you to see her photograph." I sort of grimaced inside to myself, remembering the last big fiasco involving Clemmy.

I took the photo from him, somewhat worried about what I'd say to him about this latest beast. He just stood there in his doorway, silently, glowing. But this picture turned out to be a nicely-framed, professionally-staged color photograph. Real good retouching, I suppose, because I'm telling you, this gal was absolutely drop-dead gorgeous! I mean, darn, she was pretty. She looked to be about ten years younger than Sam, but still had a look of maturity about her. He said her name was Victoria Williamson. I could quickly tell that this was a real lady. She had light brown hair, falling gracefully down to her shoulders, and lovely light brown eyes. Even in the photo, you could see the confident sparkle in those eyes of hers. They said, "I'm a refined lady, and I know it!" This Victoria had high cheek bones, and absolutely perfect makeup. She looked like a professional model. Nothing fake about this lady, I'll tell you. Sam had finally found the real McCoy, in my humble opinion.

"My gosh Sam, she's pretty," I said. "No, Sam, not just pretty, but gorgeous." And I meant it, too. Sam just beamed more. Then I said with a change of my attitude, "But for crying out loud, Sam. You're bound to have had this picture at least a day or so and now you've had me come over here tonight—through all that mess outside. I'm pretty put out with you, you know that?" I stopped and caught my breath. "But, as long as I'm over here, just go ahead and tell me all about this new lady friend of yours." I wasn't about to call her a "gal." That connotation would surely be demeaning to this lovely person.

"Well Hank," he said, ignoring my anger. "I first met her about fifteen years ago. Went to her first wedding—to a friend of mine named John Williamson down in Jacksonville, Florida. He and I were roommates in the Coast Guard together for a while. He'd been dating her quite a bit and I was one of his ushers in their wedding. He and I have more or less kept in touch over these years. It seems as though he and Victoria just drifted apart after a while. Maybe because he was away from home a lot. He's now an accident investigator for a big insurance company and is sent all over the world to investigate maritime accidents that his company has insured."

"Anyway," he happily continued, "I was just strolling along the waterfront scene down by the Cape Fear River in Wilmington one evening a few months back and there she was, with a couple of girl friends. I hadn't seen her for several years, but I'm here to tell you, Hank, time has only made her more beautiful." He grinned like a teenage boy in love for the first time as he said that.

"Wow!" was all I could say for a moment. "Sam, that sounds great. C'mon buddy, tell me more." Sam likes to be encouraged to give out more information about things. Sure, he does.

I left my wet stuff on his front porch and Sam finally invited me into his repositioned three-sofa sitting room to sit down. We sat on the pink couch. The other two are a mostly-yellow plaid and a red velvet. "We got a chance to chat and she gave me her phone number there in Wilmington and I told her I'd call," said Sam, rubbing his hand over his rapidly-expanding bald spot. Before he said that, he seemed almost in a deep trance, just as if he was thinking about something really nice. "She's living in a condominium with these two girl-friends. Both of her roommates are older than her, maybe sixtyish. One's not too bad, but the other gal has horribly-dyed light blond hair and is a real doozy." Sam was getting more excited as he was speaking. "And boy, is she a real crab? Complains about everything. And get this: She's one of these people who knows everything about everything and just will not shut up until she has lectured you all about it. You know the type?"

I thought, *Yes, Sam, I know the type. Yep, I know the type real well.*

My friend continued, "I can't stand to be around that nutty roommate of Victoria's very long at all. Nothing anybody else does is okay with her. She's always right and everybody else is wrong. Every time I get on an interesting subject and try to explain a few details, she cuts me right off with her own crummy and ignorant opinion." What got to me as he was saying this was that old Sam seemed to have no recognition of his own traits whatsoever. "A guy just can't explain anything to her. What a beast! Anyway, the other room-mate—her name is Louise—is a real pleasant lady, and sort of reminds me of my second wife … ugh … Carol." (He obviously had to hesitate momentarily to think of her name.) "Remember her? Anyway, both Victoria and Louise are easy to talk to and always seem interested in whatever I have to say."

Sam continued his rapid-fire, excited-voice explanation, "Now Victoria, she's something else again. I'm telling you, Hank, she's absolutely the greatest lady I've ever known. I think this might really be the one for me." He smoothed down the hair on the back of his head when he said that.

"She sure looks pretty, Sam, but you need to remember, 'beauty is only skin deep'." I said that trying to give him a real fatherly response. "What does she do, Sam? I mean, for a living."

"She's an upper executive with a big construction company down there in Wilmington. Earns a great salary I think, and of course, gets a steady amount of alimony from John."

"John?" I finally got a word in.

"Oh yes, John's my old roommate, the one that married her. Oh, I have already told you that, haven't I?" It was real easy to see that Sam was excited. A lot of the time I think Sam sort of gets carried away with his discussions, but sometimes it's interesting, too.

"Oh yes," Sam said as he adjusted his shirt collar, and then brushed his hair back again. "I was telling you about Victoria. We started dating and pretty soon we decided we're right for each other. At least, I know she's the one I have been looking for all my life. Kind of reminds me of my mother in a way, but I'm not sure that has anything to do with it. Maybe some shrink could have fun with that."

I said, hearing the distant boom of some thunder, "Yeah, I guess so, Sam." I was interested in Sam's stuff, but didn't want to get caught going home in a thunderstorm. Figured I may as well hear him out.

Sam continued, of course. "Perhaps it's what's known as an 'old wives tale,' but they say guys are always trying to marry somebody like their mother and gals are looking for someone like their father. Hank, if that's anywhere near true, I tell you, some of those folks out there sure must have a lousy opinion of their moms and dads."

"I can buy that," I said. "I have also heard that if you look at a girl's mother, you can see how this particular gal will look when she's that age. I can sure think of a bunch of women that seem to fit that category. But I'll say, Sam, that Bobbie sure isn't anything like her mother. Thank goodness, too. But then, if she had been, I darn sure would not have married that sweet thing." (Actually, I playfully like to call Bobbie my 'sweet thang'.) I smiled slightly while pushing back some cuticle on my left thumb, "You never did get to know her mom, did you, Sam? I mean, what she was really like."

He replied that he hadn't, as he stood up slightly and tugged gingerly where his pants were pinching his crotch. I began to perceive that my friend was pretty nervous, and I wondered if he was concerned that I might not approve of his choice.

I calmly looked him in the eye after he sat back down again. "Her mom was reasonably pleasant on the surface," I continued. "But once you got to know her well, she was a seriously mean tyrant. She dominated Bobbie's poor father like something else again. I mean, that poor guy just couldn't ever do anything to please her. Nothing. Several times I heard her call him names that you wouldn't believe. I mean, right in front of her own son-in-law, too."

You know, when Sam and I are chatting, we get on all kinds of subjects and can easily get carried away. Lots of times we more or less rap about people we mutually know, and other times, people that maybe only one of us knows. We tend to dissect their personalities. I suppose you could say we psychoanalyze them. Maybe that kind of conversation makes the two of us feel superior, because we never seem to have any of the nutty problems that other folks do. Well, not many, anyway.

"My father-in-law was a pretty nice guy," I went on, "but I darn sure don't know how he stood living with a woman like that all those years. I've wondered sometimes, and I'd never tell Bobbie this of course, if he stayed married to that old hag just because of Bobbie. You know, to keep the family together and all that. Must have been hell, listening to her gripe and complain about everything incessantly day after day, year after year. They were married a right long time before he died. And oh yeah, here's something interesting, Sam. I never really thought about it before now."

Now here's another good point I like about Sam's and my chats: We talk about things, and lots of times our conversation will open up completely new avenues of thought. It helps me expand my mind. I guess it must be the same with my good friend, because he does lead us in some real interesting directions of conversation from time to time.

I continued, "Bobbie's mother died less than two years after her father died. She just sort of withered away. The doctor never found anything seriously wrong with her. Physically, I mean, but I guess she felt that if she didn't have anybody around to gripe at and bless out and lord over, then life must not be worth living." A big flash of lightning lit up the outside and thunder exploded. Sam jumped up suddenly, looked around the room, and then sat back down.

I continued, "Maybe she just sort of willed herself to die. Know what I mean? Kind of sad in a way. Bobbie never talks about either one of them much. But hey, enough about that mess. What are your and this Victoria's plans?"

"Okay," Sam began again with a serious look on his face, peering over his glasses at me. "We're going to get married next month down in Wilmington, and you're going to be my best man." No request. Just a statement of fact. Actually, it made me feel real good to know that after all, maybe I did have Sam's respect and acceptance as a friend. "And Victoria and I have talked about it and she says it is okay if Bobbie is in the wedding too." He grinned as he adjusted his glasses. They had a tendency to slide down his nose.

"Well I don't know how she'll feel about that Sam," I said. "After all, she's never met your Victoria."

"Oh, Victoria will be up here the day after tomorrow and they can meet then. I just know they'll get along great together. It'll work out just fine." He fiddled with his belt buckle. "Well Hank, that's what I wanted you over here for," said Sam with finality.

In other words, the audience with his majesty was over. I'd been dismissed and it was time for me to go on back to my own abode. Sam wanted me over so he could tell me about Victoria. He told me. Now that was done. Quitting time.

I picked up on this hint right away. Can't fool me, boy. I know when it's time for me to leave.

So I got up, walked to the front door, happy to note that the storm had apparently quickly passed and it was only mildly drizzling. I turned back to him and said, "Gotta go now. See you later, Sam."

I wonder now if I was too abrupt. Hope I didn't hurt my buddy's feelings, leaving so soon. After all, friends respect each other's feelings, don't they?

I trotted on home through the rain. By this time, the rain had pretty much let up anyway, but I still got sort of muddy leaving Sam's house. All his front yard sod still hadn't completely grown together yet, even after about a year and a half. Oh well, I suspected it'd eventually get real pretty. If the dreaded crab grass didn't strike.

I described Victoria to Bobbie and told her Sam's story. Actually, I edited out the irrelevant stuff for her. She seemed genuinely surprised that she was "expected" to be in the wedding; maybe I should say "astonished." At first, I think I detected a spot of anger, but that quickly passed as she thought about it more. You may remember that I mentioned that Bobbie never has cared much for or respected Sam as much as I do.

Lo and behold, the next day I saw Sam out in his yard, picking up debris from the rain storm, and actually mowing his yard. Well, mowing the sod squares, anyway. I couldn't help but notice, even from as far away as my yard, that he was carefully mowing in particular directions so that the cut blades of grass from each square would sort of blow out from under the mower and drift down onto the spots where no natural grass had yet grown. I guess those cut blades of grass lying there on the dirt between squares of sod more or less made the entire yard look greener, even if it had some low spots between the sod patches. Kind of a neat idea if it had really worked, I guess. He'd probably need to do a good rake job later, though, I figured, when those cut blades of grass died and turned brown. Now that'd be an interesting yard pattern: green sod squares interspersed with spots of brown. Very unique.

Well, the next day, mid-afternoon, came the expected phone call. Sam of course. Victoria had arrived and Bobbie and I were cordially invited over to Sam's that evening for cocktails and hors d'oeuvres, "to meet Victoria." Naturally, I accepted for the two of us.

Bobbie turned to me with her hands on her lovely hips and said rather sternly, "Well, what shall we wear? Formal? Informal? Who else is invited, or is it just to be the four of us? I hope she's not going to be like that Clemmy person."

"Darned if I know," I said. So I called Sam back and explained the dilemma.

He laughed and said, "Oh, it's just the four of us and it's very informal. Just come as you are."

I relayed all this to Bobbie and she seemed relieved that I'd checked on it for her.

So what happened? Well, we showered and I slipped on a light blue golf shirt, fresh jeans and my best, least-scuffed deck shoes and Bobbie slipped on a nice tank top (with real pretty red and yellow flowers all over it) and some matching yellow shorts and sandals. I thought she looked real luscious. Then we strolled on over at the appointed time.

Get this: Sam met us at the door wearing his tuxedo! Yes, really. I could see the beautiful Victoria standing back by a window in the sitting room in a very nice, dark blue satin, formal cocktail dress. And at that point, I realized that her photo that Sam had showed me had not done her justice. This lady was absolutely stunning, slender, nicely proportioned, with a regal bearing.

But talk about being chagrinned! Sam had distinctly said informal. Even with my poor hearing, I'd made no mistake about that! And boy, were we ever informal! (But clean!) You know, I'm buddy enough with Sam so that I really didn't mind the discrepancy so much for me, but I could just "feel" Bobbie withering. As we walked in, now caught in our embarrassment, Sam proudly took Bobbie's hand and moved us over to meet Victoria.

"Barbara Ann?" exclaimed Sam's Victoria, with a surprised look on her face. "Is that really you?"

Bobbie suddenly showed a similar look of surprise and, grinning, said, "Why, Victoria! For heaven's sake. We haven't seen each other since when, Queens' graduation? You look just marvelous!"

Sam and I were dumbfounded. For crying out loud, who'd have ever guessed that my Bobbie and his Victoria would've known each other? Turns out that they were sorority sisters in Kappa Delta back in Queen's College in Charlotte. They hadn't kept in touch, so had a lot of catching up to do.

Sam went on ahead and made the formal introduction to me anyway, and I instantly found her absolutely delightful. Victoria was sharp. I mean real sharp. She spotted immediately our underdressed situation and turned to Sam. "Now Sam, you old reprobate," she said sternly, "I'll bet you set this up as a practical joke, didn't you? And let me tell you one thing: I will bet you have embarrassed and upset these nice people to no end."

Sam sort of grinned. "Well, maybe …" Actually, he had an expression on his face that maybe I'd never seen on him before. I guess you might have called it stark humiliation. I like Sam a lot, but I really didn't understand why he thought something like this would be funny. It certainly wasn't to my sweet wifey. Now, maybe Sam'll take advantage of me from time to time, but I got right mad at him embarrassing my wife. But, could it actually be that Sam had finally met his match in Victoria? She certainly called him down on it quickly enough. And as she took him aside momentarily, I could tell she was dressing him down something fierce. He deserved it, in my opinion. Sam just stood there, looking sheepish. He studied the shine on his shoes.

Victoria moved back to us and smiling broadly, took Bobbie's arm and guided her to one of the couches (the red velvet one).

"Bobbie, it's so wonderful to see you again. Actually, you do look delightful, and you must tell me where you bought that cute top. I'm not familiar with the local stores."

Bobbie seemed so much more excited to be there at Sam's, now that she learned that Sam had actually brought somebody home with some real class. I heard Victoria say to Bobbie, "We'll let the guys do their thing while you and I get caught up on old times. Do you have any idea what happened to Mary Anna Johnson? And Sarah Hartsell? Oh, this is going to be so much fun!"

As I saw the two ladies sit down, Victoria said to Bobbie, "Sam's already told me a lot about you and Harold." As I heard Victoria say "Harold," I knew that she'd quickly become my friend too. Bobbie smiled happily as I think she realized that she'd found herself with an old and pleasant friend in spite of Sam.

Sam and I grabbed a napkin-full of hors d'oeuvres and our drinks and went upstairs to "his room," where he keeps his computer. And also a couple of pretty comfortable easy chairs. (I think he got them at a two-for-the-price-of-one sale at a local easy chair establishment.) Not that I've ever been invited to spend all that much time up there in that room. We were usually found on his front porch if it wasn't too terribly cold, or else in his three-couch sitting room.

Frankly, I must admit that Sam's a lot more adaptable to cold weather than I am. What I mean is that some of those evenings we've spent on his front porch were just awfully cold. He might have on a light sweater or jacket, but I sure as heck needed a full winter coat—with gloves. You could almost not see across the porch for all the frosty breaths we were blowing out. But he'd just go right on yakking as if the ambient temperature was in the sixties. And hint as I might, I could rarely ever get him to understand my view that it was just way too cold for two idiots to be sitting casually on his front porch in rocking chairs, just nonchalantly chatting. Now I'll admit, maybe his scotch and water kept him warm, but I'm here to tell you, my cola sure didn't help me.

On the other hand, sometimes in the summers, when the mosquitoes and "no-see-ums" were out, he'd still want to stay out there. Some host. By the way, if you're uninformed, "no-see-ums" are tiny gnat-like flying bugs (officially called "ditparah gnats"), almost too small to be seen, that bite you and sting like fury. No welts, just stings. They're a really unpleasant nuisance. Anyway, here both of us would be, just rocking and talking away, and all the time, we'd be swatting and slapping away at the darn bugs. And lots of time the air hadn't had time to cool off either, so we'd be sweating like mad on top of everything else. Just two special friends enjoying each other's company. Yeah, sure.

But would he go inside where the air conditioning was nice, and where there would be no bugs? Oh no! Sam figured it'd be a nice night to sit on the porch and rock and talk, so we sat on his old porch and rocked and talked (and froze or sweated) because he wanted to. One thing, though: I sure did like my occasional break when I needed to go inside for another drink or go to the toilet. (I think Sam's bladder must be the size of a basketball.) At least I would get a couple minutes' reprieve that way. I figured out a system after a few of those evenings over there with my good friend: If I was the one who went after the drinks, I'd get a bad-weather break. So I kind of automatically became the "gofer." My choice, you see. Sam would say, "Hey, I think it is about time for another refill, don't you?"

And I would quickly jump up and say, "Hey, keep your seat. I'll go." I guess if you look objectively at that situation, you might say it was pretty belittling to me, but in all honesty, I really felt the need to get off that hot or cold porch without offending or insulting my friend.

I remember one night a couple of summers ago when we had severe weather warnings. I mean, the local weather bureau was warning our entire area to watch out for severe thunderstorms, dangerous lightning, and possible hail. It also emphasized that a tornado was possible and that all residents should be on the alert. Well, we were sure as heck on alert. Sam and I sat on that porch of his through one of the worst storms I've ever seen. I mean it was powerful, too! The whole place was lit up by such frequent and close-by lightning that you would almost have thought it was daytime. Lots of ozone smell. I'll bet the wind gusts bordered on forty-five miles per hour, too. In fact, the next day I learned that one of the big red oaks over in my yard had lost a huge limb to the storm. Luckily, however, that big limb missed the wooden backyard fence.

Anyway, there we sat on his porch through the entire storm, hail the size of marbles and all.

I said, "Sam, don't you think maybe we ought to move inside? We might get struck by lightning out here." (I deeply hoped we'd live through that awful night.)

"Nah. Not likely," Sam said, and then went on to inform me about the statistical analysis of lightning strikes during a severe thunderstorm and how being under a roof on his porch was probably about as good as being in his house proper. "And anyhow," he added. "Out on my porch we can better commune with nature, smell the nice ozone and rain and see the interesting hail falling." He also took that opportunity to instruct me on how to count the seconds between the time you see the flash and hear the boom, and then determine the approximate distance away from us each bolt of lightning happened to be at the time. Not very darn far several times, I'm telling you. So we stayed there and obviously we got through it okay. (I've conveniently forgotten the time he said. I really didn't consider that data important enough to clutter my brain.)

Nonetheless, I began to think later that maybe I ought to be a little bit more assertive in my suggestions to my good friend Sam. In reality, I can't help but realize that as a general rule, Sam never has paid too much attention to my thoughts or suggestions. Like I've said, maybe it is because he's older and has had more experience in living than me. But after all, real friends do pay attention to each other's concerns, don't they? Therefore, I know my buddy Sam would never purposely ignore or demean something I'd said or suggested. Would he?

❦   ❦   ❦

Anyway, after Bobbie had visited with Victoria, and I spent a couple of hours upstairs chatting with Sam and saying nothing in particular, Bobbie called from downstairs, "Hey honey, it's time to go home." So we did.

The rest of the evening and even the next day I think all Bobbie talked about was Victoria. Boy, she just couldn't get over seeing her again and what a nice young lady she'd been in college and in the Kappa Delta's. It was, "Victoria said, … Victoria told me, … Victoria and I …" Of course, both of them being very friendly and personable, Victoria and Bobbie had about eight thousand old friends to catch up on, so they told each other the latest they knew about everybody they could think of. Also, Bobbie and Victoria were going shopping together later that afternoon. Seems like Victoria was not just putting Bobbie on when she asked about her pretty blouse. She seriously wanted to know about the local clothing stores. Well, they went and had what I would call a "shopping good time." (A darn good time, according to the bill for Bobbie's new clothes! But I didn't complain about the cost; I liked them on her. Oh, she's a pretty thing, my Bobbie.)

The next morning our phone rang. Bobbie got it, and it turned out to be Victoria. She said she was heading on back down to Wilmington, but was "utterly delighted" to finally meet Harold and see Bobbie again. Said she'd be in touch in a week or so about her wedding plans, and was quite glad that Bobbie had accepted her invitation to be a member of her wedding party.

Late that afternoon, about dusk, Sam saw me out in my hammock and walked over. He seemed somewhat disturbed and clearly something was up. He just never comes over to see me. It's always a phone call for me to drop whatever I'm doing and go over to his house. Which I usually do.

"Hey Sam. What's up?" I said, looking up from the hammock. Since this time I was king and he was the guest, I told him to pull up a lawn chair, while I just continued to enjoy my hammock. (Incidentally, I don't have a front porch on my house like Sam does.) Frankly, I can't remember when Sam last came over to my house without a formal invitation, so I immediately knew something was up. I'm real perceptive that way.

Sam pulled the chair close to my hammock and I adjusted my pillow to where I could more easily look at him without getting up. I figured that it was a nice host-like thing I was doing, so I could more easily have a good conversation with my guest.

"I've got a slight technical problem with Victoria, Hank." He spoke with a great deal of seriousness in his voice and a very wrinkled forehead. He sat on the edge of that chair with his fingers interlaced.

"Hey buddy," I replied, "What's happening? Tell me all about it." Now I just have to admit that something going on here really did make me feel good. I mean, I usually seem to be the one in the subordinate spot, although I do consider him my best friend, so I don't really mind (much). But here he is, in my yard, confessing his problems to me. I mean, holy cow!

"Victoria wants to redo my house."

I cleared my throat. "So, Sam, what's wrong with that?" I spoke in as much of an authoritarian voice as I could muster.

"Well, for one thing, she wants to take one of my sitting room couches out and move it to the hallway beside the stair landing. And she wants to shift a bunch of my wall pictures around, and clean out my dining room, and change my bedroom arrangement, and take my master bathroom shower down, and clean out the attic, and put better lighting down in the basement, and tear up all the sod and replant the lawn, and tear down my old car shed, and rework my shop, and …"

At this point I think he had to stop and grab a quick breath. I felt it might be a good time to step in a little bit.

I raised my head off the back of the hammock pillow and looked him straight in the eye. "Sam, I really don't see anything much wrong with her suggestions. I realize that you've lived by yourself for several years and are pretty comfortable the way things are now, but after all, old buddy, you're marrying a terrifically nice lady and part of your new job is to please her. Right?"

"Yeah, I know all that, but I'm not sure I want to change everything anyway, just to please her." He sat back in the lawn chair and unclasped his hands. I noticed that he kept rubbing his palms on his pants. "After all, I have some rights too, don't I? Do you understand what I'm saying Hank?" Boy, Sam was really serious and frantic by all this. I've seen my friend upset and angry numerous times, but I think this situation really had him baffled. I'd never before seen him in a mood like this. Here he was, apparently in serious love with a truly wonderful lady. He knew, as did Bobbie and I, that they had the potential for a fine, lasting marriage. Sam had made the verbal commitment. He had decided to spend the rest of his life with Victoria. But now he was obviously asking himself if he really did want to alter his bachelor lifestyle for her. Was she, or rather, was the relationship, worth it? Most unlike my friend to be confronted with such decisions, at least from all he'd told me in the past.

Sam is one of these guys that always feels like he has to be in control. Or maybe that is just the way he has always been with me and, just possibly, other guys, too.

But now I believe that maybe Victoria's charms had taken control of Sam's life. He was just sitting there, sweating up a storm.

Although I really didn't know her all that well yet, I do really give a great deal of credit to my sweet wifey. She had told me, "I really can't understand why Sam deserves her, because Victoria's a very smart person. I'll say, though, that he's getting a really nice and wonderful lady for a wife this time." As I was nodding my head in complete agreement, Bobbie continued, "You know, after leaving Queens, she went on to Duke and got her MBA."

My Bobbie has this innate ability to make quick, yet uncannily accurate appraisals about people she meets. And when Barbara says she likes somebody, you'd sure better believe that person is okay. No question. And, since she'd known Victoria for quite a few years earlier, the deal with Sam would be okay. Bobbie said so.

So I think even Sam realized what a gem he had in Victoria and that, maybe for the first time, he'd have to kowtow to somebody else's wishes. Clearly, from what he told me, Victoria had been rather adamant about straightening his place up. And boy, was my Bobbie elated to hear about that! Maybe, at last, Sam's place would start looking better, with Victoria's personal touch. At least that was Bobbie's view. I personally never did see all that much wrong with Sam's house. Well, maybe his lawn looked a little peculiar, and it's true that shed in his backyard looked a little shabby, what with the broken door hinges and sagging roof. And there was his swamp in the far back yard gully. But maybe guys just don't look at things the same way that women do.

Anyway, Sam apparently finally got it through his thick skull that I was more on Victoria's side in this situation than his. I told him in the most fatherly voice I could muster, "Do whatever it takes to keep Victoria happy. You can't afford to lose that fine woman." Imagine me saying something that dogmatic to Sam! And I'll be darned if it didn't seem to settle in on him.

"Hank, I appreciate your advice. I guess maybe I'd better do what she wants, if you say so. Thanks," he said seriously. And with that he got up from the lawn chair and actually shook my hand. Well boy-oh-boy if that wasn't a first! Now, I have to say this was a big breakthrough. It floored me. Sam thanking me. Me! Unbelievable. And he started on home, his head tilted down as if in real deep thought. Walked straight through his cocklebur-infested weed patch.

So whatever caused it, me or Victoria, it worked. (Probably Victoria, let me point out.) So, over the next couple of weeks, did we ever see some changes going on over there? Dear, sweet Bobbie was so excited. Personally, I found it more interesting than exciting.

First, the shed came down. Actually, Sam borrowed my big sledgehammer again and really went at it. It only took two days of swinging that thing to knock it all down. He hired what looked like a teenager to help him stack up the broken boards, old variegated shingles, and oil drums. He didn't call me to help. Then he had a dump truck back up and they loaded it about a dozen times in getting rid of all that stuff. I saw several ladies from the Preservation Society, as well as a couple members of the Town Board riding by looking at what he was doing. Sam complained to me later about the high cost of the cleanup. "Had to pay extra to get rid of those toxic chemicals," he declared. "Just for Victoria." (I remained silent at that point.)

After the decrepit shed came down, a series of blank spots of oily dirt where each of his old cars and that big truck had been stored were thus exposed. Bobbie didn't care much for that of course, but I assured her that, eventually, those spots would be fixed.

In a couple of days the landscaping people arrived and I couldn't help but wonder what they thought about Sam's patchwork lawn. I'd be willing to bet that they got a bunch of good laughs about it—behind Sam's back of course. Actually, I strongly suspect that Sam was pretty well embarrassed about even letting a real landscape architect see what he'd done. I watched from my hammock as their front-end loader just sort of scooped those pieces of sod right up. It surprised me how easily they came up, even though they'd been lying there, nailed down for some time. Sam told me later that the landscapers said he hadn't done his initial preparation correctly. He never did tell me what other mistakes they told me he had made, but he sure paid dearly for such errors.

Now let me tell you about what became of Sam's dam, puddle and swamp. Sam and I were sitting in my front yard again, and get this: We were both sipping on minted iced tea. He said, "When I took Victoria on a tour of my back acreage, and she saw my dam and pond, she said, 'Interesting.' That's what she said." He seemed sort of chagrinned while he was telling me this, but actually, I already knew most of it. Bobbie and Victoria had previously discussed it and Bobbie relayed it all to me.

He continued, "Victoria said, 'Although I can see that you've done a lot of work here, it's such a beautiful site, maybe we can make it even better.'" Apparently, by this time, she had accepted the fact that my buddy would occasionally go off one tangent or another, some of which didn't work out too well. (Little did she know how many.) I remained silent and nodded my head a lot in acceptance of what he told me.

She made arrangements for a contractor to come out and look at it with them. Two days later a bunch of great big trucks were hauling huge concrete culverts, rocks and fill dirt to his dam site. Lo and behold if they didn't fill that entire gully in—dam, puddle, swamp and all. They bulldozed a big gap right in the middle of his dam and laid in these big culverts first of course. The contracting company even had one of those big motorized machines that pack down the dirt, like they use when building a highway. They did a really nice professional job of it, and I'll bet it cost poor Sam or Victoria a penny or two. Actually, if the truth were known, it should have come out of Sam's pocket, in my opinion. Only had to cut down four big trees and just a few smaller ones.

Then, to top things off, she had a full sized tennis court built right there on top of all that packed dirt. Asphalt top, proper fencing, painted green with white lines and all. Boy was it nice! And more than that, she even had that hill terraced and nicely grassed in so one could take a couple of lawn chairs there and look down on the players. I'll tell you one thing: Victoria quickly proved to me (and Sam) that she was one classy and smart lady. They used sod, and it was not checker boarded.

After they got the new lawn seeded—and I must admit, it did look better when the new grass started emerging from the good earth—they did the backyard too, where the sheds had been. Also, to Bobbie's relief, they seeded the side yard between our two houses.

Next came the painters. I don't think Sam picked out the color, because let me tell you something: When they finished the paint job on that old house, it was a pure work of art. Took about three weeks, by the time they scraped off layer after layer of old paint. I suppose Victoria told the painters that she wanted it painted as close to the original color as possible, which was what I think they call "white-on-white." I mean when they finished, it was simply gorgeous. Bobbie, needless to say, was absolutely thrilled to live next door to what now appeared to be a first class mansion. I have to admit that after seeing how good Sam's house turned out, I was looking with a jaundiced eye at our own abode. It is a blond brick 1920s era job. Bobbie didn't say anything about painting our wooden trim, so I guess I dodged that bullet. We did become some mighty proud neighbors at this point, though. I have to say, Victoria really turned Sam's home into a real showplace. Bobbie told me the Preservation Society was utterly delighted and wanted to invite Victoria to join. They even asked Victoria if they could put Sam's house on the annual Aquaville House Tour.

I was over on Sam's porch about dusk a few days later and we were talking about how Victoria now wanted the attic and basement cleaned out.

"You know," Sam said, "she wants to get rid of all those old magazines, newspapers and things I've saved. She calls it junk. Heck, I haven't even gotten around to reading some of it yet." Well, this desire of Victoria's apparently turned into another confrontation that Sam lost to her.

Continuing along this line of conversation, he told me, "It's been my idea to just have it all hauled down to the front yard and have a big yard sale with all those old magazines and newspapers. I figure that I'm shrewd enough where I can make several hundred dollars that way. I suspect some folks would pay me big bucks for a few of those older magazines."

He probably would've, too, but I think Victoria vetoed that plan.

Two days later a paper-shredding truck as well as a big Salvation Army truck pulled up in front of his house and all that stuff quickly disappeared. No sloppy yard sales for Victoria, no siree! Sam told me later that she felt that such sales didn't show sufficient "class" for someone of Sam's stature in the community. How do you argue with logic like that?

CHAPTER 23

Wilmington

Bobbie and Victoria had been corresponding for a couple of weeks, as well as making numerous phone calls back and forth. Also, Victoria had been back next door a couple of times and she and Bobbie had spent even more time renewing their friendship. Bobbie says they have many similar tastes. In fact, the only real difference between the two that I can observe is that Victoria loves Sam and Bobbie hates him. Well, maybe that's a tad too strong. Maybe Bobbie probably doesn't actually "hate" him, but she sure as heck doesn't care a lot for him. Bobbie, being the sweet individual that she is, however, would never tell Victoria how she really feels about Sam. She's real tactful that way. Better maybe, to tell a white lie than to disturb or otherwise upset a friend.

Bobbie even went down to Wilmington a couple of times to visit Victoria in her condo. It seems as though Victoria wanted Bobbie to be her matron of honor. What a nice gesture! Bobbie said she found that Victoria had a very nice place and a couple of pleasant, but boring, roommates. And oh yes, Bobbie mentioned that one of them kind of reminded her of Sam somehow.

At last came the wedding day. Sam had rented a suite up on the top floor at what was apparently the nicest hotel in Wilmington, and Bobbie and I were given one of the suite's bedrooms. I'll tell you, Sam went all out for this wedding; nice, very nice. Actually, he kept pretty much out of our way, as he was out doing "wedding things," I suppose. Bobbie had a couple of errands to run.

Even though I was Sam's best man, I had little to do, so I was glad that I'd brought a new novel from home to read. Kind of missed my hammock, though. Our hotel room overlooked the Cape Fear River, so I had a pretty good time watching the ocean-going cargo ships and various other boats down there on the water. Kind of interesting. I had a real good view of an old World War II battleship, *The North Carolina,* that they have permanently moored down there on the river.

Bobbie and I went over to the church about an hour early, so she could get all set with Victoria and I could maybe keep Sam settled down.

Sitting in a straight-back chair in the church anteroom Sam said to me, "You know, Hank. Do you think you could run out and find me a nice glass of sherry? That'd work well right now and maybe help settle my nerves."

"No way, Sam," I told him firmly. "You're going into those vows with Victoria stone cold sober. You understand me good?"

"Aw Hank," Sam replied, pulling on my coat sleeve. "Just one."

I said, "Not on your life, boy." (Always wanted to say that; you know, "life-boy"—like an old bath soap that smelled so medicinal, *Life Buoy.*)

Sam remained quiet for a moment or so, while we heard the organist beginning to play out in the main sanctuary.

"Hank," Sam said, looking up at me frowning. He had his fists clenched. "Maybe this is all just a big mistake. I screwed up two marriages. What if I do it again?"

"Now Sam, relax," I told my friend. "This is no mistake, believe me. Victoria's a marvelous lady and you two'll have a fine marriage."

Sam reached down and rubbed the shine of his shoes slightly. Then he nervously rubbed his hands over his enlarging bald spot. "I hope so, Hank. I really hope you're right." Then he looked around the room anxiously and started to stand.

I put my hands on his shoulders and eased him back into his chair. I didn't take my hand off his shoulder for a while either; at least not until he stopped trying to stand up again and he had started breathing more steadily. I mean to tell you, to have Sam under my thumb for a while certainly was a change, and I was enjoying every darn minute of it. For certain, I'd never before seen him so nervous and unsure of himself.

In a little while I was able to sneak a peek out the door to the sanctuary where everybody was filing in and being seated by the ushers. And when I say "everybody," I mean everybody. I swear, it looked as though the entire population of Wilmington came. I'd never before seen standing room only at a wedding, and it was a huge church, the largest in the city. Darned if it didn't appear to me as though Victoria sure was one popular lady down there in Wilmington.

After a little while, one of the ushers stopped by the anteroom where Sam and I were waiting. "Just to check on you two," he said. As I peeked out the slightly-opened door again, the young man mentioned that his home was Wilmington and he pointed out several special people. For instance, there were several prominent doctors, the mayor, the head of the Chamber of Commerce, a United States Senator, a movie producer, and even a couple of movie stars. I even saw our Governor out there. No infants. Wow!

I won't go into the actual wedding here, but just let me say it was magnificent. It reminded me of the wedding scene in the movie, *The Sound of Music*, except there were no Nazi's or nuns—that I could spot, at least. Victoria was just as beautiful a bride as I've ever seen. Darn, she looked nice. Sam in his cutaway looked right good himself and real noble, too. I really think he'd finally figured out that he was one lucky guy to get a lady as nice as Victoria.

And Bobbie, as Victoria's Matron of Honor, sure did look scrumptious herself. I was real proud of her. I felt a tad awkward in my own cutaway, but endured.

❧   ❧   ❧

The reception at a local country club was just as nice as could be. Needless to say, it was all super. First class. All kinds of hot and cold hors d'oeuvres, wines, champagne. They even had hired a string quartet from the North Carolina Symphony which played real fine classical music.

Whoo-ee! I determined that wedding and reception must have set Victoria's daddy back a penny or two. I figured at the time that he'd be making payments for at least a couple of years.

After that reception, Sam and Victoria took off for the Wilmington International Airport—in a gleaming white stretch limousine yet—and then they flew to Europe. Sam had told me they were going to honeymoon in Monaco, of all places. Boy, I'll bet that cost him a bundle. Apparently, old buddy Sam finally figured that since he had such a delightful new wife, he'd spare no expense to please her. *Good for him*, is what I have to say about that. I'll have to admit that Sam has shown a tendency to be a little tight-fisted with his dollars over the years, but boy, not this time.

A month later, Bobbie and I finally saw Sam and Victoria return to their home next door to us there in Aquaville. When a couple of hours had passed, Bobbie called over there and asked if we could come over for a short visit. Hearing an affirmative answer, Bobbie immediately drove downtown and picked up a real nice arrangement of flowers. When she returned, we went on over. We dressed in smart casual this time.

Goodness gracious, you just wouldn't believe the difference in the house. We hadn't been over there since the interior renovations were completed, and boy, it sure did have a woman's touch. I mean, after rearranging (and re-covering) Sam's furnishings and bringing a lot of Victoria's furniture up from Wilmington, and what with the newly painted interior and Victoria's rearranging of the wall pictures, it looked just like a movie setting. You could have filmed *Gone With The Wind* there and not have known the difference. I was tempted to look around for Rhett Butler and Scarlett O'Hara. Really, the place was just magnificent.

And Sam and Victoria looked fabulous. They had real solid suntans and both were still beaming, just like nearly all newlyweds. After a little bit of conversation, Bobbie and I decided to leave them alone, with the admonition to call us when they were really settled in.

The next day Sam, and I parked ourselves in the rocking chairs on his front porch. I was kind of glad that Victoria let Sam keep those comfortable rocking chairs. For a moment or two, I watched a pair of cardinals talking to each other in a bush out at the street. The grass on Sam and Victoria's lawn was emerging. Sam sipped on a soda!

Then the conversation began. It seems that Sam really walked into something (by marrying Victoria) that he didn't really mind at all, but didn't expect. Now, I'll have to admit that my sweet wifey had already clued me in on a lot about Victoria, but I hadn't mentioned this fact to my buddy Sam. Bobbie told me that when she and Victoria were schoolmates at Queens, Victoria's father was station manager and disc jockey at a small radio station somewhere over in the eastern part of North Carolina. He was earning a fairly decent salary obviously, because Victoria always had very nice clothes and stuff. That's what Bobbie said. Bobbie's folks could just barely manage to keep her there the entire four years, she told me. In fact, Bobbie worked part-time in the college cafeteria the whole time while she was there. And she still made Dean's List every semester. Graduated *Magna Cum Laude,* too! I told you my wife was smart.

I think I mentioned earlier that Sam said Victoria was a successful executive down there in Wilmington. Okay, here's what he subsequently learned about her, that she apparently failed to mention to him when they were courting: Her dad now owns six television stations, four radio stations and a chain of daily newspapers. In other words, he has become fabulously wealthy. Her parents live in a mansion down in Palm Beach part of the year and also have a multi-million dollar home on Figure Eight Island (a privately owned beach resort for the wealthy), just up the road from Wilmington. He has a private jet with its own crew, and they keep a married couple as chauffeur and housekeeper at both places. Not only that, he owns a ninety foot luxury yacht with a crew on standby, too. I mean, Sam married into an enormous amount of money! But smart Victoria, as I would expect after Bobbie told me all about her, didn't let Sam know anything about all that until after they were married. Probably didn't want to ever think that my good friend had married her for her money. Maybe he could have figured something out considering the size of the wedding, but then, Sam was pretty nervous at that time. While we sat on his porch and nonchalantly watched an occasional car drive by, Sam casually mentioned to me that Victoria had a "sizable" trust fund at this point, and was in line to inherit a "tidy sum," plus controlling interest in her father's businesses at some point in the future.

But anyway, Sam told me that Victoria was just "outstanding" (his word). She was doing everything she could to please him and, catch this, Sam said he was doing likewise to please her. I must admit that my pal has shown a slight tendency over the years, to be just a little bit self-centered and selfish. I, being his good friend, have certainly learned to accept this trait, and I never really did let it bother me—well, not much anyway. Bobbie, of course, saw these characteristics right away too. Maybe that is why she never seemed to develop a fondness for him. But Sam told me that he was beginning to look back on his life and his previous marriages, and that he realized that maybe, just maybe, mind you, he hadn't given sufficient efforts to the concerns of other people in the past.

"What do you think about that, Hank?" he said, uncrossing his legs and turning to me, not grinning, but with a curious smile on his lips.

Boy, talk about putting a guy on the spot. Here's my best friend asking me to verify some of his bad traits. And I sure didn't want to hurt his feelings.

I pondered that for a few moments, and finally said, "Well, Sam, if you look back over your life and find some things that you're not particularly happy that you said or did, I don't think that you need to dwell on them. But I would also say that you might want to take the opportunity to make sure you don't do such things in the future. That way, you're bound to become a better person in this old world of ours. Think so?"

After that deep philosophical response by yours truly, Sam just sat there quietly for a few moments. I watched a squirrel gingerly walk across a power line out over the street.

Finally he turned his chair toward me, reached out, shook my hand and spoke up. "Harold, you're the best friend a man could ever have. Thanks."

Hearing that remark, I darn near fainted. I was Sam's best friend! He said so! I'd had some suspicions about it when he made me his best man in his wedding, but now, he really confirmed it! *Damn!*

Sam and Victoria are now living a full and happy life next door to us, traveling widely around the world. Sam never again has called me Hank. I've become "Harold" at last.

Bobbie and I had several long conversations a little later about Sam's and my relationship. She said, "Harold, I find it very hard to understand why you felt like you had to have Sam as a so-called 'best friend.' You certainly have a great personality. Besides, you have plenty of friends around here in addition to him. All your employees at your lab can be called your friends, can't they? And at our country club?"

Somewhat humbled, I replied, "Honey, I'm not absolutely sure myself why I assigned that declaration to Sam. You know, after Terry died, I was sort of left in the dark for a while. I felt like I had nobody at all. I badly wanted somebody—maybe anybody—to like me."

She replied soothingly, "Yes, honey. I remember when that happened, and I was also saddened at Terry's dying."

"I felt completely lost. I assumed that nobody would like me; they all admired Terry so much."

During this discussion with Bobbie, I felt a great deal of recalled remorse, and tears began forming in my eyes. She moved over beside me and hugged me tenderly.

I sniffed, then continued, "If you remember, I was very shy back then. I was afraid to speak out much or make my opinions known. It concerned me that I'd get laughed at if I didn't know the right answers or responses. I saw other guys that had close pals and I sort of envied them. I wanted somebody like that. I wanted to belong. Can you understand that, honey? I just wanted to be liked by my peers—and respected."

"Dear Harold," she said quietly.

That's all I ever wanted—to be respected. And somehow, I subconsciously decided that I'd have to have a 'best friend' to get that respect. I now realize that didn't really make much sense, but it's the way I felt."

I said nothing for a few brief moments. Bobbie remained quiet.

"I saw how popular Terry was and how he and Sam were so close. I felt maybe I should have the same thing. When Terry 'offered' Sam as my 'big brother,' I thought it would answer all my needs. Little did I realize that that was the wrong response. I simply needed somebody to be my closest friend. That way I felt as though I had some security. Sam'd be there for me just like Terry was. But I now realize all that was pretty naïve and immature."

Bobbie continued to let me drone on in my summation of my feelings.

"Obviously I went overboard. I realize now that it was pretty immature and unrealistic of me to set Sam up that way. He may not have even realized it himself. But I now think that maturity and self-sufficiency are the important things; much more then 'friendship.'"

So I changed. And Sam (maybe Victoria) perceived my change of attitude and changed his perspective of me also, I think. He treats me more like an equal now. Doesn't call and demand that I go over, but rather, may call and ask for my opinions, and occasionally, even come over to my yard. And lo and behold, now he actually listens to me, and frequently—okay, sometimes—follows my advice.

Sam's never yet thanked Bobbie and me for saving his life that time, and has never apologized for trying to dominate me so much, but that's okay. He's still my friend and I'll accept his foibles.

Although we aren't doing any more offshore fishing together, Sam and Victoria invite us to her dad's mansion on Figure Eight Island from time to time. Sometimes Sam and I do some surf fishing then. On a few occasions her dad takes us out on his yacht, but not for fishing. Hanging a couple of lines off the stern of that humongous vessel would look pretty pitiful.

Bobbie and Victoria enjoy hitting the Wilmington stores, which is just fine. Victoria knows the owners of several upscale ladies' stores and has been delighted to show sweet wifey around. Bobbie has purchased some very classy outfits there.

Incidentally, Bobbie and I noticed Sam's grammar improve immediately following his association with Victoria.

❧   ❧   ❧

A couple of weeks ago as I was walking out to my trusty hammock, I noted with some regret that my grass was looking rather puny. I'd accumulated an infestation of crab grass, and saw numerous bare spots. Hmm. I wondered if sod might be an answer. Maybe if I called Sam …

THE END

978-0-595-44262-1
0-595-44262-5

CPSIA information can be obtained
at www.ICGtesting.com
Printed in the USA
FSOW01n0416081217
42102FS